U0153229

實用 第二版
航空英語

五南圖書出版公司 印行

Practical English for the Airline Industry

陳淑娟・編著

ENGLISH

Preface 二版序言

夢想的路上，你／妳仍然堅持目標，不曾放棄嗎？

　　我想是的！如果此刻你／妳正翻開這本書，或者，已經買下這本書，與它相伴同行一段時間了，我相信，你翱翔天際的夢想，一直都在，而且仍然努力不懈。

　　兩年的時光荏苒，謝謝每一位因此書與我結緣的人。當我們在不同的地方，各自為了理想繼續前行時，無論識與不識，我的感謝和祝福，會一直存在字裡行間，分享圓夢路程上的一步一腳印。

　　為能不負所託與信任，再版之前，針對所有內容的編排，進行了更縝密的檢查與校對。音檔的部分，亦進行大範圍的錄音重製，以符合航空專業性要求。希望無論是在課堂上的講授與學習，或是個人自學準備參加航空從業人員的考試，這本書，都能成為最適用的工具。

　　現在與未來的我，依舊會堅守在教育的崗位上，激勵和守護年輕孩子勇敢築夢追夢。這本書，是我送給自己和你／妳們的禮物。敬請

所有先進予以賜教不吝斧正，讀者們與我分享心得，讓我和這本書，都能繼續成長、繼續進步。繼續，陪伴圓夢。

陳淑娟 謹誌

2018 新春

Preface 初版序言

你/妳願意為夢想，付出多少時間和努力？

　　翱翔天際，是人類從未放棄過的夢想。而飛機的發明，讓夢想與現實終能合一。從飛行器的演進一日千里，到航空產業的蓬勃發展，需求與供給兩造的相輔相成，如今，無論是以飛機做為主要交通工具，或是搭機從事休閒旅遊活動，「飛行」已然成為許多人不可或缺的生活經驗和生命體驗。

　　和其它產業一樣，景氣循環與內外在條件，對於航空業的發展，存在著顯著影響力。但島國如台灣，無論是我們想走向世界，或歡迎世界進入我們，航空公司提供的飛航相關服務，皆扮演著至關緊要的橋樑角色。也因為這樣的居中聯結角色特性，語言能力，尤其是英語，成為航空業從業人員不可或缺的必要條件。

　　薪資福利優、搭機旅行便捷、工作內容專業度高、工作場域全球化及多元化、職業形象佳、易與世界接軌，以上種種描述，正是航空業吸引各方菁英，努力經過層層關卡，加入成為其中一員的重要動機。由於航空公司招考多設有年齡限制，想達成夢想成為「航空人」，務必及早開始準備。航空公司每年多於三月開始徵才活動，經過數月的篩選，於畢業季後，七月一日報到受訓。大專院校的莘莘學

子們，若想自數千名競爭對手中脫穎而出，你/妳還有多久可以準備的時間？

　　航空專業涵蓋層面深度與廣度兼備，選擇正確有效的入門磚，學習過程才能獲致事半功倍的成效。本書融合作者十年航空業實務專業，及交通運輸研究之學術專長，為所有在學大專院校學生、社會新鮮人、和仍在航空產業門檻外，尋求入門之鑰的年輕人，設計內容自淺而深，包含三大部份共16章的航空英文專業教材。第一部份提供訂位、購票、機場劃位、客艙服務等基礎互動情境之單字片語對話；第二部份涵蓋航空專業術語、航空器構造、飛行衛教等兼具專業及實用的進階航空知識；最後輔以撰寫履歷自傳及求職面試之必備要略，內容豐富易懂、範例完整詳盡。無論你/妳選擇只扮演「需求面」的消費者（旅客），或想同時取得「供給面」（航空業從業人員）及「需求面」兩種角色，這本大專航空英文專書，皆可謂量身打造的實用工具。

　　現在，打開航空業之門的鑰匙已經交到你/妳的手中了，翻開書頁，循序漸進地朝夢想前進吧！

　　祝你/妳成功。

陳淑娟　謹誌

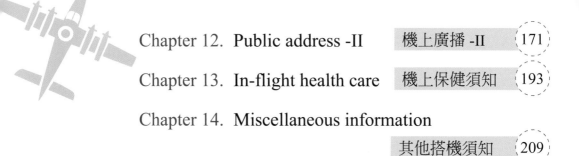

Part I **Practical English for the Airline Industry**

航空業實用會話

Chapter 1. Making a reservation 訂位

▶ Outline: 介紹預訂機位之基礎單字、實用片語及情境對話。另整理機場代碼、城市代碼、航空公司代碼及機型代號以供參考。

▶ Learning Goals: 熟記必備單字、片語。能夠流暢進行情境對話及角色扮演。熟悉各項航空相關代碼。

Ⓐ Basic Vocabulary 基礎必備單字

❶ airfare ⓀⓀ [ˈɛrfɛr] ⓓⒿ [ˈeəfeə] 機票票價 (n.)

英文釋義 fare for travel by airplane; ticket price for air trip

- low airfare, discount airfare 折扣票價
- How much is the round-trip airfare? 來回機票一共多少錢？

❷ assignment ⓀⓀ [əˈsaɪnmənt] ⓓⒿ [əˈsaɪnmənt] 指派 (n.)（工作或座位）

英文釋義 a specified task or amount of work（指派的工作）；allocation（分配座位）

- give students assignments 指派學生作業
- He left for his assignment in the U.S.. 他為工作赴美。
- Are you satisfied with your seat assignment? 你對座位安排滿意嗎？

❸ available ⓀⓀ [əˈveləbḷ] ⓓⒿ [əˈveiləbl] 可行的；可用的；可取得的 (a.)

英文釋義 ready for use or service

同義字 obtainable; accessible

- There are three seats available in the business class. 商務艙有三個空位。

❹ book ⓀⓀ [bʊk] ⓓⒿ [buk] 預訂；訂位 (v.)

英文釋義 to register (as a name) for some future activity or condition; to reserve in advance

同義字 reserve; hold

• The agent booked tickets to the show for the whole family.　工作人員為全家人預訂了看秀的票。

❺ flight KK [flaɪt] DJ [flait]　飛行；航班 (n.)

英文釋義 the act of flying or leaving

• direct flight　直飛

• connecting flight　轉乘班機

• There are more than three direct flights departing for Hong Kong every day.　每天有超過三班直飛香港的班機。

❻ itinerary KK [aɪˈtɪnəˌrɛrɪ] DJ [aiˈtinərəri]　清單；明細 (n.)

英文釋義 the route of a journey or tour（旅行路線）；travel diary（旅行日誌）；traveler's guidebook（旅行指南）

• One moment, please. Your itinerary has been taken care.　請稍等，你的旅程明細表已經在處理中。

❼ nonstop KK [nɑnˈstɑp] DJ [nɔnˈstɔp]　直達 (n. a.)

同義字 direct

• nonstop flight: a flight made without intermediate stops between source and destination　直達航班

• How many nonstops are there to Paris?　飛巴黎的直達班機有幾班？

❽ passenger KK [ˈpæsn̩dʒɚ] DJ [ˈpæsindʒə]　旅客；乘客 (n.)

英文釋義 a person who is traveling from one place to another in a car, bus, train, ship, airplane or other transportation devices

• There are 250 passengers on board.　機上有250位乘客。

❾ preferable KK ['prɛfərəbl] DJ ['prefərəbl]　較喜歡的 (a.)

英文釋義 more desirable than another

同義字 preferred

- Tea is preferable to coffee.　和咖啡比起來，較喜歡喝茶。

❿ reconfirmation KK [ˌrikənfə'meʃən] DJ [ˌriːkənfə'meiʃən]　再確認 (n.)

英文釋義 additional proof for something that was believed is correct; to confirm something such as an airline or hotel reservation again

- The reconfirmation of your booking has been done.　你的預約已經再次確認過了。

⓫ reservation KK [ˌrɛzə'veʃən] DJ [ˌrezə'veiʃən]　預約 (n.)

英文釋義 something reserved in advance

同義字 prearrangement

- I would like to make a reservation for dinner.　我要預約晚餐。

⓬ staff KK [stæf] DJ [stɑːf]　職員；工作人員 (n.)（為集合名詞，單複數同形）

英文釋義 a group of people who work for an organization or business

- ground staff　地勤人員
- Don't worry. Our staff will help you fill out the application form.　別擔心，我們的工作人員會協助你填寫申請表的。

⓭ stopover KK ['stɑpˌovɚ] DJ ['stɔpˌəuvə]　中途停留 (n.)

英文釋義 a stopping place on a journey

- There is a stopover to change planes in Dallas.　在達拉斯會停留更換飛機。

⓮ timetable ㊄ ['taɪmˌtebl̩] ⓓ ['taɪmˌteibl̩]　時刻表 (n.)

英文釋義 a schedule of times of arrivals and departures

同義字 schedule

・Where can I get the timetable?　哪裡可以拿到時刻表？

⓯ validate ㊄ ['væləˌdet] ⓓ ['vælideit]　使生效 (v.)

英文釋義 make legally; confirm the validity

同義字 confirm; endorse

・This ticket has been validated.　這張票已經生效。

Ⓑ Phrase 片語

❶ accident insurance　意外險

❷ all set　都處理好了

❸ budget ticket　折扣票

❹ charter flight　包機

❺ direct flight　直航班次

❻ domestic flight　國內航班（國內線）

❼ electronic ticket　電子機票

❽ first class　頭等艙 / business class　商務艙 / economy class　經濟艙

❾ IT (Inclusive Tour) / package tour　全包式旅行

❿ independent traveler　散客

⓫ international (overseas) flight　國際航班（國際線）

⓬ jumbo jet　巨無霸噴射客機

⓭ make a reservation for　訂位

⓮ non-transferable　不可轉讓的

⓯ one-way　單程 / round trip　來回

⓰ outbound tour　出境旅行 / inbound tour　入境旅行

⓱ RWT (round the world tour)　環球旅行

⓲ seat assignment　劃位

ⓒ Dialog 情境對話

S ：staff   P ：passenger

情境 I ▷ 01-1

S Good morning, sir! May I help you?

P Yes, I would like to make a reservation for two to Seattle.

S What date, please?

P March the 9th. Are there flights departing in the morning?

S Yes, we have a flight leaving Taiwan at 11 a.m., arriving in Seattle at about seven the next morning.

P Is there any seat available in economy class?

S Yes, but they are all in the rear section of the cabin. I'm afraid that you don't have sufficient options for now. Is it fine with you?

P No problem, as long as it's not over the wing. I have to get back by Monday, anyway.

S Would it be a round-trip or one-way?

P Round trip, please.

譯 文

員工 先生您早，有甚麼我能幫忙的嗎？

乘客 我想預約兩個到西雅圖的機位。

員工 請問出發日期幾號？

乘客 三月九日。有早上起飛的班機嗎？

員工 有一班上午11點台北起飛，隔日上午七點抵達西雅圖的班次。

乘客 經濟艙還有空位嗎？

員工 有的，不過沒有太多選擇性，已經剩下機艙後段的位置了。您覺得可以嗎？

乘客 沒問題，只要不在機翼附近的位置就好，反正我非得周一前趕回去。

員工 請問是單程還是來回呢？

乘客 來回。

情境 II 01-2

P Good afternoon. I want to go to Madrid. Would you please check and see which way I can take to get there?

S Please wait for a moment......well, you can get there by KLM via Amsterdam or by Singapore Airlines via Singapore.

P I prefer going by Singapore Airlines. Can you tell me the itinerary?

S There is one leaving for Singapore at 9:30 Friday morning and the connecting flight would be 4 o'clock in the afternoon directly for Madrid.

P How much is the fare for business class?

S USD 5,000 for round trip.

P Should I make the reservation now?

S It's better doing so. The flights in July are usually full.

P Thank you very much. Please arrange the reservation for me.

S Certainly, madam. I will do it right away.

譯 文

乘客 午安,我要前往馬德里,請幫我查看看有哪些班次。

員工 請稍等。您可以搭乘荷航於阿姆斯特丹轉機,或新航於新加坡轉機。

乘客 我想搭新航。能給我航班詳細資料嗎?

員工 有一班星期五上午9點半出發前往新加坡,下午4點從新加坡直飛馬德里。

乘客 商務艙票價多少?

員工 來回票五仟美金。

乘客 需要現在立刻訂位嗎?

員工 最好是的。七月的航班通常客滿。

乘客 謝謝你。那就麻煩你幫我處理一下。

員工 沒問題。我現在馬上處理。

情境Ⅲ 01-3

S EVA Airways. May I help you?

P Yes, I would like to make a reservation.

S May I have your name, madam?

P Yes. My name is Jenny Fox.

S All right. Ms. Fox. Where are you planning to go?

P I would like to fly from Taipei to New York.

S Would it be a one-way or a round-trip?

P A one way, please.

S Which class would you prefer?

P Make it economy class, please.

S When will you leave, Ms. Fox?

P I plan to go on Saturday afternoon, that's June 4th, if possible.

S I'll check for you right away. One moment, please.

P Thank you!

S Ms. Fox. Your reservation is on June 4th, Saturday evening. Your flight

is BR-32, leaving at 7:05 PM and arriving in New York JFK international airport at 10 PM local time.

P Perfect. Thank you very much.

S Wish you a wonderful trip.

譯 文

員工 長榮航空您好，需要甚麼服務呢？

乘客 我想預約航班。

員工 請問小姐怎麼稱呼？

乘客 我的名字是珍妮福克斯。

員工 沒問題，福克斯小姐。請問您要去哪裡？

乘客 我要從台北飛紐約。

員工 請問單程還是來回？

乘客 單程。

員工 甚麼艙等呢？

乘客 經濟艙。

員工 甚麼時候出發？

乘客 計劃是六月四號星期六下午離開。

員工 請您稍等，我立刻幫您查詢。

乘客 謝謝你。

員工 福克斯小姐，您預約的班次是六月四日星期六傍晚出發的航班。七點五分從台北起飛，當地時間晚上十點鐘抵達紐約甘迺迪國際機場。

乘客 太好了，非常謝謝你。

員工 祝您旅途愉快。

Airline Humor（航空幽默小品）!!

A flight attendant, struggling a little with her English, was heard to announce: "We hope you have had a present fright and that you will fry with us again......"

某位英文發音不佳的空服員，掙扎地說出以下的廣播稿內容：
我們希望今天的飛行讓您覺得很「驚恐」，也期待您能再次和我們一起「煎煮」……

Appendix   附 錄

❶ City / Airport Codes   城市／機場代碼

城市名／機場（中文）	城市名（英文）	代號
奧克蘭	Auckland	AKL
阿姆斯特丹	Amsterdam	AMS
安哥拉治	Anchorage	ANC
雅典	Athens	ATH
亞庇（沙巴）	Kota Kinabalu	BKI
曼谷	Bangkok	BKK
布里斯本	Brisbane	BNE
波士頓	Boston	BOS
廣州	Guangzhou	CAN
坎培拉	Canberra	CBR
巴黎戴高樂機場	Charles-de-Gaulle	CDG
宿霧	Cebu	CEB
基督城	Christchurch	CHC
芝加哥	Chicago	CHI
濟州島	Jeju	CJU
重慶	Chongqing	CKG
清邁	Chiang Mai	CNX
札幌	Chitose	CTS
成都	Chengdu	CTU
德里	Delhi	DEL

城市名／機場（中文）	城市名（英文）	代號
大連	Dalian	DLC
峇里島	Denpasar	DPS
底特律	Detroit	DTW
杜拜	Dubai	DXB
紐約紐華克機場	Newark Airport	EWR
福州	Fuzhou	FOC
法蘭克福	Frankfurt	FRA
福岡	Fukuoka	FUK
關島	Guam	GUM
河內	Hanoi	HAN
杭州	Hangchow	HGH
東京羽田機場	Haneda	HND
香港	Hong Kong	HKG
普吉島	Phuket	HKT
檀香山	Honolulu	HNL
哈爾濱	Harbin	HRB
銀川河東機場	Hedong Airport	INC
紐約甘迺迪機場	John F. Kennedy Airport	JFK
雅加達	Jakarta	JKT
高雄	Kaohsiung	KHH
大阪關西機場	Kansai	KIX
昆明	Kunming	KMG
熊本	Kumamoto	KMJ
鹿兒島機場	Kagoshima	KOJ

城市名／機場（中文）	城市名（英文）	代號
吉隆坡	Kuala Lumpur	KUL
佬沃	Laoag	LAO
洛杉磯	Los Angeles	LAX
倫敦希斯羅機場	Heathrow Airport	LHR
里斯本	Lisbon	LIS
倫敦	London	LON
馬德里	Madrid	MAD
墨爾本	Melbourne	MEL
澳門	Macau	MFM
米蘭	Milan	MIL
馬尼拉	Manila	MNL
寧波	Ningbo	NGB
名古屋	Nagoya	NGO
長崎	Nagasaki	NGS
南京	Nanking	NKG
南寧	Nanning	NNG
東京成田機場	Narita	NRT
紐約	New York	NYC
琉球	Okinawa	OKA
大阪	Osaka	OSA
巴黎	Paris	PAR
北京	Beijing	PEK
檳城	Penang	PEN
釜山	Pusan	PUS

城市名／機場（中文）	城市名（英文）	代號
浦東國際機場	Pudong	PVG
仰光	Rangoon	RGN
羅馬	Rome	ROM
帛琉	Palau	ROR
西雅圖	Seattle	SEA
首爾	Seoul	SEL
舊金山	San Francisco	SFO
胡志明市	Saigon	SGN
上海	Shanghai	SHA
瀋陽	Shenyang	SHE
新加坡	Singapore	SIN
泗水	Surabaya	SUB
雪梨	Sydney	SYD
三亞	Sanya	SYX
青島	Qingdao	TAO
濟南	Jinan	TNA
台南	Tainan	TNN
台北	Taipei	TPE
桃園國際機場	Taoyuan International Airport	TPE
台北松山機場	Songshan Airport	TSA
天津	Tianjin	TSN
台中	Taichung	TXG
東京	Tokyo	TYO
維也納	Vienna	VIE

城市名／機場（中文）	城市名（英文）	代號
華盛頓	Washington	WAS
溫州	Wenzhou	WNZ
武漢	Wuhan	WUH
無錫	Wuxi	WUX
廈門	Xiamen	XMN
渥太華	Ottawa	YOW
溫哥華	Vancouver	YVR
多倫多	Toronto	YTO
蘇黎世	Zurich	ZRH

❷ Aircraft Types　飛機機型

【波音公司系列】The Boeing company

734　Boeing 737-400

737　Boeing 737 All Series Passenger

738　Boeing 737-800

747　Boeing 747 All Series Passenger（如：744　Boeing 747-400）

757　Boeing 757-200 / Boeing 757-300

767　Boeing 767 All Series

777　Boeing 777-200 / Boeing 777-300

787　Boeing 787-8 / Boeing 787-9 / Boeing 787-10

【空中巴士公司系列】The Airbus company

A310

A320

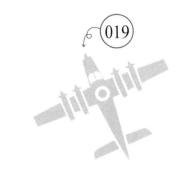

A330（如：333　A330-300）

A340（如：343　A340-300）

A350

A380

【其它公司生產機型】

ATR (Avions de Transport Regional / Aerei da Trasporto Regionale)

ATR 72- 600

Embraer

ERJ – 190

ERJ – 195

McDonnell Douglas

M11　MD-11 All Series

MD 82

MD 83

❸ Carriers Codes　航空公司代碼

航空公司（中文名）	航空公司（英文名）	代碼
美國航空	American Airlines	AA
華信航空	Mandarin Airlines	AE
馬來西亞亞洲航空	Air Asia Berhad	AK
義大利航空	Alitalia	AZ
英國航空	British Airways	BA
長榮航空	EVA Airways	BR
釜山航空	Air Busan	BX

航空公司（中文名）	航空公司（英文名）	代碼
立榮航空	Uni Air	B7
中國民航	Air China	CA
中華航空	China Airlines	CI
國泰航空	Cathay Pacific Airways	CX
中國南方航空	China Southern Airlines	CZ
達美航空	Delta Air Lines	DL
全亞洲航空	AirAsia X	D7
阿酋航空	Emirates Airlines	EK
遠東航空	Far Eastern Air Transport	FE
上海航空	Shanghai Airlines	FM
聯邦快遞	FedEx Corporation	FX
印尼國家航空	Garuda Indonesia	GA
夏威夷航空	Hawaiian Airlines	HA
海南航空	Hainan Airlines	HU
香港航空	HongKong Airlines	HX
日本亞洲航空	AirAsia Japan	JW
日本航空	Japan Airlines	JL
港龍航空	Dragon Airlines	KA
大韓航空	Korean Air	KE
荷蘭航空	KLM Royal Dutch Airlines	KL
廈門航空	Xiamen Airlines	MF
馬來西亞航空	Malaysia Airlines	MH
樂桃航空	Peach Aviation	MM
中國東方航空	China Eastern	MU

航空公司（中文名）	航空公司（英文名）	代碼
全日空航空	All Nippon Airways	NH
澳門航空	Air Macau	NX
西北航空	Northwest Airlines	NW
紐西蘭航空	Air New Zealand	NZ
捷克航空	CSA Czech Airlines	OK
韓亞航空	Asiana Airlines	OZ
菲律賓航空	Philippine Airlines	PR
澳洲航空	Qantas Airways	QF
卡達航空	Qatar Airways	QR
新加坡航空	Singapore Airlines	SQ
瑞士航空	Swissair	SR
泰國航空	Thai Airways	TG
虎航	Tigerair	TR
酷航	Scoot	TZ
聯合航空	United Airlines	UA
俄羅斯洲際航空	Transaero Airlines	UN
全美航空	US Airways	US
越南航空	Vietnam Airlines	VN
深圳航空	Shenzhen Airlines	ZH
捷星亞洲航空	Jetstar Asia	3K
四川航空	Sichuan Airlines	3U
宿霧太平洋航空	Cebu Pacific Air	5J
春秋航空	Spring Airlines	9C

Chapter 2. Purchasing tickets 購票

▶ Outline: 介紹購買機票相關之基礎單字、實用片語及情境對話。另補充機票有關規定及條例。

▶ Learning Goals: 熟記必備單字、片語。瞭解機票相關規定及附加條款。

Ⓐ Basic Vocabulary 基礎必備單字

❶ annual ㊎ ['ænjʊəl] ㊒ ['ænjuəl] 一年一度的；一整年的 (a.)

〈英文釋義〉 occurring or payable every year; happening once a year

• annual income 全年收入

• an annual reunion 一年一度的團聚

• Everyone looks forward to the coming of the annual celebration. 每個人都期待著周年慶的到來。

❷ applicable ㊎ ['æplɪkəbl̩] ㊒ ['æplikəbl] 可用的；合用的

〈英文釋義〉 something that is appropriate or relevant to practice

〈同義字〉 apposite, suitable

• This rule is not applicable to foreigners. 這個規定對外國人不適用。

❸ carrier ㊎ ['kærɪ⋅] ㊒ ['kæriə] 運送人、運送組織、運送工具 (n.)

〈英文釋義〉 person: involves carrying something（e.g. mail, newspaper, disease 郵差、送報生、帶原者）

group: persons or firms in the business of transporting people or goods or messages 交通運輸事業體

artifact: vehicle or ship designed to carry something 車、船、飛機等運輸工具

- aircraft carrier　航空母艦
- Southwest Airlines is the largest domestic carrier in the U.S..　西南航空是美國最大的國內線航空公司。

❹ commencement ㊀ [kə'mɛnsmənt] ㊁ [kə'mensmənt]　開始 (n.)

英文釋義 time of beginning something; the ceremonies or the day for conferring degrees or diplomas

同義字 start; begin

- People celebrate the annual event at the commencement of spring. 人們在春天開始時，慶祝這個年度盛事。

❺ destination ㊀ [ˌdɛstə'neʃən] ㊁ [ˌdesti'neiʃən]　終點站；目的地 (n.)

英文釋義 the place where one is heading for or directed; the predetermined end of a journey

- My destination is San Francisco. I plan to go study there.　我的目的地是舊金山，我計劃去那兒讀書。

❻ dispatch ㊀ [dɪ'spætʃ] ㊁ [di'spætʃ]　派遣；發送；迅速處理 (v. n.)

英文釋義 complete or carry out; to send off something with promptness or speed

- dispatcher　簽派員
- We must get it done with dispatch.　我們要立刻完成這件事。

❼ embody ㊀ [ɪm'bɑdɪ] ㊁ [im'bɔdi]　具體化；包含 (v.)

英文釋義 represent or express something abstract in tangible form; consist of

同義字 objectify; contain

- He successfully embodies the feeling of the hometown in his novel. 他成功地在小說中具體呈現了懷鄉之情。

• This book embodies the works of many young writers.　這本書收錄了許多年輕作家的作品。

❽ endorse ⓚⓚ [ɪn'dɔrs] ⓓⓙ [in'dɔːs]　同意；背書；簽名 (v.)

endorsement (n.)

英文釋義 support something; formal and explicit approval; a signature that endorses something

同義字 sanction; warrant (n.)

• endorse a check　於支票上簽名

• I completely endorse your remarks on this issue.　我完全同意你對這件事的評論。

❾ identification ⓚⓚ [aɪ,dɛntəfə'keʃən] ⓓⓙ [ai,dentifi'keiʃən]　身分證；識別 (n.)

英文釋義 documents represent who you are and current status

• What data may be seen on an ID?　身分證上有哪些資料？

(ID = identification)

❿ incidental ⓚⓚ [,ɪnsə'dɛntl̩] ⓓⓙ [,insi'dentl̩]　附加的；額外的 (a.)

英文釋義 an item or point or condition which is not essential and prime

同義字 additional

• These are incidental conditions to the contract.　這些是契約的附加條款。

⓫ liability ⓚⓚ [,laɪə'bɪlətɪ] ⓓⓙ [,laiə'biliti]　義務 (n.)

英文釋義 something that someone is responsible for

同義字 obligation; a debt

- In Taiwan, performing military service is the liability to all male. 在台灣，服兵役是所有男性的義務。

⑫ negligence 🔴 ['nɛglɪdʒəns] 🔵 ['neglidʒəns] 忽略 (n.)

英文釋義 lacking concern; without paying necessary attention

同義字 ignorance; carelessness

- The accident was caused by the negligence of the driver. 這個意外肇因於駕駛的疏忽。

⑬ obtain 🔴 [əb'ten] 🔵 [əb'tein] 取得；獲得 (v.)

英文釋義 receive something as return for effort

同義字 gain; acquire

- How did you obtain the visa? 你是怎麼取得簽證的？

⑭ overbooked 🔴 [ˌovɚ'bʊkt] 🔵 [ˌəuvə'bʊkt] 超訂的 (a.)

英文釋義 promise to give something more than you have; to issue reservations in excess of the space available

- I am sorry. This flight is overbooked. 很抱歉，這個航班已經超額訂位了。

⑮ omit 🔴 [o'mɪt] 🔵 [əu'mit] 刪去；遺漏；省略 (v.)

英文釋義 to leave out or take out someone or something

同義字 exclude; drop; miss; neglect

- Don't omit his name from the list. 請別從名單上將他的名字刪除。

⑯ proven 🔴 ['pruvn̩] 🔵 ['pru:vən] 被驗證的；被證明的 (a.)

英文釋義 has been proved or tested

同義字 verified

- The validation of this ticket is proven.　這張機票已被驗證有效。

⑰ representative ⓚⓚ [rɛprɪ'zɛntətɪv] ⓓⓙ [repri'zentətiv]　代表 (n.)

英文釋義 person who represents a group or company（e.g. station manager, insurance councilor　航站經理；保險公司專員）

- John is selected as the representative to attend the conference.　約翰被選為參加研討會的代表。

⑱ tariff ⓚⓚ ['tærɪf] ⓓⓙ ['tærif]　關稅 (n.)

英文釋義 a government tax on imports or exports

同義字 duty; tax

- The government plans to lower the tariff on imported goods.　政府計畫降低進口貨物關稅。

⑲ ultimate ⓚⓚ ['ʌltəmɪt] ⓓⓙ ['ʌltimit]　終極的；最高的；最基本的 (a.)

英文釋義 furthest or highest in degree or order; the best or most extreme of its kind; original and fundamental facts of nature

同義字 farthest; utmost; eventual; basic; fundamental

- Captain is the ultimate one who commands the flight.　機長是航班的最高指揮者。

⑳ undertake ⓚⓚ [ˌʌndə'tek] ⓓⓙ [ˌʌndə'teik]　試圖；從事；著手做；同意

英文釋義 accept as a charge attempt; take on, start doing something; agree with something

同義字 attempt; endeavor

- We undertook a trip to the east.　我們到東部旅行。
- The project is undertaken.　這個計劃正在進行中。

B Phrase 片語

❶ comply with　遵守

❷ traveler check　旅行支票

❸ service charge　服務費

❹ on standby　候補中

❺ onward passenger
繼續航程的乘客

❻ peak (tourist) season　旅遊旺季 /
off-peak (light) season　旅遊淡季

❼ be affected by　受……影響

❽ be equivalent to　等同於……

❾ be subject to　受……規範

❿ reference code　訂位代號

⓫ prior to　在……之前

C Dialog 情境對話

S：staff   P：passenger

情境 02-1

P How much is it altogether?

S With the return flight, that comes to $650. Would you like to pay by cash or credit card?

P Credit card, please.

S Please sign your name below. Here is your ticket and receipt.

P Thank you very much.

S It's my honor to serve you. Wish you a delightful trip.

譯文

乘客 一共多少錢？

員工 連同回程機票，一共是六百五十元美金。請問您付現還是刷卡？

乘客 刷卡。

員工 請在下方簽名。這是您的機票和收據。

乘客 謝謝你。

員工 很榮幸爲您服務。祝您旅途愉快。

Ⓓ Ticket Information 　（機票資訊）

Advice to international passengers on Limitation of Liability

國際航線乘客有關運輸責任限制之訊息

- If the passenger's journey involves an ultimate destination or stop in a country other than the country of departure, the Warsaw Convention may be applicable and the Convention governs and in most cases limits the liability of carriers for death or personal injury and in respect of loss of or damage to baggage.

  只要旅客航程之終點或接駁站非出發國，即可適用華沙公約之規定。多數情況下，華沙公約條款對於航空運輸公司有關旅客傷亡、行李遺失損害等相關責任，皆有一定限制規範。

- Additional protection can usually be obtained by purchasing insurance from a private company. Such insurance is not affected by any limitation of the carrier's liability under the Warsaw Convention or such special contracts of carriage. For further information please consult your airline or insurance company representative.

  額外保障通常可經由私人保險公司購得，其保額上限不受華沙公約條款或其他特殊運輸協定約束。更多訊息可洽詢航空公司或保險公司代表。

- This ticket is good for carriage for one year from date of issue, except as otherwise provided in this ticket, in carrier's tariffs, conditions of carriage, or related regulations. The fare for carriage hereunder is subject to change prior to commencement of carriage. Carrier may refuse transportation if the applicable fare has not been paid.

除非因關稅、運輸條件或其他另有規定,機票自開立起,有效期限為一年。於航程開始前,票價保有變動的可能性。若適用票款未被付清,航空公司有權拒載。

- Carrier undertakes to use its best efforts to carry the passenger and baggage with reasonable dispatch. Times shown in timetables or elsewhere are not guaranteed.

  航空公司保證盡最大努力,於合理時間內運送乘客及行李至目的地,但時刻表上載明之航班起訖時間,並非絕對。

- Passenger shall comply with Government travel requirements, present exit, entry and other required documents and arrive at airport by time fixed by carrier or, if no time is fixed, early enough to complete departure procedure.

  乘客必須遵守政府旅遊相關要求,於航空公司規定的時間內至機場辦理手續,並出示入出境之必要證件。若航空公司無明文規定時間,則應盡早抵達機場以完成所有出境手續。

- If you return a wholly unused ticket for refund, you may be assessed a fee for that refund.

  若您申退一張完全未使用的機票,仍可能被收取手續費。

- If you have a ticket which is partially used, there may be little or no refund on the unused portion.

  已經使用機票上的部分航段,若申退未使用的部分,可能退還少許票價,或完全無法退費。

Airline Humor（航空幽默小品）!!

airline abbreviations　航空公司代號—縮寫篇

AA (American Airlines) - Always Another（美國航空—永遠是另一個）

AI (Air India) - Allah Informed（印度航空—阿拉發話了）

TWA (Trans World Air) - Took Wrong Airline; Terrorist Welcome Aboard;

Travel Without Arrival; Teenie Weenie Airlines

（環球航空—搭錯家了、歡迎恐怖份子上機、永不到達、小小小

小…的航空公司）

Chapter 3. Airport service—I 機場服務—I

▶ Outline: 介紹機場劃位櫃台作業相關之基礎單字、實用片語及情境對話。

▶ Learning Goals: 熟記必備單字、片語。能夠流暢進行情境對話及角色扮演。

Ⓐ Basic Vocabulary 基礎必備單字

❶ agent ㏍ ['edʒənt] ㏈ ['eidʒənt] 代理人（商）；仲介人 (n.)

英文釋義 a person who acts on behalf of or does business for another person

- federal agent 聯邦雇員
- secret agent (spy) 間諜
- ground agent 地勤
- travel agent 旅行社代表
- The ground agent has taken care of the check-in procedure. 地勤已經處理好登機手續了。

❷ approach ㏍ [ə'protʃ] ㏈ [ə'prəutʃ] 靠近 (v.)；策略 (n.)

英文釋義 come near; strategy to handle

- instrument approach 儀器進場（儀降）
- They became silent when I approached. 我一走近他們就安靜下來了。
- The best approach to learn a foreign language is to keep practicing. 學外語最好的方法就是不斷練習。

❸ belongings ㏍ [bə'lɔŋɪŋz] ㏈ [bi'lɔŋɪŋz] 所有物；行李 (n.)

英文釋義 something owned by someone

同義字 property; possessions; assets

• I have nothing but personal belongings. 我只有個人物品。

❹ charge ㊎ [tʃɑrdʒ] ㊙ [tʃɑ:dʒ] 收費 (v.)

英文釋義 request for payment

• All transactions have been charged to your account. 所有交易已自您的帳戶扣款。

❺ clerk ㊎ [klɜk] ㊙ [klɑ:k] 雇員；辦事員 (n.)

英文釋義 one who works at a sales or service counter

• bank clerk 銀行行員

• She works as an accounting clerk in a local company. 她在一家當地的公司從事記帳員的工作。

❻ departure ㊎ [dɪ'pɑrtʃə] ㊙ [di'pɑ:tʃə] 出發 (n.)

英文釋義 act of leaving

反義字 arrival

• The approximate date of his departure is next month. 他大概下個月出發。

❼ luggage ㊎ ['lʌgɪdʒ] ㊙ ['lʌgɪdʒ] 行李 (n.)（不可數名詞）

英文釋義 suitcases for a traveler's belongings

同義字 baggage

• a piece of luggage 一件行李；two pieces of luggage 兩件行李

• I have two pieces of hand-carry luggage. 我有兩件手提行李。

❽ option ㊎ ['ɑpʃən] ㊙ ['ɔpʃən] 選項 (n.)

英文釋義 one of a number of things from which you can choose

同義字 selection; choice

- You have to pay them since you have no option.　你除了付他們錢外別無選擇。

⑨ overweight ⓚ ['ovɚ‚wet] ⓓ ['əuvəweit]　超重 (v. n. adj.)

英文釋義 weight over and above what is required or allowed

- overweight luggage　超重行李
- Being overweight has become a serious issue for many kids and adults in several countries.　許多國家皆有成人及孩童體重過重的問題。

⑩ passport ⓚ ['pæs‚port] ⓓ ['pɑːs‚pɔːt]　護照 (n.)

英文釋義 a document issued by a country to a citizen allowing him/her to travel abroad and re-enter the home country

- The passport must be valid for at least six months.　護照效期最少要半年以上。

⑪ scale ⓚ [skel] ⓓ [skeil]　磅秤 (n.)；秤重 (v.)

英文釋義 a system of measurement

- He scales 86 kilograms.　他的體重是86公斤。
- Would you mind putting the baggage on the scale?　您介意將行李放上磅秤嗎？

⑫ suitcase ⓚ ['sut‚kes] ⓓ ['suːtkeis]　行李箱 (n.)

英文釋義 a portable rectangular traveling bag for carrying clothes

- My clothes won't all go into that tiny suitcase.　我的衣服塞不進那個小行李箱裡。

⑬ supervisor ⓚ [‚supɚ'vaɪzɚ] ⓓ [‚sjuːpə'vaizə]　督導；管理者 (n.)

英文釋義 the one who supervises the operation

同義字 director; boss

- We have to submit the reports to the supervisor by 5 PM. today. 今天下午五點前要將報告交給督導。

❹ terminal ㏍ ['tɝmənl̩] ㏒ ['tə:minl] 航站；終點 (n.) 最終的 (a.)

英文釋義 either end of a carrier line having facilities for the handling of freight and passengers

同義字 final; last

- terminal cancer 癌症末期
- computer terminal 電腦終端機
- Passengers are transported by bus to the air terminal. 乘客搭巴士前往航站。

❺ transport ㏍ ['træns,pɔrt] ㏒ ['træns,pɔ:t] 運輸；載運 (v. n.)

英文釋義 move something or somebody around

同義字 convey

- There is no doubt that this city has to improve the public transport system. 毫無疑問地，這城市應該改善大眾交通系統。

⑧ Phrase 片語

❶ baggage claim 行李條
❷ boarding pass 登機證
❸ check-in 劃位
❹ currency exchange 外幣兌換處
❺ flight information board 班機資訊看板
❻ authorized personnel only 閒人勿入
❼ not valid before (after) 在之前／之後無效
❽ free luggage allowance 免費行李限額

❾ ground crew　地勤人員
❿ over the limit　超過規定上限

⓫ passport inspection area
　護照檢查區

Ⓒ Dialog 情境對話

Ⓐ：Agent　Ⓟ：Passenger

情境 Ⅰ　03-1

Ⓐ Next one in line, please.

Ⓟ Hello.

Ⓐ Good morning, sir. May I have your passport and ticket, please?

Ⓟ Sure, here you are.

Ⓐ Do you have any check-in luggage?

Ⓟ Yes, I have one suitcase and a golf bag.

Ⓐ Did you pack your baggage all by yourself?

Ⓟ Yes, I did pack the baggage by myself.

Ⓐ Have you ever left your baggage unattended?

Ⓟ No, I carry them all the time.

Ⓐ I am sorry that I have to make sure again. Has anyone at any time asked you to transport something for them?

P No one has approached me about carrying anything for them.

A Thank you very much. Please place them on the scale one at a time.

P OK.

A Here is your passport, boarding pass and baggage claim receipt. Enjoy your flight.

譯文

地勤 麻煩下一位。

乘客 你好。

地勤 早安。請給我您的機票和護照。

乘客 沒問題,在這裡。

地勤 您有需要託運的行李嗎?

乘客 一只箱子和一個高爾夫球袋。

地勤 這個箱子是您自己打包的嗎?

乘客 行李是我自己打包的。

地勤 您曾經讓行李離開過您的視線範圍嗎?

乘客 沒有,我一直帶著它們。

地勤 很抱歉,我必須再確認一下。有沒有任何人請您代運任何東西呢?

乘客 沒有,沒有任何人請我幫忙帶東西。

地勤 謝謝您。麻煩您將行李一件一件地放上磅秤。

乘客 好的。

地勤 這是您的護照、登機證和行李條。祝您飛行愉快。

情境 II ▶ 🎵03-2

A I'm sorry, sir, but your suitcase is overweight.

P Are you sure? What should I do?

A This is a shopping bag. You can either take out some belongings to carry as hand baggage, or you can pay the overweight baggage fee.

P I think I'd better save some money for the trip.

A That's right. Here is your passport and boarding pass. Your flight will be leaving from Gate 21 at 4:30 PM, and boarding time is 4 PM.

P Great.

A Thank you for choosing China Airlines and have a good flight.

譯文 ▶

地勤 先生很抱歉，您的行李超重了。

乘客 是嗎？那怎麼辦？

地勤 這是一個購物袋，您可以將一些行李放進來手提上機，或者，付行李超重費。

乘客 我想我還是省點錢的好。

地勤 沒錯！這裡是您的登機證和護照。今天的登機門是21號，起飛時間下午四點三十分，四點整開始登機。

乘客 太好了。

地勤 謝謝您選擇中華航空。祝您飛行愉快。

Airline Humor（航空幽默小品）!!

During the final days at Denver's old Stapleton airport, a crowded United flight was canceled. A single agent was re-booking a long line of inconvenienced travelers. Suddenly, an angry passenger pushed his way to the desk. He slapped his ticket down on the counter and said, "I HAVE to be on this flight and it has to be FIRST CLASS!"

The agent replied, "I'm sorry, sir. I'll be happy to try to help you, but I've got to help these folks first, and I'm sure we'll be able to work something out."

The passenger was unimpressed. He asked loudly, so that the passengers behind him could hear: "Do you have any idea who I am?"

Without hesitating, the gate agent smiled and grabbed her public address microphone. "May I have your attention please?" she began, her voice bellowing through the terminal. "We have a passenger here at the gate WHO DOES NOT KNOW WHO HE IS. If anyone can help him find his identity, please come to gate 17."

With the folks behind him laughing in line hysterically, the man glared at the United agent, gritted his teeth and swore "F--- you." Without flinching, she smiled and said, "I'm sorry sir, but you will have to stand in line for that too."

丹佛史特普爾頓舊機場翻新前，一架滿載的聯航班機因故取消了，櫃檯只有一位地勤人員正為了長長一列的旅客重新劃位。此時，一位憤怒的旅客排開眾人直抵櫃檯前，他將機票用力甩在桌面，說：

「我一定要搭上這班飛機，而且是頭等艙的座位。」

地勤回答他：

「很抱歉，這位先生。我很願意協助您，但我必須先處理這些排隊旅客的座位，我確信您的要求不會有問題的。」

乘客並不買帳，他以所有人都聽得見的音量大聲說：

「妳知道我是誰嗎？」

毫不遲疑地，地勤面帶微笑地拿起麥克風做廣播，聲音傳遍了整個航廈大廳：

「請注意，這裡有位乘客不知道自己的身份。如果您可以協助指認，請前來17號登機門。」

身後排隊的乘客全都笑翻了，惱羞成怒的乘客瞪著地勤人員，咬牙切齒地罵出了三字經的國罵。毫不畏縮的地勤人員笑著回答他：

「對不起，這位先生，就算您想那麼做，也得排隊慢慢來。」

Appendix　附　錄

Sample of boarding pass　登機證範本

(1)　(2)　(3)　(4)　(5)

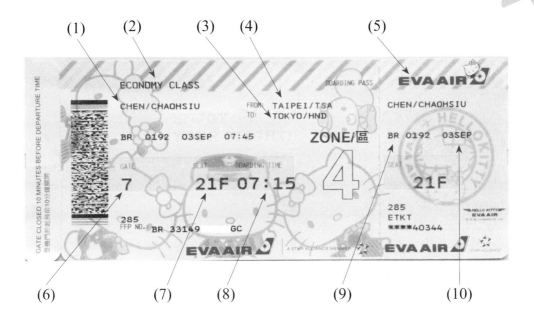

(6)　(7)　(8)　(9)　(10)

(1) passenger name（乘客姓名）

(2) class（艙等）：economy class（經濟艙）

(3) destination（目的地）：Haneda airport（東京羽田機場）

(4) departure city（起飛城市）：SongShan airport（台北松山機場）

(5) airlines（航空公司）：EVA airways（長榮航空）

(6) boarding gate number（登機門號碼）

(7) seat number（座位號碼）

(8) boarding time（登機時間）

(9) flight number（班機號碼）

(10) date（日期）

Chapter 4.　Airport service—II　　機場服務—II

▶ Outline: 介紹機場安檢及候機室等候登機相關之基礎單字、實用片語、情境對話及登機廣播。

▶ Learning Goals: 熟記必備單字、片語。能夠流暢進行情境對話及登機廣播。

Ⓐ Basic Vocabulary　基礎必備單字

❶ aid ⓀⓀ [ed] ⓓⓙ [eid]　幫助；救助 (n.)

英文釋義 the act or result of helping

同義字 help; assistance

- first aid kit　急救箱
- The nurse gave first aid to the wounded.　護士為傷兵急救。

❷ allow ⓀⓀ [ə'laʊ] ⓓⓙ [ə'lau]　允許 (v.)

英文釋義 to let happen or give permission to do something

同義字 permit

- It is not allowed to bring sharp objects onboard an airplane.　不允許攜帶尖銳物品上機。

❸ announcement ⓀⓀ [ə'naʊnsmənt] ⓓⓙ [ə'naunsmənt]　通知；宣告 (n.)

英文釋義 public or formal statement that tells people about something

- make an announcement　進行廣播
- An important announcement will be made in a couple of days.　再過幾天會有重大事情宣布。

❹ attention ⓀⓀ [ə'tɛnʃən] ⓓⓙ [ə'tenʃən]　注意；專心 (n.)

英文釋義 a close or careful observing or listening

- pay attention to something/someone　注意某事 / 某人
- This agenda has caught my attention.　這個議題引起我的注意。

❺ boarding 🄺 ['bordɪŋ] 🄓 ['bɔːdiŋ]　上機（船）；寄宿（膳）(n.)

英文釋義 the act of getting on an airplane or a ship

- The boarding gate is packed with passengers.　登機門邊擠滿了人。

❻ bound 🄺 [baʊnd] 🄓 [baund]　跳躍；跳起；註定 (v.)

英文釋義 a springy jump; be destined to happen

同義字 jump; leap

- Without sufficient practice, this team is bounded to lose.　練習得不夠充分，這個隊伍註定會輸。

❼ convenience 🄺 [kən'vinjəns] 🄓 [kən'viːnjəns]　便利 (n.)

英文釋義 anything being suitable to one's comfort, purposes, or needs

- I would like to schedule a meeting at your convenience.　依您方便的時間，我想預約一次會面。

❽ cooperation 🄺 [ko,ɑpə'reʃən] 🄓 [kəu,ɔpə'reiʃən]　合作 (n.)

英文釋義 people work together to do something; someone being helpful by doing what is wanted or asked

- The success of the project relies on the cooperation among all members.　這個企畫案的成功端賴所有成員的通力合作。

❾ crew 🄺 [kru] 🄓 [kruː]　全體船員（組員）(n.)

英文釋義 a group of people who work together

- Air crew consists of cockpit crew and cabin crew.　空勤組員包括駕駛艙及客艙組員。

❿ dispose 🆉 [dɪ'spoz] 🆉 [di'spəuz]　處置；去除 (v.)

英文釋義 to put something in a proper order; get rid of

• Mom asks me to dispose of garbage.　媽要我去丟垃圾。

⓫ patience 🆉 ['peʃəns] 🆉 ['peiʃəns]　耐性 (n.)

英文釋義 the ability of one's tolerance of delay or incompetence

• You need a lot of patience to work on board.　在機上工作需要充分耐性。

⓬ proceed 🆉 [prə'sid] 🆉 [prə'si:d]　繼續進行；開始著手 (v.)

英文釋義 to go forward or onward, especially after an interruption

同義字 make a start; set in motion

• You should proceed with much caution.　你應該更小心地進行這件事。

⓭ scanner 🆉 ['skænɚ] 🆉 ['skænə]　掃描機 (n.)

英文釋義 a device that is used to see inside something

• Those engineers are working on a new type of scanner.　那些工程師正在開發新的掃描機。

⓮ security 🆉 [sɪ'kjʊrətɪ] 🆉 [si'kju:riti]　安全；安全感；安檢處 (n.)

英文釋義 the state of being protected or safe from danger; the area in a place (e.g. airport) where people go through some inspection (to make sure that nothing illegal or danger is being carried)

• It takes about half an hour to go through the security check in the airport.　通過機場安檢程序大約需要半小時。

B Phrase 片語

❶ carry-on luggage/hand luggage
手提行李

❷ dispose of 丟棄

❸ proceed with 進行

❹ speed up 加速

❺ due to 因為

❻ inform of 通知

❼ pay attention to 注意

ⓒ Dialog 情境對話

Ⓢ：security officer　Ⓟ：passenger

情 境　04-1

Ⓢ Place your carry-on luggage inside the security scanner, please. Your laptop has to be removed from the bag.

Ⓟ Sure, no problem.

Ⓢ Sir, you're only allowed to bring three ounces of liquids, aerosols, or gels. You have to dispose of the water bottle.

Ⓟ Yeah, I know.

Ⓢ Please remove all metal objects and put them inside the tray before walking through the security scanner on the right.

Ⓟ Alright!

譯 文

安檢員 請將您的手提行李放上掃描輸送帶，手提電腦必須拿出來。

乘 客 好的，沒問題。

安檢員 先生，您只能帶3盎司的液體、噴霧或凝膠上機。這個裝水的寶特瓶必須丟掉。

乘　客 喔，我瞭解。

安檢員 請將您身上所有金屬物品拿出來放進托盤內。從右方的安檢掃描機通過。

乘　客 好的。

Ⓓ Boarding announcement 登機廣播

廣 播 🎵 04-2

❶ Good (morning/afternoon/evening), Ladies and gentlemen,

Welcome to _____ Airlines/Airways flight _____ to _____.

In a few minutes we will proceed with boarding process. Passengers with special aid will be boarding first, followed by first class and business class passengers. Economy class passengers please remain seated until your seat numbers have been called. Thank you for the cooperation.

各位貴賓，早安 / 午安 / 晚安：

歡迎搭乘__（航空公司名）__航空__（班機號碼）__號班機前往__（目的地名）__。再過幾分鐘我們將開始登機，有特殊需求的旅客請您優先登機。之後是頭等艙及商務艙的旅客。經濟艙的旅客請您暫時留在座位上，我們會廣播告知您座位的登機順序。謝謝您的合作。

廣 播 🎵 04-3

❷ Ladies and gentlemen,

Attention please, passengers bound for _____ on _____ flight _____ , your flight will be boarding in 15 minutes. In order to speed up boarding, please have your boarding pass ready. Thank you for your cooperation.

各位貴賓：

搭乘__（航空公司名）__（班機號碼）__班機前往__（目的地名）__的旅客請注意，您的班機將於15分鐘後開始登機。為了加速登機作業時間，請準備好您的登機證，謝謝您的合作。

廣播　♪04-4

❸ Ladies and gentlemen,

Due to bad weather conditions, all flights will be delayed departure. We truly feel sorry for the inconvenience, which may cause you. Thank you for the cooperation and patience. We will inform you of the new departure time as soon as possible. Thank you for your attention.

各位貴賓：

因為天候狀況不佳，目前所有航班將延遲起飛，很抱歉造成您的不便。謝謝您的合作與耐心等待。我們會盡速通知您最新的起飛時間，謝謝。

Airline Humor（航空幽默小品）!!

After flights, maintenance crews are required to log the details of the action taken to solve the pilots "squawks." (P = The problem logged by the pilot / S = The solution and action taken by the maintenance engineers

飛行結束後，維修人員必須在維修紀錄表中，針對機師提出的飛機操作時出現的狀況，載明所有執行的動作。以下紀錄，P指機師登錄的問題；S指機務維修人員採取的行動。

P - Left inside main tire almost needs replacement.
S - Almost replaced left inside main tire.
問題：左邊內側的主機輪差不多該換了。
處理：左邊內側的主機輪差不多已經換了。

P - Test flight OK, except auto land very rough.

S - Auto land not installed on this aircraft.

問題：除了自動降落功能操作不順外，試飛沒有問題。

處理：本機並未裝設自動降落功能。

P - Suspected crack in windshield.

S - Suspect you are right.

問題：駕駛艙窗戶玻璃有可疑裂紋。

處理：你的懷疑很可能是正確的。

P - Evidence of a leak on right main landing gear.

S - Evidence removed.

問題：右側主機輪有漏油事證。

處理：漏油事證已被移除。

Chapter 5.   In-flight service—I   機上服務—I

▶ Outline: 介紹乘客上機至飛機起飛前的各種情境會話及對話，並羅列相關基礎單字及實用片語。

▶ Learning Goals: 熟記必備單字、片語。能夠流暢陳述服務應對會話及進行情境對話與角色扮演。

Ⓐ Basic Vocabulary 基礎必備單字

❶ announcement ㏍ [ə'naʊnsmənt] ㄐ [ə'naʊnsmənt] 廣播；宣布 (n.)

英文釋義 a public notification or declaration

- make an announcement = announce   進行廣播
- Attention, please. I have an announcement to make.   請注意，我要宣布一件事。

❷ cockpit ㏍ ['kɑk'pɪt] ㄐ ['kɔkpit] 駕駛艙 (n.)

英文釋義 a space or compartment in a usually small vehicle, from which it is steered, piloted, or driven

- Only aircrew members are allowed to enter the cockpit.   只有空勤組員被允許進入駕駛艙。

❸ compartment ㏍ [kəm'pɑrtmənt] ㄐ [kəm'pɑ:tmənt] 隔間 (n.)

英文釋義 a part or separated room in a space

同義字 partition; division

- Please be careful when you open the overhead compartment.   打開頭頂置物櫃時，請小心。

❹ detector ㏍ [dɪ'tɛktə] ㄐ [di'tektə] 偵測器 (n.)

英文釋義 a device for detecting the presence of electromagnetic waves or of radioactivity

- smoke detector　煙霧偵測器
- A handy detector must be operationally simple and reliable.　好用的偵測器應該容易操作且性能可靠。

❺ embarkation KK ['ɛmbɑr'keʃən] DJ ['embɑ:'keiʃən]　出發；開始 (n.)

英文釋義 to go on board a vehicle for transportation; to make a start

反義字 disembarkation

- Please provide the local lodging information on your embarkation card.　請在入境表上填入當地的住宿資料。

❻ facility KK [fə'sɪlətɪ] DJ [fə'siliti]　設施 (n.)

英文釋義 something that is built to serve a particular purpose

- Most of people are not familiar with cabin facility.　大多數人對客艙設備並不熟悉。

❼ fasten KK ['fæsn̩] DJ ['fæsn]　繫緊；紮牢 (v.)

英文釋義 to make something stay firmly in place

- For your own safety, please fasten seat belt tightly.　爲了您自身的安全，請繫緊安全帶。

❽ hesitate KK ['hɛzə'tet] DJ ['heziteit]　遲疑；躊躇 (v.)

英文釋義 to hold back in doubt or indecision

- Please don’t hesitate to ask me if you need anything.　若您需要任何東西，請不要遲疑，可以告訴我。

❾ instrument KK ['ɪnstrəmənt] DJ ['instrumənt]　儀器；器具 (n.)

英文釋義 a device or tool used for a particular purpose

同義字 device; tool; apparatus

- Language is an essential instrument for communication. 語言是溝通的主要工具。

❿ interference KK ['ɪntə'fɪrəns] DJ [intə'fiərəns] 干擾；阻礙 (n.)

英文釋義 the act of or something that obstructs or hinders others

同義字 blocking; hampering

- I can't hear the radio program well because of too much interference. 因爲太多的頻率干擾，我無法收聽廣播節目。

⓫ jet lag KK [dʒɛt'læg] DJ [dʒɛt'læg] 時差感（病）(n.)

英文釋義 various physical and psychological conditions caused by long hours flight

- I suffer from jet lag after a long haul flight. 長途飛行後，我的時差病很嚴重。

⓬ occupied KK ['ɑkjʊpaɪd] DJ ['ɔkjupaid] 已占用的；使用中的 (a.)

英文釋義 being taken or used

反義字 vacant

- All lavatories are currently occupied. 所有化妝室目前皆有人使用。

⓭ positive KK ['pɑzətɪv] DJ ['pɔzitiv] 確定的；正面的 (n.)

英文釋義 completely sure; involving advantage or good

反義字 negative

- There is positive proof that she stole it. 有確切證據證明她偷了東西。
- He has a positive attitude towards life. 他的生命態度是正向的。
- Please give me a positive answer. 請給我肯定的答案。

⓮ vacant 🅚🅚 ['vekənt] 🅓🅙 ['veikənt]　空的；空白的 (a.)

　英文釋義 not being used or taken

　同義字 unoccupied

　• There are still vacant rooms for rent.　仍有空房待租。

Ⓑ Phrase　片語

❶ life vest (jacket)　救生衣

❷ call button　服務鈴

❸ cabin attendant = flight attendant
空服員（客艙組員）

❹ overhead compartment /cabinet /
bin　頭頂置物櫃

❺ public address system　機上廣播
系統

❻ safety demonstration　安全示範

❼ emergency exit　緊急逃生出口

● Conversation 會話

Cabin attendant (CA)

❶ Greeting passengers　迎賓　🎧05-1

CA: Welcome aboard.

歡迎登機！

May I see your boarding pass?

我可以看一下您的登機證嗎？

May I help you with your carry-on (luggage)?

需要幫您處理手提行李嗎？

May I hang up your coat?

需要幫您掛外套嗎？

Do you have any valuables in your coat?

您的外套裡有貴重物品嗎？

May I stow this suitcase for you? Is there any fragile object inside?

需要幫您放置行李箱嗎？裡頭有甚麼易碎品嗎？

❷ Ground service　地面服務　🎧05-2

CA: Would you like to read a newspaper/magazine?

請問您要看報紙／雜誌嗎？

We have_____, _____, _____ and _____.

機上有　雜誌名　，　雜誌名　，　雜誌名　，和　雜誌名　。

I'm sorry, but another passenger is reading it now. Would you mind if I brought it to you later?

對不起，有其他乘客正在閱讀那本雜誌。您介不介意我待會兒拿過來？

I'm sorry, we don't have _____ on board. Would you care for another magazine instead?

不好意思，機上沒有_____雜誌。您想看另一本嗎？

Here is your hot towel, please be careful.

這是您的熱毛巾，小心燙。

Here is the headset for the in-flight entertainment.

這是機上娛樂服務專用的耳機。

❸ Safety check　安全檢查 ♪05-3

CA: Please place your baggage in the overhead compartment.

請將您的手提行李放在上方的行李廂內。

Please place your baggage under the seat in front of you.

請將您的手提行李放在前方座位下。

Excuse me, sir/ma'am, your baggage may not block the emergency exit/the aisle. Would you please put it in the overhead compartment?

對不起，先生／女士，您的行李擋住了緊急逃生出口／走道，能請您放在上方行李箱裡嗎？

We'll be taking off very soon. Would you please fasten your seat belt tightly/firmly?

我們即將起飛，能否請將您的安全帶繫緊？

I will bring an extension belt for you.

我會拿一條加長型安全帶來。

Excuse me. Please put/return your seat back to the upright position/its original place.

對不起，請將您的椅背豎直／歸位。

For the safety reason, please turn off your cellular phone or switch it to the airplane mode.

為了安全理由，請將您的手機關機，或調整至飛航模式。

Please turn off your cellular phone to avoid causing interference with the cockpit instruments.

請將您的手機關機，以避免對駕駛艙儀器造成干擾。

Ⓓ Dialog 情境對話

Ⓒ：Cabin attendant　Ⓟ：Passenger

情境 ▷ 🎵05-4

Ⓒ Do you know where your seat is?

Ⓟ No. Can you help me?

Ⓒ Certainly. Your seat number is 40K. It's a window seat in the rear section of the cabin. Please go straight and turn right.

Ⓟ I see. Thank you.

Ⓒ You're welcome. Please do not hesitate to ask for help.

譯文 ▷

空服員 您知道座位在哪裡嗎？

乘客 不知道，可以幫我忙嗎？

空服員 當然可以。您的座位號碼是40K，靠窗，在客艙的後段，請您直走右轉。

乘客 我知道了，謝謝您。

空服員 不客氣，有甚麼需要協助的地方請盡管說。

Airline Humor（航空幽默小品）!!

Occasionally, airline attendants make an effort to make the "in-flight safety lecture" a bit more entertaining. Here are some real examples that have been heard or reported:

"There may be 50 ways to leave your lover, but there are only 4 ways out of this airplane..."

"Your seat cushions can be used for floatation, and in the event of an emergency water landing, please take them with our compliments."

"We do feature a smoking section on this flight; if you must smoke, contact a member of the cabin crew and we will escort you to the wing of the airplane."

"Smoking in the lavatories is prohibited. Any person caught smoking in the lavatories will be asked to leave the plane immediately."

空服員偶爾會努力為機上的安全示範，增加一些娛樂效果。以下就是幾個實例：

「離開愛人的方法也許高達50種，但離開飛機的方法一共只有四種……」

「在水上迫降的緊急狀況發生時，您的座墊可以當作浮板使用。萬一出事時，座墊就當作航空公司的免費贈品囉！」

「飛機上確實是有吸菸區的。如果你想抽菸，請告知空服人員，會有人護送你到機翼上抽菸的。」

「機上的化妝室內絕對禁菸。如果有人被發現在廁所內吸菸，他必須立刻離開飛機機艙。」

Chapter 6.　　In-flight service—II　　機上服務—II

▶ Outline: 介紹乘客機上服務的各種情境會話及對話，並羅列相關基礎
單字及實用片語。

▶ Learning Goals: 熟記必備單字、片語。能夠流暢陳述服務應對會話
及進行情境對話與角色扮演。

Ⓐ Basic Vocabulary　基礎必備單字

❶ altitude ㎉ ['æltə'tjud] ㏈ ['ælti'tju:d]　高度 (n.)

英文釋義 the vertical elevation of an object above a surface

• The aircraft has reached its cruising altitude of about 37,000 feet.
飛機飛抵三萬七千英呎的巡航高度。

❷ aperitif ㎉ [ɑperi'tif] ㏈ [ɑperi'ti:f]　開胃酒；餐前酒 (n.)

英文釋義 alcoholic beverage, usually a cocktail, that is specifically served
before a meal

• Would you like an aperitif before your meal?　餐前想喝杯開胃酒嗎？

❸ appetizer ㎉ ['æpə'taɪzə] ㏈ ['æpitaizə]　開胃菜 (n.)

英文釋義 a small portion of food served before a main course to stimulate
the appetite

同義字 hors d'oeuvre; starter

• Would you like to order an appetizer?　您想點份開胃菜嗎？

❹ attitude ㎉ ['ætətjud] ㏈ ['ætitju:d]　態度 (n.)

英文釋義 a feeling or emotion toward a fact or state

• service attitude　服務態度

• positive attitude v.s. negative attitude　正向態度 v.s. 負面態度

- His irresponsible attitude drives everyone crazy. 他不負責任的態度把每個人氣瘋了。

❺ beverage 🔤 ['bɛvərɪdʒ] 🔤 ['bevəridʒ] 飲料 (n.)

英文釋義 drink (other than water)

- Beverage is not allowed on an MRT. 捷運上不能喝飲料。

❻ captain 🔤 ['kæptɪn] 🔤 ['kæptin] 機長 (n.)

英文釋義 a senior pilot who commands the crew of an airplane

- PIC: pilot in command 航班中，職級最高的機長
- The captain makes the announcement to greet passengers on board. 機長廣播歡迎乘客搭機。

❼ co-pilot 🔤 [ko'paɪlət] 🔤 [ko'pailət] 副機師 (n.)

英文釋義 a pilot who is second in command of an aircraft

同義字 first officer

- leader ←→ co-leader 領導 ←→ 副領導
- The co-pilot was at the controls when the plane landed. 降落時是由副駕駛操控飛機的。

❽ deport 🔤 [dɪ'port] 🔤 [di'pɔ:t] 遣返 (v.)

英文釋義 to send out of the country by legal

- deportee 遭遣返的人
- Those people were deported for entering the country illegally. 那些人因為非法入境遭到遣返。

❾ disembark 🔤 ['dɪsɪm'bɑrk] 🔤 ['disim'bɑ:k] 下機；下船；下車 (v.)
disembarkation (n.)

英文釋義 to leave a vehicle, airplane or ship

同義字 deplane

- All passengers please disembark from the No. 2 door on the left.　所有乘客請從左邊二號門下機。

⑩ entrée 🅺🅺 ['ɑntre]　（法文）主餐 (n.)

英文釋義 a dish served as the main course of a meal

同義字 main dish

- What would you like for tonight's entrée?　您今晚想吃甚麼主餐？

⑪ original 🅺🅺 [ə'rɪdʒən̩l] 🅳🅹 [ə'ridʒən̩l]　最初的；原始的 (a.)

英文釋義 the earliest form of something; something is viewed as different and unique

同義字 primary; initial

- The original price of the house was way too high.　這屋子的原價實在太高了。
- She is an original artist.　她是個具原創性的藝術家。

⑫ purchase 🅺🅺 ['pɝtʃəs] 🅳🅹 ['pə:tʃəs]　購買 (v. n.)

英文釋義 to buy a product or service

- make a purchase　購買
- They consider to purchase a house in the suburbs after retirement.　他們考慮退休後在郊區買棟房子。

⑬ purser 🅺🅺 ['pɝsə] 🅳🅹 ['pə:sə]　事務長 (n.)

英文釋義 a senior cabin attendant who commands the cabin crew

- chief purser = cabin chief　事務長；座艙長
- deputy purser　副事務長

- The chief purser is always ready to help passengers during a flight.

飛行中，座艙長總是隨時準備好提供乘客協助。

❶❹ recline ⓚⓚ [rɪ'klaɪn] ⓓⓙ [ri'klain]　傾斜；放倒 (v.)

英文釋義 to lean or incline backwards

- You may recline the seat back to take a break.　您可以斜放椅背稍做休息。

❶❺ recommend ⓚⓚ [rɛkə'mɛnd] ⓓⓙ ['rekə'mend]　推薦；介紹 (v.)

英文釋義 to advice or suggest a choice to others

- propose a recommendation　提出建議

- I recommend that we have lunch in the China town.　我建議我們到中國城吃午餐。

❶❻ seniority ⓚⓚ [sin'jɔrətɪ] ⓓⓙ ['si:ni'ɔ:rəti]　年資 (n.)

英文釋義 a privileged status attained by length of continuous service

- There is a debate regarding whether promotion should be through merit or seniority.　晉升該依功績或年資仍在討論中。

❶❼ upright ⓚⓚ ['ʌp,raɪt] ⓓⓙ [ʌp'rait]　垂直的（地）；直立；豎直 (a. adv. v. n.)

英文釋義 a vertical position or direction; something raised upward

- Please upright your seatback to its original position.　請將您的椅背豎直回原位。

071

B Phrase 片語

❶ head set 耳機

❷ wall mounted bassinet

嵌入式搖籃

❸ duty free sales 免稅品販賣

❹ call button 服務鈴

❺ air show 飛航訊息

❻ international Date Line

國際換日線

❼ on the rocks 加冰塊（飲料）

❽ ahead of 提早

❾ time difference 時差

© Conversation 會話

❶ Aperitif/Meal service 餐飲服務 🔊06-1

CA: Here is your menu and wine list, sir/ma'am. I will be back to take your order later.

先生 / 女士，這是您的菜單和酒單。等會兒我再回來替您點餐。

Would you care for/like an aperitif before dinner/lunch?

晚餐 / 午餐前，您想喝些餐前酒嗎？

Can I get you something to drink?

您想喝些甚麼嗎？

I am sorry to keep you waiting. Here is your whisky/brandy on the rocks.

對不起讓您久等了。這是您的威士忌 / 白蘭地加冰塊。

What would you like for tonight's dinner?

今天晚餐您想吃甚麼？

I am sorry. I am afraid that we are out of _____. Would you care for _____ instead?

對不起，已經沒有_____了。您願不願意換成_____？

We have breakfast in Chinese style and Western style.

我們有中式和西式的早餐。

Excuse me, sir. Have you finished with this? May I take this plate away?

對不起，請問您用完了嗎？我可以收回餐盤了嗎？

❷ D/F Sales 免稅品販售 🔊06-2

CA: Would you like to purchase any duty-free items?

您想買免稅品嗎？

The in-flight magazine shows the selections we have.

機上雜誌有我們的選項。

How would you like to pay? Cash or credit card, sir/ma'am?

先生 / 小姐，您想怎麼付款？付現或信用卡？

It comes to_____dollars altogether.

總共_____元。

❸ **Flight Information　航班資訊**　🎵06-3

CA: Our scheduled flight time today is _____ hours and _____

minutes.

我們表訂的飛行時間是_____小時_____分鐘。

We expect to arrive at　城市名　on time.

我們預定準時抵達　城市名　。

We are a little ahead of/behind schedule.

我們比表訂時間提早一些 / 延後一些。

Because we cross the International Date Line,　目的地　is one day

behind/ahead of　出發地　.

因為我們跨越國際換日線，　目的地　比　出發地　晚一天 / 早一

天。

The time difference between _____ and _____ is _____

hours.

　目的地　和　出發地　的時差是　數字　小時。

We are flying over　地名　now. You should be able to see　景觀

out of the window on your right/left.

我們正飛過 地名 的上空，您可以從右/左邊的窗外看見 景觀 。

You might like to know that there is an air-show program on channel 頻道號碼 . We have all flying information on it.

您可以在第 號碼 頻道收看飛航資訊節目，上面會顯示所有與本航班有關的飛行資料。

❹ Safety check/Landing　安全檢查 / 著陸　♪06-4

CA:　Please upright your seat back and return the seat table to the original position.

請將您的椅背豎直，桌子收好。

Open the window shade, please.

請將遮陽板打開。

Please keep your seat belt fastened until the aircraft has come to a complete stop.

在飛機尚未完全停妥前，請保持繫緊安全帶。

❺ Disembarkation　下機　♪06-5

CA:　Thank you. We hope that you have enjoyed the flight with us.

謝謝，希望您滿意今天的服務。

Have a pleasant stay in 目的地 .

希望您在 目的地 玩得愉快。

Thank you for flying 航空公司 .

謝謝您選擇 航空公司 。

Hope to see you soon/again.

希望很快能再次為您服務。

D Dialog 情境對話

C ：Cabin attendant　P ：Passenger

情境 I　　🎵06-6

C Excuse me, sir. Would you like some beverage to drink?

P I'd like to have some juice with ice.

C We have apple, orange and tomato juices. Which one would you like?

P Orange juice, please.

C Sure. Here you are.

譯文

空服員 不好意思，先生，請問您要喝點甚麼飲料嗎？

乘　客 麻煩果汁加冰塊。

空服員 我們有蘋果汁、柳橙汁和番茄汁，請問您要哪一種？

乘　客 我要柳橙汁。

空服員 好的，這是您的柳橙汁。

情境 II　06-7

C Hello ma'am. Today we have beef with noodle and chicken with rice for the entrée. Which one would you prefer?

P What would you recommend?

C Both main dishes are delicious. Personally I prefer noodle to rice. So I'd go with beef.

P Good. I'll have beef then.

C Certainly. Here is your beef. Would you like to have some drink with your meal?

P Red wine, please.

譯文

空服員 小姐您好。今天的主餐選擇是牛肉配麵和雞肉配飯,請問您要吃哪一種?

乘　客 你推薦哪一種呢?

空服員 兩種主餐都很可口,不過我個人喜歡吃麵,所以我會選牛肉。

乘　客　那我就吃牛肉吧。

空服員　好的，這是您的牛肉。要不要喝點甚麼呢？

乘　客　麻煩給我紅酒。

Airline Humor（航空幽默小品）‼

On a Continental Flight with a very "senior" flight attendant crew, the pilot said, "Ladies and gentlemen, we've reached cruising altitude and will be turning down the cabin lights. This is for your comfort and to enhance the appearance of your flight attendants."

在大陸航空的一架班機上，有一位非常「資深」的空服員，機長於是廣播說道：各位貴賓，我們已經飛抵巡航高度，現在我們將調暗客艙的燈光。如此一是爲了您的舒適，二是爲了讓空服員看起來更美些。

Chapter 7.　C. I. Q.　　　　　　機場通關

▶ Outline: 介紹乘客下機後，於機場通過移民、海關、檢疫等各種入境檢查的情境，羅列相關單字、片語及對話。

▶ Learning Goals: 熟記必備單字、片語。能夠流暢進行情境對話與角色扮演。

Ⓐ Basic Vocabulary　基礎必備單字

❶ approximate ㏍ [ə'prɑksəmɪt] ㏈ [ə'prɔksimit]　大概的；約略的；粗估 (a. v.)

英文釋義 not completely accurate but very close estimation

同義字 estimated; near

- We approximated the distance at 100 miles.　我們粗估距離大約是100英哩。

❷ carrousel (carousel) ㏍ [ˌkærʊ'zɛl] ㏈ [ˌkæru'zel]　旋轉木馬；行李轉盤 (n.)

英文釋義 a conveyer belt for air travelers to claim their check-in baggage

同義字 merry-go-round　旋轉木馬；baggage claim　行李提領處

- It always takes a long time to wait the luggage coming on the carrousel.　每次等行李輸送帶上的託運行李，都得等好久。

❸ compensation ㏍ [ˌkɑmpən'seʃən] ㏈ [ˌkɔmpen'seiʃən]　賠償（金）；彌補 (n.)

英文釋義 something (payment) that is done or offered to make up for damage, trouble, loss, and so on.

- compensation for damage　損害賠償

• According to the contract, you may receive USD. 200 as the compensation.　根據合約，您可以獲得200美元的賠償金。

❹ conference ⓀⓀ [ˈkɑnfərəns] ⒹⒿ [ˈkɔnfərəns]　研討會；會議 (n.)

英文釋義 a large meeting gathering people who are interested in a particular subject to exchange and discuss ideas, usually lasting a few days; meeting of representatives of organization

• academic conference　學術研討會

• I plan to attend the conference in Singapore next year.　我計畫參加明年在新加坡的研討會。

❺ Customs ⓀⓀ [ˈkʌstəmz] ⒹⒿ [ˈkʌstəmz]　海關 (n.)

英文釋義 the official department, located at a port, airport or frontier, that administers and collects the duties on imported goods, also check travelers and baggage.

• You have to pass through the Customs after retrieving your check-in luggage.　領到託運行李後，你必須通過海關檢查。

❻ declaration ⓀⓀ [ˌdɛkləˈreʃən] ⒹⒿ [ˌdɛkləˈreiʃən]　申報；聲明；宣告 (n.)

英文釋義 the act of declaring something; make an official announcement

同義字 statement

• the Declaration of Independence　宣告獨立

• All arriving passengers have to fill out a Customs declaration.　所有入境旅客都要填寫海關申報單。

❼ Immigration ⓀⓀ [ˌɪməˈgreʃən] ⒹⒿ [ˌimiˈgreiʃən]　入出境移民署 (n.)

英文釋義 the place at an airport (and sea port) where officials check the travel documents of everyone who enters the country

- The Immigration officers will check passengers' travel documents.
機場移民署官員會檢查乘客的旅行證件。

❽ intend 🄚🄚 [ɪn'tɛnd] 🄳🄹 [in'tend]　意欲；打算 (v.)

英文釋義 plan to so something; have something in mind

同義字 mean; plan

- I intend to go home.　我打算回家。
- Are you intended?　你是故意的嗎？
- He intends no harm.　他沒有惡意。

❾ liquor 🄚🄚 ['lɪkɚ] 🄳🄹 ['likə]　含酒精飲料（烈酒）(n.)

英文釋義 alcoholic beverage made by distillation

同義字 spirit

- He was liquored up in the reunion party.　他在同學會上被灌醉了。

❿ prohibit 🄚🄚 [prə'hɪbɪt] 🄳🄹 [prə'hibit]　禁止（依法規定）(v.)

英文釋義 to prevent someone from doing something

同義字 prevent; forbid

- Smoking is prohibited indoors.　室內禁止吸菸。

⓫ Quarantine 🄚🄚 ['kwɔrən'tin] 🄳🄹 ['kwɔrənti:n]　檢疫；隔離 (n.)

英文釋義 official inspections in airports, sea ports or designated places for preventing the spread of contagious diseases or harmful insects from entering into a country

- The Quarantine dogs are on patrol in the baggage claim area.　檢疫犬在行李轉盤附近巡邏。

⓬ surname 🄚🄚 ['sɝ͵nem] 🄳🄹 ['sə:neim]　姓氏 (n.)

英文釋義 a name shared in common to identify that a group of people are members of a family

同義字 family name; last name

- They assumed that I was German from my surname.　他們從我的姓氏推斷我是德國人。

⓭ timepiece KK ['taɪmˌpis] DJ ['taimpi:s]　計時器；鐘；錶 (n.)

英文釋義 an instrument to measure or show the progress of time

- The pricy timepiece has to be declared in Customs.　高價的計時器須在海關處申報。

⓮ vaccination KK [ˌvæksn̩'eʃən] DJ [ˌvæksi'neiʃən]　接種；疫苗 (n.)

英文釋義 a substance usually injected into people or animals to protect against a particular disease

- You'd better perform vaccinations before leaving for the Africa.　你最好在前往非洲前，完成疫苗的接種。

Ⓑ Phrase 片語

❶ baggage claim　行李提領處

❷ baggage inspection　行李檢查

❸ on a visit/vacation　訪友探親行程／渡假行程

❹ business trip　商務旅行

❺ toilet article　梳妝用品——perfume 香水、comb 梳子、cosmetics 化妝品、shaver 刮鬍用品，etc.

❻ personal effect = personal article　個人用品

❼ hazardous material/ dangerous goods　危險品

❽ prohibited item　違禁品

❾ Quarantine bins　檢疫箱

❿ date issued　核發日

⓫ time off　休假

⓬ C. I. Q. = Customs, Immigration, Quarantine　機場通關縮寫

⓭ E/D Card = Embarkation / Disembarkation card　入境表格

⓮ Customs Declaration Form　海關申報單

ⓒ Dialog 情境對話

O ：officer P ：passenger

情境 I   07-1

O May I see your passport please.

P Yes, here you are.

O What's the purpose of your visit?

P I am here on a vacation.

O How long do you plan to stay?

P About 10 days.

O Where are you going to stay during your trip?

P The local hotels.

O Are you traveling alone?

P Yes.

O Do you have any relatives living here?

P No.

O Do you intend to work or study here?

P No. I just want to enjoy my time off and have a stress-free trip.

O Thank you. Wish you a good time.

譯　文

移民局官員	請出示護照。
乘　客	在這裡。
移民局官員	您此次的旅行目的是？
乘　客	渡假。
移民局官員	預計待幾天呢？
乘　客	10天左右。
移民局官員	旅行期間的住所是？
乘　客	當地飯店。
移民局官員	一個人旅行嗎？
乘　客	是的。
移民局官員	有沒有親戚住這裡？
乘　客	沒有？
移民局官員	你打算留在這裡工作或念書嗎？
乘　客	不，我只想好好地享受我的假期。
移民局官員	謝謝你，祝你旅途愉快。

情境 II 07-2

O Please put your baggage through baggage inspection.

P Ok.

O Do you have any prohibited items?

P No.

O What is inside your baggage?

P Most items are for personal use.

O Please open your baggage. What are these?

P These are gifts for friends.

O Do you bring any spirits, tobacco or fruits, plants?

P Yes, I have got a bottle of whiskey and a carton of cigarettes. I bought them on board. Do I have to pay tax on them?

O No, it's below the limit.

譯 文

海關人員	請將行李放上檢查檯。
乘 客	好的。
海關人員	有沒有帶任何違禁品？
乘 客	沒有。
海關人員	箱子裡裝得是甚麼東西？
乘 客	大多是個人用品。
海關人員	麻煩打開行李箱。這些是甚麼呢？
乘 客	是帶給朋友的禮物。
海關人員	你是否攜帶菸酒、水果或植物？
乘 客	是的。我帶了一瓶威士忌和一條菸，是機上買的。要付稅嗎？
海關人員	不用，並沒有超過額度。

S ：staff P ：passenger

情境Ⅲ 07-3

P Excuse me. I'm reporting a missing suitcase.

S May I see your baggage claim tag, please?

P Yes, here you are.

S Can you roughly describe the suitcase?

P It's a medium-sized black suitcase with wheels.

S Sorry ma'am. Your suitcase seems to have been misplaced.

P Oh no! I have got something important in it!

S I am terribly sorry. I promise that we'll do our best to get it back to you as soon as possible. Would you please fill out this claim form? When we find your suitcase, we'll contact you immediately and deliver it to your hotel.

P What if you can't find it?

S The airline will pay you a compensation fee.

P I see. Please send it to my hotel once you find it.

譯 文

乘客 不好意思，我要申報一只遺失的行李箱。

地勤 能不能出示一下您的行李條？

乘客 好的，在這裡。

地勤 可以大致描述一下您行李的樣子嗎？

乘客 是一只黑色的中型行李箱，有輪子的。

地勤 很抱歉，小姐。您的行李應該是被誤送到其他地方了。

乘客 啊！我裡頭有很重要的東西耶。

地勤 真的很抱歉。我們一定盡全力盡快地將行李送回給您。麻煩您填一下行李遺失單。找到行李後會立刻聯絡您，將它送到飯店。

乘客 那萬一找不到呢？

地勤 航空公司會給付您賠償金的。

乘客 我知道了。一找到行李，請馬上送到旅館給我。

Airline Humor（航空幽默小品）!!

Should the cabin lose pressure, oxygen masks will drop from the overhead area. Stop screaming, grab the mask, and pull it over your face before assisting children or adults acting like children. If you have a small child traveling with you, secure your mask before assisting with theirs. If you are traveling with two small children, decide now which one you love more.

當客艙失壓時，氧氣面罩會從頭頂自動落下。停止尖叫、拉下面罩、戴上面罩然後協助孩童，或者行為舉止與孩童無異的成人。如果你有幼童隨行，先將自己的面罩戴好後再幫他們戴上。如果你

有兩名同行的孩子，現在就決定，你比較愛哪一個。

Passengers waiting for a flight began to get anxious when the airplane hadn't arrived half an hour after it was scheduled to depart. The harried agent finally told us that our plane had been diverted and that arrangements had been made for us to travel with a rival airline. By the time we sprinted to the other side of the terminal, frustration levels were high. Finally we were airborne, and drinks were served. A passenger complained that the other airline served complimentary peanuts. A flight attendant lightened the mood considerably when she quipped, "With them you get peanuts. With us you get transportation!"

乘客們在表訂起飛時間的半小時後，仍在等待尚未降落的飛機，因此越發急躁。受夠乘客抱怨的地勤人員最後告訴我們，飛機已經轉降其它機場，所有乘客將被轉至「友航」的航班。等我們氣急敗壞地衝到航廈的另一側搭機時，所有不滿情緒已經飽和。終於飛機起飛了，開始飲料的服務。某位乘客開始抱怨，另一家航空公司有免費的花生可以配飲料。一名空服員聽見後，得意洋洋地嘲諷這位乘客說道：

「跟著他們你可以有花生吃，可是跟著我們有飛機搭！」

Appendix　附　錄

⊸ References for Duty Free Allowance　各國免稅品參考限額

❶ Taiwan　台灣

Duty free rules and regulations are subject to change without notice.
免稅品規定及條例可能未經事前告知即更動。

- A reasonable quantity of perfume for your own use in relation to the length of your visit.　就您停留時間的長短為依據，合理份量的香水。

- Allowances for those over the age of 20: Presents, gifts and personal belongings up to but not exceeding TWD 20,000 (New Taiwan Dollar or NT$)　20歲以上旅客的限額：新台幣兩萬元以下的禮物及個人用品。

- Allowances for those under the age of 20: Presents, gifts and personal belongings up to but not exceeding TWD 10,000 (New Taiwan Dollar or NT$)　20歲以下旅客的限額：新台幣一萬元以下的禮物及個人用品。

- 200 Cigarettes OR 25 Cigars OR 454 gms of rolling tobacco. (only for air travelers who are 20 years of age or older)　200根香菸、25支雪茄、454克菸草，僅限20歲以上的搭機旅客。

- 1 bottle, not exceeding 1 liter, of alcohol (only for air travelers who are 20 years of age or older)　不超過一公升的一瓶酒精性飲料，僅限20歲以上的搭機旅客。

❷ U.S.　美國

The following goods may be imported by visitors over 21 years of age.
以下免稅限額對象為21歲以上造訪美國的旅客：

- 200 cigarettes or 100 cigars.　200支菸或100支雪茄。
- 1L of alcoholic beverage.　1公升酒精飲料。
- Goods up to a value of US$800 (returning residents who have been out of the country for at least 48 hours; this limit is applicable once every 30 days and is reduced to US$200 for travelers who have already used the allowance or have been out of the USA for less than 48 hours).
  美金800元以下的物品。唯此金額係指返國旅客若離境時間超過48小時可適用。若離境時間不足48小時，或30天內離境超過一次的旅客，則限額降至美金200元。
- Goods up to a value of US$100 (non-residents visiting the USA for at least 72 hours). Travelers arriving from certain Caribbean and Latin American countries may import up to 2L of alcoholic beverages, as long as at least 1L was produced in one of the applicable countries.
  非美國籍旅客，入境時間超過72小時者，可攜帶美金100元以下的物品。此外，自特定加勒比海或拉丁區國家入境的旅客，可攜帶2公升的酒精飲料，但其中1公升飲料必須是這些特定國家所製造的。
- US residents returning from a US insular possession (American Samoa, Guam or US Virgin Islands) have a duty-free allowance of US$1,600, including up to 1,000 cigarettes (at least 800 of which must have been bought in the insular possession) and 5L of alcoholic beverages, one of which must be a product of the insular possession.
  隸屬美國的島嶼居民，如薩摩亞、關島、維爾京群島，可攜帶達美金一千六百元的免稅品，包括1000支菸，其中半數需購自以上幾個島國；5公升酒精飲料，其中一瓶需為以上島國所製造。

❸ European Union　歐盟

An air traveler arriving in the EU from a non EU country could import:
所有自非歐盟國家入境歐盟各國時，可攜帶的免稅品限額為：

- 200 cigarettes or 100 cigarillos or 50 cigars or 250 grams of tobacco
  200支菸、或100支小雪茄菸、或50支雪茄、或250克菸草。

- 1 litre of spirits, 4 litres of wine, 16 litres of beer　一公升烈酒、四公升葡萄酒、16公升啤酒。

- €430 of other goods (toys, perfume, electronic devices, etc.).　價值達430歐元的物品，包括玩具、香水、電子產品等等。

- Taxes and customs duties will be applied on the value of goods exceeding those limits. However, the value of an individual item may not be split up.　超出額度的物品會被課稅，單一項物品的價格不可分開計算。

❹ Japan　日本

The following goods may be imported into Japan by travelers 20 years of age and older:　以下限額為20歲以上入境日本旅客：

- 400 cigarettes or 100 cigars or 500g of tobacco or 500g of a combination of these.　400支菸、100支雪茄、500克菸草或總計不超過500克的各類菸品。

- 3 bottles (approximately 750ml each) of alcohol.　三瓶酒精飲料，每瓶約750毫升。

- 60ml of perfume.　60毫升香水。

- Other goods up to the value of ¥200,000.　其他物品總價達20萬日幣。

❺ China　中國大陸

- 400 cigarettes or 100 cigars or 500g of tobacco.　400支菸、100支雪茄或500克菸草。

- 1.5L of alcoholic beverages with 12% or more alcoholic content. 酒精濃度超過12%的飲料1.5公升。

- Personal articles up to a value of ¥5,000 for Chinese residents. 中國大陸國民之個人物品，價值低於人民幣5000元。

- Personal articles which will be left in China up to a value of ¥2,000 for non-residents. 非中國大陸國民之旅客，其個人物品，若爲停留時間所使用/不再攜帶出境者，價值應低於人民幣2000元。

❻ Thailand 泰國

- 200 cigarettes or 250g of cigars or tobacco. 200支菸或250克雪茄、菸草。

- 1L of alcohol. 1公升酒精飲料。

- Goods to the value of ฿10,000. 其他物品總價達1萬泰銖。

❼ Malaysia 馬來西亞

- 200 cigarettes or 225g of tobacco. 200支菸或250克菸草。

- 1L of alcohol. 1公升酒精飲料。

- Food up to the value of RM75. 不超過75元馬幣的食物。

- 3 pieces of new clothing and 1 new pair of shoes. 三件新衣、一雙新鞋。

- 1 portable electronic item for personal care. 一件個人用電子產品。

- Other goods up to the value of RM400. To be eligible for these duty-free allowances, residents must have been out of the country for at least 72 hours and non-residents must plan to visit Malaysia for at least 72 hours. 其他物品總價400元馬幣以下。以上免稅規定適用於離境至少72小時的馬來西亞公民，或入境停留超過72小時的外籍旅客。

❽ Australia　澳洲

The following items may be imported into Australia by travelers over 18 years of age:　以下規定適用於18歲以上入境澳洲的旅客：

- 50 cigarettes or 50g of tobacco or cigars.　50支菸或50克雪茄、菸草。
- 2.25L of alcoholic drinks.　2.25公升酒精飲料。
- Articles for personal hygiene and clothing, not including perfume or fur apparel.　個人衛生用品或衣物，但不包括香水及皮革衣物。
- Other goods to a value of A$900 (A$450 if under 18).　其他物品價值900元澳幣以下。若18歲以下旅客則為450元澳幣限額。

❾ New Zealand　紐西蘭

The following items may be imported into New Zealand by persons of 17 years of age and over:　以下規定項目為17歲以上入境紐西蘭之旅客：

- 200 cigarettes or 50 cigars or 250g tobacco or a mixture of all three weighing no more than 250g.　200支菸或50克雪茄或250克菸草，或三種菸品總數不超過250克。
- 4.5L of wine or beer.　4.5公升葡萄酒或啤酒。
- 3 bottles of 1.125L of spirits or liqueurs.　三瓶1.125公升烈酒或甜酒。
- Other goods to the value of NZ$700.　其他物品不超過700元紐幣。

E/D Cards and Customs Forms 入境表格及海關申報單

❶ the U.S. E/D Card 美國入境表

DEPARTMENT OF HOMELAND SECURITY
U.S. Customs and Border Protection

OMB No. 1651-0111

Welcome to the United States
I-94 Arrival/Departure Record
Instructions

This form must be completed by all persons except U.S. Citizens, returning resident aliens, aliens with immigrant visas, and Canadian Citizens visiting or in transit.

Type or print legibly with pen in ALL CAPITAL LETTERS. Use English. Do not write on the back of this form.

This form is in two parts. Please complete both the Arrival Record (Items 1 through 17) and the Departure Record (Items 18 through 21).

When all items are completed, present this form to the CBP Officer.

Item 9 - If you are entering the United States by land, enter LAND in this space. If you are entering the United States by ship, enter SEA in this space.

5 U.S.C. § 552a(e)(3) Privacy Act Notice: Information collected on this form is required by Title 8 of the U.S. Code, including the INA (8 U.S.C. 1103, 1187), and 8 CFR 235.1, 264, and 1235.1. The purposes for this collection are to give the terms of admission and document the arrival and departure of nonimmigrant aliens to the U.S. The information solicited on this form may be made available to other government agencies for law enforcement purposes or to assist DHS in determining your admissibility. All nonimmigrant aliens seeking admission to the U.S., unless otherwise exempted, must provide this information. Failure to provide this information may deny you entry to the United States and result in your removal.

CBP Form I-94 (05/08)
OMB No. 1651-0111

Arrival Record

Admission Number

804412492 28

1. Family Name
2. First (Given) Name
3. Birth Date (DD/MM/YY)
4. Country of Citizenship
5. Sex (Male or Female)
6. Passport Issue Date (DD/MM/YY)
7. Passport Expiration Date (DD/MM/YY)
8. Passport Number
9. Airline and Flight Number
10. Country Where You Live
11. Country Where You Boarded
12. City Where Visa Was Issued
13. Date Issued (DD/MM/YY)
14. Address While in the United States (Number and Street)
15. City and State
16. Telephone Number in the U.S. Where You Can Be Reached
17. Email Address

CBP Form I-94 (05/08)

DEPARTMENT OF HOMELAND SECURITY
U.S. Customs and Border Protection

OMB No. 1651-0111

Departure Record

Admission Number

804412492 28

18. Family Name
19. First (Given) Name
20. Birth Date (DD/MM/YY)
21. Country of Citizenship

CBP Form I-94 (05/08)

See Other Side

STAPLE HERE

This Side For Government Use Only
Primary Inspection

Applicant's Name

Date Referred ___ Time ___ Insp. # ___

Reason Referred

☐ 212A ☐ ☐ ☐ PP ☐ Visa ☐ Parole ☐ L/O ☐ TWOV

Other

Secondary Inspection

End Secondary Time ___ Insp. # ___

Disposition

22. Occupation
23. Waivers
24. CIS A Number
A-
25. CIS FCO
26. Petition Number
27. Program Number
28. ☐ Bond
29. ☐ Prospective Student
30. Itinerary/Comments

31. TWOV Ticket Number

Paperwork Reduction Act Statement: An agency may not conduct or sponsor an information collection and a person is not required to respond to this information unless it displays a current valid OMB control number. The control number for this collection is 1651-0111. The estimated average time to complete this application is 8 minutes per respondent. If you have any comments regarding the burden estimate you can write to U.S. Customs and Border Protection, Asset Management, 1300 Pennsylvania Avenue, NW, Washington DC 20229

Warning A nonimmigrant who accepts unauthorized employment is subject to deportation.
Important Retain this permit in your possession; *you must surrender it when you leave the U.S.* Failure to do so may delay your entry into the U.S. in the future.
You are authorized to stay in the U.S. only until the date written on this form. To remain past this date, without permission from Department of Homeland Security authorities, is a violation of the law.
Surrender this permit when you leave the U.S.:
  - By sea or air, to the transportation line;
  - Across the Canadian border, to a Canadian Official;
  - Across the Mexican border, to a U.S. Official
Students planning to reenter the U.S. within 30 days to return to the same school, see "Arrival-Departure" on page 2 of Form I-20 prior to surrendering this permit.

Record of Changes

Departure Record

Port:
Date:
Carrier:
Flight No./ Ship Name:

❷ the Republic of Indonesia Customs Form　印尼海關申報單

Ministry of Finance of the Republic of Indonesia
Directorate General of Customs and Excise

CUSTOMS DECLARATION
(BC 2.2)

Each arriving Passenger/Crew must submit Customs Declaration (only one Customs Declaration per family is required)

1. Full Name
2. Date of Birth　Date　Month　Year
3. Occupation
4. Nationality
5. Passport Number
6. Address in Indonesia (hotel name/residence address)

7. Flight or Voyage number
8. Date of Arrival　Day　Month　Year
9. Number of family members traveling with you (only for Passenger)
10. a. Number of accompanied baggage　PKG
　　b. Number of unaccompanied baggage (if any, and see the reverse side of this form)　PKG
11. I am (We are) bringing:　　　　　　　Yes (√)　No (√)
　　a. Animals, fish and plants including their products (vegetables, food, etc.).
　　b. Narcotics, psychotropic substances, precursor, drugs, fire arms, air gun, sharp object (ie, sword, knife), ammunition, explosives, pornographic articles.
　　c. Currency and/or bearer negotiable instruments in Rupiah or other currencies which equals to the amount of 100 million Rupiah or more.
　　d. More than 200 cigarettes or 25 cigars or 100 grams of sliced tobacco, and 1 liter drinks containing ethyl alcohol (for passenger); or more than 40 cigarettes or 10 cigars or 40 grams of sliced tobacco, and 350 milliliter drinks containing ethyl alcohol (for crew).
　　e. Commercial merchandise (articles for sale, sample used for soliciting orders, materials or components used for industrial purposes, and/or goods that are not considered as personal effect).
　　f. Goods purchased/obtained abroad and will remain in Indonesia with total value exceeding USD 50.00 per person (for Crew); or USD 250.00 per person or USD 1,000.00 per family (for Passenger).

If you tick "Yes" to any of the questions number 11 above, please notify on the reverse side of this form and please go to RED CHANNEL. If you tick "No" to all of the questions above, please go to GREEN CHANNEL.

I HAVE READ THE INFORMATION ON THE REVERSE SIDE OF THIS FORM AND HAVE MADE A TRUTHFUL DECLARATION

(SIGNATURE)　　　　DATE (DAY/MONTH/YEAR)

Welcome to Indonesia

Directorate General of Customs and Excise would like to thank you for your kind cooperation during the inspection to identify narcotics, illegal drugs any articles which are related to terrorism activities, currency and/or bearer negotiable instruments associating with money laundering, and/or smuggling activities, that violate state laws and regulations of Indonesia.

Illicitly bringing those goods into Indonesia and/or doing smuggling activities, may subject to penalties and legal actions.

Passenger who brings/carries goods for personal use that were purchased or obtained abroad and will remain in Indonesia, is entitled to an exemption of import duties, excise, and taxes of those goods at the most:
◦ USD 250.00 per person or USD 1,000.00 per family per arrival, and
❖ 200 cigarettes or 25 cigars or 100 grams of sliced tobacco or other tobacco product, and 1 liter drinks containing ethyl alcohol for every adult.

Crew who brings/carries goods for personal use that were purchased or obtained abroad and will remain in Indonesia, is entitled to an exemption of import duties, excise, and taxes of those goods at the most:
◦ USD 50.00 per person per arrival, and
❖ 40 cigarettes or 10 cigars or 40 grams of sliced tobacco or other tobacco products, and 350 milliliter drinks containing ethyl alcohol.

If you are bringing commercial merchandise into Indonesia, the merchandise is subject to import duty and other import taxes.

Please notify Customs Officer, in case you are bringing currency and/or bearer negotiable instruments (cheque, travellers cheque, promissory notes, giro) in Rupiah or other currencies which equal to the amount of 100 million Rupiah or more.

Should you have unaccompanied baggages, please duplicate this Customs Declaration and request an approval to Customs Officer for claiming the unaccompanied baggages.

To expedite the customs services, please notify the goods that you are bringing/carrying completely and correctly in this form, then submit it to Customs Officer.

Making a false declaration constitutes serious offences which attract penalties or punishment in accordance with laws and regulation.

SIGN ON THE OPPOSITE SIDE OF THIS FORM AFTER YOU HAVE READ THE INFORMATION ABOVE AND MADE A TRUTHFUL DECLARATION.

Goods Declared

Description of Goods	Qty	Value

For official use only

Chapter 8.　In-flight passenger handling
機上旅客狀況處理

▶ Outline: 介紹客艙服務可能遭遇之旅客異常狀況，此類事件雖不至於影響飛航安全，但處理方式若不當，可能直接造成旅客的身心不適，需及時提供建議或協助。

▶ Learning Goals: 熟記必備單字、片語。能夠流暢進行情境對話與角色扮演。

Ⓐ Basic Vocabulary　基礎必備單字

❶ abnormal ᴋᴋ [æb'nɔrml̩] ᴅᴊ [æb'nɔ:məl]　不尋常的；反常的 (a.)

英文釋義 different from what is usual or average

反義字 normal; regular

• The abnormal situation should be carefully monitored.　這個反常的狀況應該被小心監控。

❷ allergic ᴋᴋ [ə'lɜˋdʒɪk] ᴅᴊ [ə'lə:dʒik]　過敏的；對……討厭的 (a.)

英文釋義 immune system reacts to a foreign substance in a way to cause someone becoming sick after eating, touching, or breathing something

• He is allergic to all kinds of nuts.　他對全部的核果類食物過敏。

❸ apology ᴋᴋ [ə'pɑlədʒɪ] ᴅᴊ [ə'pɔlədʒi]　道歉 (n.)

英文釋義 a written or spoken statement expressing that one person is sorry about something

• make an apology = apologize

• I owe you an apology for my misunderstanding.　因為我的誤解，該向你道歉的。

❹ arrest ㎄ [ə'rɛst] ㎅ [ə'rest]　逮捕；拘留 (v.)

英文釋義 an action of taking or keeping of a person in custody by legal

- The police arrested him on charges of murder.　警察因謀殺罪嫌逮捕他。

❺ descend ㎄ [dɪ'sɛnd] ㎅ [di'send]　下降 (v.)

英文釋義 move from a higher place to a lower one; go down

- The airplane descended to a safe altitude.　飛機降到安全高度。

❻ detain ㎄ [dɪ'ten] ㎅ [di'tein]　扣留；拘留；留置 (v.)

英文釋義 to hold or keep someone in a place or officially refrain someone from leaving a place

- The unexpected thunderstorm detained us for several hours.　這場意料之外的雷雨耽誤了我們好幾個小時的時間。

❼ extinguish ㎄ [ɪk'stɪŋgwɪʃ] ㎅ [iks'tiŋgwiʃ]　終結；熄滅 (v.)

英文釋義 to bring to an end; put out

- fire extinguisher　滅火器
- The fire fighters have tried so hard to extinguish fire within 30 minutes. 消防員很努力地在30分鐘內滅火。

❽ fault ㎄ [fɔlt] ㎅ [fɔ:lt]　缺點；錯誤 (n.)　挑毛病 (v.)

英文釋義 a problem or bad part of something

同義字 defect; mistake; flaw

- Please accept my apology. It's all my fault.　這都是我的錯，請接受我的道歉。

❾ first-aid 🔤 [ˈfɝstˈed] 🔤 [ˈfəːstˈeid]　急救 (n.)

英文釋義 provide sick or injured person emergency treatment

- call in somebody's aid　請求某人協助
- The proper first-aid was given to the wounded woman before the ambulance arrived.　救護車到達前，受傷的女人已得到適當的急救。

❿ humming 🔤 [ˈhʌmɪŋ] 🔤 [ˈhʌmiŋ]　嗡嗡聲的；忙碌的 (a.)；耳鳴 (n.)

英文釋義 be very active or busy; a continuous low droning sound

- humming bird　蜂鳥
- hum and haw　支支吾吾；嗯嗯啊啊─猶豫不決的樣貌
- The classroom is humming with activities.　教室裡大家因為各種活動而忙碌著。
- I have a constant humming all day long.　我整天都覺得耳鳴。

⓫ journey 🔤 [ˈdʒɝnɪ] 🔤 [ˈdʒəːni]　旅行 (n.)

英文釋義 traveling from one place to another

同義字 tour; trip

- I feel exhausted after the long journey.　長途旅行後我累壞了。

⓬ stain 🔤 [sten] 🔤 [stein]　污漬 (n.)；污染 (v.)

英文釋義 to leave a discoloration on something

- without a stain on his character　他的人格零瑕疵。
- The ink stain is hard to be removed.　墨水污漬很難被清除。

⓭ tablet 🔤 [ˈtæblɪt] 🔤 [ˈtæblit]　藥片 (n.)

英文釋義 compressed powdered drug for swallowing

- You have to take the tablets twice a day.　你一天要吃兩次藥片。

⓮ wheelchair ㊎ [ˈhwilˈtʃɛr] ㊊ [ˈhwiːlˈtʃɛə] 輪椅 (n.)

英文釋義 a chair with wheels that is used by an individual with a mobility disability

• Wheelchair service is available in the airport.　機場內提供輪椅服務。

Ⓑ Phrase　片語

❶ first-aid kit　急救箱

❷ doctor kit　醫療箱

❸ refrain from　避免

❹ vegetarian meal　素食餐

C Conversation 會話

❶ Making an apology　致歉 🎵08-1

CA: I am very sorry to have caused you trouble. We want to pay the cleaning charge for your suit.

眞的很抱歉造成您的麻煩。我們會付給您衣服的清潔費。

I am terribly sorry to keep you waiting.

非常抱歉讓您久等了。

I am sorry to have troubled you so much.

對不起，造成您許多困擾。

Please accept my apology.

請您接受我的道歉。

Excuse me, Mr./Mrs./Ms.＿姓氏＿. It's all our fault. If there is anything we can do to make your journey smoother, please do not hesitate to tell us.

對不起，＿姓氏＿先生／太太／小姐，這都是我們的錯。如果我們能做甚麼讓您的旅途較爲舒適自在，請務必讓我們知道。

Ladies and gentlemen,

Due to air traffic congestion, the arrival time is estimated to be 20 minutes behind schedule. We are sincerely sorry for the unexpected inconvenience.

各位貴賓：

因爲目前空中交通壅塞，抵達時間將比表訂時間延遲20分鐘。對於這突發狀況造成的不便，我們謹此致上眞誠的歉意。

❷ **Special order　乘客特殊要求**　🎵08-2

CA: Mrs. Chen, this is your vegetarian meal. Enjoy it.

陳太太，這是您的素食餐，請慢用。

I am sorry, ma'am. We don't serve instant noodle this flight. Would you like to have a sandwich for snack?

對不起，女士。這趟航班沒有提供泡麵的服務，您的點心想吃三明治嗎？

Excuse me, sir. Smoking is strictly prohibited on board. Please do not intend to smoke anywhere in the cabin. Passengers found to be smoking will be fined, and at worst be arrested and detained upon landing.

這位先生，對不起，機上是嚴格禁止吸菸的。請不要試圖在客艙的任何地方抽菸。乘客若在客艙內吸菸，輕則會遭到罰鍰，重則在降落後，將被拘留或逮捕。

Please don't worry, Mr. Webber. We will prepare a wheelchair for you upon arrival.

韋伯先生，請不要擔心，降落後在機艙外，我們會為您準備輪椅的。

D Dialog 情境對話

C ：cabin attendant　　P ：passenger

情境 I 08-3

C Yes, May I help you?

P I am not feeling well. Do you have any medicine/tablets in the aircraft?

C Yes, we do. How do you feel now?

P I have got a terrible headache.

C Please wait for a minute. I will show you what we have. Are you allergic to any medicine?

P No, I don't think so. Do you have Panadol or aspirin on board?

C Yes, we do have aspirin. Give me one second. I will be right back.

P Thank you.

C Here is the aspirin and water. I will bring another blanket for you.

P All right.

C Would you like me to recline your seat? I think that it would be more comfortable.

P It's very caring of you. Thank you.

譯 文

空服員 需要幫什麼忙嗎？

乘 客 我有點不舒服，請問機上有甚麼藥品嗎？

空服員 有的。您覺得哪裡不舒服？

乘 客 我頭痛欲裂。

空服員 請稍等，我去拿機上的藥物過來讓您看一下。您有任何藥物過
　　　　敏的病史嗎？

乘 客 沒有。機上有普拿疼或阿斯匹靈嗎？

空服員 我們有阿斯匹靈。請等我一下，我立刻為您準備。

乘 客 謝謝。

空服員 這是阿斯匹靈和水。我再幫您多拿一件毯子過來。

乘 客 好的。

空服員 要不要將椅背向後倒？這樣可能會覺得舒服一點？

乘 客 謝謝你。你真貼心。

情境 II 08-4

P Excuse me, Miss, can you give me some water? My ears are humming terribly.

C It's due to the change of altitude pressure. I'll get you the water immediately.

P Please.

C Here is your water, sir.

P Thank you. By the way, do you know anything to reduce the discomfort?

C Sure. First please relax, then open your mouth and slowly take a deep breath for a couple of times. How do you feel?

P I do feel much better now.

C That's great. Maybe you need some sweets, it can also ease the pain.

P Oh, really? That will be wonderful. Can I have an extra blanket? I feel a little bit cold.

C Certainly, I'll bring another one for you. Please wait for a minute. Here is your sweets and blanket, sir.

P Thank you very much.

C You are welcome.

譯 文

乘 客 對不起，小姐，能給我一杯水嗎？我耳鳴的厲害。

空服員 這是因為氣壓改變的關係。我馬上幫您拿杯水來。

乘 客 麻煩你了。

空服員 先生，這是您的水。

乘 客 謝謝。對了，你知道有甚麼可以緩解耳鳴的方法嗎？

空服員 是的。請您先放鬆身體，然後把嘴張大，慢慢地做幾次深呼吸
的動作，怎麼樣？覺得好些了嗎？

乘 客 嗯，的確好多了。

空服員 那就好。您也可以吃點糖，這樣也能減輕耳鳴的不適。

乘 客 是嗎？那太好了。可以再給我一件毯子嗎？我覺得有點冷。

空服員 當然沒問題，請稍等一下，我去拿過來給您。這是您的糖和毛
毯。

乘 客 謝謝你。

空服員 別客氣。

Airline Humor（航空幽默小品）!!

• As you exit the plane, please make sure to gather all of your belongings.
Anything left behind will be distributed evenly among the flight
attendants. Please do not leave children or spouses. Last one off the
plane must clean it.

下機時，請記得攜帶您所有的隨身物品。所有留下的東西將會被空服員均分。請勿遺失您的小孩或另一半。最後下機的乘客必須清潔機艙。

- A flight Attendant's comment on a less than perfect landing: "We ask you to please remain seated as Captain Kangaroo bounces us to the terminal."

一位空服員對於機長不太完美的落地下了這樣的評論：請您留在座位上，直到袋鼠機長帶領我們跳回航廈為止。

- As we waited just off the runway for another airliner to cross in front of us, some of the passengers were beginning to retrieve luggage from the overhead bins. The head attendant announced on the intercom, "This aircraft is equipped with a video surveillance system that monitors the cabin during taxiing. Any passengers not remaining in their seats until the aircraft comes to a full and complete stop at the gate will be strip-searched as they leave the aircraft."

降落後，就在飛機剛離開跑道，正等待另一架飛機通過的當兒，有些乘客已迫不及待地開始從頭上置物櫃中拿出行李。座艙長於是做了以下的廣播：

「這架飛機配備有監視系統，可以在飛機滑行時，監控客艙的情況。在飛機完全停妥前，任何乘客只要離開座位，下機時都會被要求脫光衣服檢查。」

Part Ⅱ Aviation English

航空專業英語

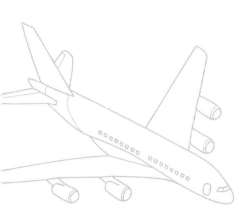

Chapter 9.　Airline jargon　　航空術語

▶ Outline: 整理航空業業務範圍中，重要相關組織、單位以及與旅客服務有關之特殊專業用語和縮寫。

▶ Learning Goals: 航空術語乃從事航空業之基礎專業知識，需完全熟記。

【A】

❶ Air carrier ㊚ [ɛr] [ˈkærɪɚ] ㊐ [ɛə] [ˈkæriə]

英文釋義 An airline authorized by the government to engage in the transportation business of passengers and cargo.

◆ 經政府授權經營乘客和貨物運輸事業的航空公司。

❷ Airborne ㊚ [ˈɛrˌborn] ㊐ [ˈɛəbɔːn]

英文釋義 It refers to the period of time when an aircraft is free of contact with the ground.

◆ 係指飛機起飛後於空中飛行的時間。

❸ All-call ㊚ [ˈɔlˌkɔl] ㊐ [ˈɔːlˌkɔːl]

英文釋義 Code called by cabin chief to request all flight attendants verifying each of the cabin doors being locked and armed for departures, or disarmed when arriving at the gate.

◆ 座艙長以機內廣播系統呼叫空服員「all-call」，代表飛機機門關閉後，要求空服員將機門設定於「開啓後滑梯自動充氣」狀態；以及降落停妥後，將機門解除滑梯自動充氣的設定。

❹ Apron ㊚ [ˈeprən] ㊐ [ˈeiprən]

英文釋義 Also known as "Ramp". It refers to the area in the airport where

airplanes are parked, refueled, loaded and unloaded baggage and cargo, or for passenger boarding.

◆ 停機坪，為機場管制區，飛機停靠、加油、上下乘客及貨物的地方。

❺ ATC – Air Traffic Control ⓚ [ɛr] ['træfɪk] [kən'trol]
　　　　　　　　　　　　ⓓ [ɛə] ['træfɪk] [kən'trɔul]

英文釋義 basically means the vast network of radio communication facilities responsible for the safe guidance of aircrafts flying through the nation's air space, and on airport taxiways and runways. It can be a tower located at the airport.

◆ 空中交通管制係指為維護飛航安全，地面的航管人員藉由無線通訊設備，協調指導通過該國空域的航空器飛航路線，以防止於空中或地面發生意外。於機場內通常可見ATC塔台。

❻ AVML - Asian Vegetarian Meal ⓚ ['eʃən] [ˌvɛdʒə'tɛrɪən] [mil]
　　　　　　　　　　　　　　ⓓ ['eiʃən] [ˌvedʒi'tɛərɪən] [mi:l]

英文釋義 Special designed menu for Chinese vegetarian meal. No animal-origin food is allowed. No onion, garlic, spring onion, chives to be used in cooking.

◆ 亞洲素食餐。無任何動物製品。不加洋蔥、蒜、青蔥等香料。

【B】

❶ BBML – Baby meal
◆ 嬰兒餐。為襁褓中或已開始食用副食品的嬰兒所準備的特別餐點。

❷ Belly ⓚ ['bɛlɪ] ⓓ ['beli]
英文釋義 It refers to the lower lobe of an aircraft, designed to hold cargo

containers and landing gear.

◆ 機腹。係指飛機下半部圓弧型的部分，主要使用於裝載貨艙及放置起落架。

❸ Briefing ㊚ ['brifɪŋ] ㊙ ['bri:fɪŋ]

英文釋義 A short meeting of the crew members of a flight to discuss the details of the flight (usually takes half an hour). The purposes of the meeting are also to review emergency procedures, equipment, service procedures, and special flight information.

◆ 飛行前簡報。通常歷時30分鐘。主要目的為討論該次飛行任務的細節資料，並複習緊急逃生步驟、設備用品、服務步驟及特殊資訊。

❹ Budget airlines ['bʌdʒɪt] ['ɛrˌlaɪns] ㊙ ['bʌdʒɪt] ['ɛəlains]

英文釋義 airlines target at short-haul flights with limited service, usually connecting secondary airports. They provide passengers with alternative for lower but non-flexible fare.

◆ 低成本航空。主要飛航短程航線，通常連接次級機場，提供有限的服務，以低票價吸引旅客。

❺ Bulkhead ㊚ ['bʌlkˌhɛd] ㊙ ['bʌlkhed]

英文釋義 A wall or partition dividing the passenger cabin.

◆ 隔板，用以將客艙分隔成數段。「bulkhead seat」係指每一段客艙的中間第一排座位，通常會預留給帶嬰兒旅行的父母，以方便設置嬰兒床。

❻ Bump ㊚ [bʌmp] ㊙ [bʌmp]

英文釋義 "Get bumped" means that cabin seats are oversold and some passengers have to be put on the next available flight. Very seldom one may get lucky to be bumped up to business or first class.

◆ 因機位超賣，某些無法上機的旅客必須被迫改搭下一班次。偶爾當商務艙或頭等艙有空位時，可能可以幸運地升等。

【C】

❶ Carry-on ㏚ [ˈkærɪˌɑn] ㏈ [ˈkærɪˌɔn]

英文釋義 hand-luggage or baggage that has not been checked-in.

◆ 手提上機的行李。

❷ Casserole ㏚ [ˈkæsəˈrol] ㏈ [ˈkæsərəul]

英文釋義 Container which the main course is in. It is made of a hard plastic or china which enables us to heat and / or cook the main meal.

◆ 空廚用以裝盛飛機餐點主餐之容器。通常材質為瓷器或硬塑料，方便放入機上廚房烤箱內加熱。

❸ Charter ㏚ [ˈtʃɑrtɚ] ㏈ [ˈtʃɑːtə]

英文釋義 Charter means "contract". A charter describes a non-scheduled flight which only operates on demand by a particular agency, group or individual.

◆ 非定期航班，乃針對特殊旅遊目的或地點，依簽約內容飛航的包機。

❹ Check-in ㏚ [ˈtʃɛkˌɪn] ㏈ [ˈtʃekˌɪn]

英文釋義 the procedure of issuing boarding pass and handling checked baggage for passengers. Usually airlines require passengers to show up at the airport two hours before take-off to go through the process.

◆ 劃位手續。旅客搭乘飛機旅行時，需於航站之劃位櫃檯完成行李託運及取得登機證等程序，才能通過安檢登機。國際航線一般要求乘客於起飛前兩小時抵達櫃檯，以便順利完成劃位手續。

❺ CHML – Child Meal
- ◆ 兒童餐。為搭機兒童準備的特別餐點，內容通常為漢堡、炸雞、義大利麵等。

❻ Coat tag ⓚ [kot] [tæg] ⓓ [kəut] [tæg]
- 英文釋義 A small tag used for checking passengers' coats and garment bags. Seat number and destination are written on it and hung over the hanger in the coat room.
- ◆ 外套掛牌。為乘客掛外套或長型大衣袋時，於標示牌上寫明座位號碼及目的地，再將衣物掛入衣櫥內。

❼ Configuration ⓚ [kən,fɪgjə'reʃən] ⓓ [kən,fɪgju'reiʃən]
- 英文釋義 The arrangement of seats and other cabin features of the interior of an aircraft.
- ◆ 指飛機內部硬體結構的排列方式，包括座位安排、置物空間等等。

❽ Cross-check ⓚ ['krɔs,tʃɛk] ⓓ ['krɔ:s,tʃɛk]
- 英文釋義 Cross-check is taken by aircrew members to double check what have been done for each other, in order to verify that the actions are completed.
- ◆ 互相檢查的程序，是空勤組員（包括機師及客艙組員）為確保每一個動作的執行無誤，於完成個人動作後，左右交換為對方進行再次檢視的動作（如機門操作）。

【D】

❶ DBML – Diabetic Meal ⓚ [,daɪə'bɛtɪk] [mil] ⓓ [,daiə'betik] [mi:l]
- 英文釋義 Meal particularly made for diabetic passengers, usually serving

them lean meats, low fat and high fiber foods, e.g. fresh fruits, vegetables and whole grain breads and cereals.

◆ 專為糖尿病病患準備的特別餐。其食材通常包含瘦肉、低油高纖食品，例如新鮮蔬果及全麥雜糧。

❷ Deadhead crew ⓚⓚ ['dɛdˌhɛd] [kru] ⓓⓙ ['dedhed] [kru:]

英文釋義 Cockpit and cabin crews flying as passengers for connecting to their next service duty.

◆ 空勤組員當趟以乘客身分於機上休息，主要為飛往目的地，執行其下一階段的指定勤務。又稱為PNC – position crew。

❸ Decompression ⓚⓚ [ˌdikəm'prɛʃən] ⓓⓙ [ˌdi:kəm'preʃən]

英文釋義 The act or process of releasing from pressure or compression in general; Loss of cabin pressurization

◆ 失壓。指飛機因機體結構受損，或加壓系統故障，導致於高空飛行時，客艙內無法維持一定高度的壓力。此時機艙內的所有人必須盡快戴上氧氣面罩，且機師會盡速降低飛行高度，以避免因為高空氧氣不足而使機上人員出現缺氧症的症狀。

❹ Deploy ⓚⓚ [dɪ'plɔɪ] ⓓⓙ [di'plɔi]

英文釋義 The act of inflating an emergency evacuation slide.

◆ 緊急逃生時，救生滑梯自動充氣的動作。

❺ Dispatcher ⓚⓚ [dɪ'spætʃɚ] ⓓⓙ [di'spætʃə]

英文釋義 Airline employees who are in charge of the routing and scheduling of an aircraft.

◆ 簽派員。航空從業人員中，專職每個航班飛行計畫的製作和簽放。需領有民航局核發的專業證照。

❻ Ditching KK ['dɪtʃɪŋ] DJ ['ditʃiŋ]

英文釋義 Making an emergency landing on water

◆ 指飛行器因故障或任何其他因素迫降在水裡。

❼ Divert KK [daɪ'vɝt] DJ [dai'və:t]

英文釋義 A flight, due to any reason, is operated from the scheduled departing point to a point other than the scheduled destination in the carrier's published schedule.

◆ 因為任何因素，班機未照原表訂飛行計畫飛抵目的地，而轉改降另一個機場。

【E】

❶ ETA – Estimated Time of Arrival KK ['ɛstə,metɪd] [taɪm] [ɑv] [ə'raɪvl̩] DJ ['estimeitid] [taim] [ɔv] [ə'raivəl]

◆ 表訂降落時間

❷ ETD – Estimated Time of Departure KK ['ɛstə,metɪd] [taɪm] [ɑv] [dɪ'partʃɚ] DJ ['estimeitid] [taim] [ɔv] [di'pɑ:tʃə]

◆ 表訂起飛時間

❸ Evacuation KK [ɪ,vækjʊ'eʃən] DJ [i,vækju'eiʃən]

英文釋義 Process of leaving an aircraft immediately under emergency situations.

◆ 緊急狀況下立即撤離飛機的流程。

【F】

❶ FAA – Federal Aviation Administration KK ['fɛdərəl] ['evɪ'eʃən] [əd,mɪnə'streʃən] DJ ['fedərəl] [,eivi'eiʃən] [əd,mini'streiʃən]

英文釋義 The federal regulatory agency responsible for the safety and emergency procedures of the U.S. air transportation system.

◆ 美國聯邦航空總署。負責美國航空運輸安全及緊急狀況處理之所有管理工作。

❷ FAR – Federal Aviation Regulations KK ['fɛdərəl] [ˌɛvɪ'eʃən] [ˌrɛgjə'leʃənz] DJ ['fedərəl] [ˌeivi'eiʃən] [ˌregju'leiʃənz]

英文釋義 Rules established for the airlines by the FAA to guard against potential safety hazards.

◆ 美國聯邦航空法規。由聯邦航空總署所制定的航空運輸相關規範條例，目地在防範所有潛在的危險。

❸ Ferry Flight KK ['fɛrɪ] [flaɪt] DJ ['feri] [flait]

英文釋義 A flight which is just positioning an aircraft in another city and not for revenue. There are no passengers on these flights, only crew members.

◆ 空機運渡飛航。非一般載客營利的航班。乃為以下三種目的執行飛行工作：1. 將飛機飛回基地。2. 將飛機自某地運送他處。 3. 將飛機飛往或飛離修護基地。

❹ Flight Crew KK [flaɪt] [kru] DJ [flait] [kru:]

英文釋義 The professional crew members who are in charge of aircraft operation, consist of captain (Capt.), first officer (F/O,) and flight engineer (F/E).

◆ 駕駛艙組員。負責執行操作飛航任務的專業機組人員，包括正駕駛（caption, pilot）、副駕駛（F/O, co-pilot）及飛航工程師（F/E，新型飛機已無需F/E一職）

❺ Flight deck ㊊ [flaɪt] [dɛk] ㊌ [flait] [dek]

英文釋義 The small space locates in the forward fuselage, where flight crew conducts the flight operations.

◆ 駕駛艙，又稱cockpit。機師座位及操控飛機之所在。

❻ Flight number ㊊ [flaɪt] [ˈnʌmbɚ] ㊌ [flait] [ˈnʌmbə]

英文釋義 The numerical designation of a flight. Usually, even numbers are for eastbound flights and odd numbers are for westbound ones.

◆ 班機號碼，通常往東飛為偶數號碼，往西為奇數號碼。

❼ FRML- Fruit Meal

◆ 水果餐。機上可經事前要求提供的特殊餐點之一。

【G】

❶ Galley ㊊ [ˈgælɪ] ㊌ [ˈgæli]

英文釋義 The kitchen of a ship or airplane

◆ 飛機上的廚房。

❷ GMT - Greenwich Mean Time ㊊ [ˈgrinwɪtʃ] [min] [taɪm] ㊌ [ˈgriːnwitʃ] [miːn] [taim]

英文釋義 The original term referred to the mean solar time at the Royal Observatory in Greenwich, London. Now it is commonly used in the United Kingdom and countries of Commonwealth.

◆ 格林威治標準時間。過往全球24個時區以此為對照基準，目前大英國協各國仍採用GMT做為標準時間之依據。

【H】

❶ Hangar 🔊 ['hæŋɚ] 🔊 ['hæŋə]

英文釋義 A covered and usually enclosed building in which aircraft are housed, maintained and repaired.

◆ 飛機維修棚。多於機場場域內建造的大型棚廠，可停機及進行飛機維修工作。

❷ Head winds 🔊 [hɛd] [wɪndz] 🔊 [hed] [windz]

英文釋義 Winds that move to the opposite direction of the aircraft, which may slows its rate of speed.

◆ 頂風。與飛機航向相反，會減低飛行速度。

❸ Hub 🔊 [hʌb] 🔊 [hʌb]

英文釋義 a major airport served as the connecting point for different routes, where most of airlines have passengers and goods transported from the original airports and transferred to smaller destinations.

◆ 樞紐機場。乃以航空運輸軸幅網路概念形成的轉運中心。為各國主要城市的最大機場，航空公司將旅客及貨物從其他機場運至樞紐機場進行轉機，再前往最終目的地。

【I】

❶ IATA - International Air Transport Association 🔊 [ˌɪntɚ'næʃənl̩] [ɛr] [ˌtræns'pɔrt] [əˌsosɪ'eʃən] 🔊 [ˌintə'næʃənəl] [ɛə] ['træns.pɔ:t] [ə'səusiˌeiʃən]

英文釋義 A private organization (trade association) representing and serving the airline industry world-wide, majorly aims at promoting cooperation among the world's scheduled airlines to ensure safe, secure, reliable and economical air services.

◆ 國際航空運輸協會。為一非官方性質之航空企業的行業聯盟組織，於各國政府授權下，制定運價及清算，致力於協調溝通各國政府間，國際空運相關政策及實際運作之困難，以期共同提供安全可靠經濟之空運服務。

❷ ICAO - International Civil Aviation Organization ㉚ [ˌɪntɚˈnæʃn̩l] [ˈsɪvl̩] [ˌevɪˈeʃn̩] [ˌɔrgənəˈzeʃən] ㉛ [ˌintəˈnæʃnəl] [ˈsivil] [ˌevɪˈeʃn] [ˌɔ:gənaiˈzeiʃən]

英文釋義 An intergovernmental specialized agency associated with the United Nations. It is established to provide standards, regulations and procedures for international aviation. The organization is dedicated to developing safe and efficient international air transport for every state to operate international airlines.

◆ 國際民航組織。乃隸屬於聯合國的一跨政府組織。主要成立目的為提供國際民航運作之標準條例及方式。致力於推動全球國際民航業者，齊心建立安全且高效率的航空運輸產業。

❸ Interphone ㉚ [ˈɪntɚˌfon] ㉛ [ˈintəˌfəun]

英文釋義 The system used for inter-station communication among cockpit and/or cabin crew members on board the aircraft. It is also used for PA (public address).

◆ 機內的通話設備。駕駛艙、每個空服員座位上及某些廚房內，備有同電話聽筒的設備，可供組員互相聯絡或進行機內廣播用途。

❹ Inventory ㉚ [ˈɪnvənˌtorɪ] ㉛ [ˈinvəntri]

英文釋義 The itemized list to keep record of drinks and duty free items loaded on board.

◆ 機內載有飲料服務及免稅物品銷售服務之所有物品的清單。

【J】

❶ Jetway 🆗 [ˈdʒɛtwe] 🆔 [ˈdʒetwei]

英文釋義 A tunnel-like, enclosed walkway connecting an airport terminal and an aircraft, used for passengers boarding and disembarkation. It is also termed as aerobridge, boarding bridge or jet bridge.

◆ 空橋。連接機場航站登機門和飛機機門的密閉式走道。

❷ Joint fare 🆗 [dʒɔɪnt] [fɛr] 🆔 [dʒɔint] [fɛə]

英文釋義 The airfare charged for travel that utilizes more than one airline. The total amount of fares are negotiated by the airlines involved.

◆ 聯運票價。旅程使用超過一家以上的航空公司機票，其票價由所有承運的航空公司共同協調確認。

【K】

❶ KSML – Kosher Meal 🆗 [ˈkoʃɚ] [mil] 🆔 [ˈkəuʃə] [mi:l]

英文釋義 All foods should be prepared and served according to Jewish dietary laws.

◆ 猶太餐。是一種宗教類的特殊餐點。餐點所有準備過程必須遵照猶太教之飲食規範。

【L】

❶ Layover 🆗 [ˈleˌovɚ] 🆔 [ˈleiˌəuvə]

英文釋義 Crew rest break between flight assignments.

◆ 外站過夜。指組員飛至外站後，於服勤回程航班前，在外站的過夜停留。

❷ LCC – Low Cost Carrier ⓚ [lo] [kɔst] [ˈkærɪɚ] ⓓ [ləu] [kɔst] [ˈkærɪə]

◆ 同「Budget airlines」低成本航空。

❸ LFML – Low Fat Meal ⓚ [lo] [fæt] [mil] ⓓ [ləu] [fæt] [mi:l]
◆ 低脂餐。可於訂位時預訂之特殊餐點。提供低油脂低熱量的食物。

❹ Logbook ⓚ [ˈlɔɡˌbʊk] ⓓ [ˈlɔɡbuk]
英文釋義 It is used for keeping record. There are several kinds of logbooks in the airline industry. For instance, Maintenance Logbook is particularly designed to allow flight attendants to note down any broken facilities or equipment in the cabin.

◆ 用以記錄的冊子。例如，維修紀錄冊乃提供空服員於發現機內物品或設備，出現故障或需替換的狀況時，登錄實際情形，以便飛機降落後，維修人員可順利接手工作。

❺ Long haul flight ⓚ [lɔŋ] [hɔl] [flaɪt] ⓓ [lɔŋ] [hɔ:l] [flait]
英文釋義 There is no definite way to classify short, medium or long-haul flight. A long-haul flight takes considerable flight time and distance, usually requires meal service twice.

◆ 長程飛行。如何界定短程、中程、長程飛行，並無絕對標準。長程飛行費時長、距離遠，通常機上會提供兩段餐點的服務。

❻ LSML – Low Sodium Meal ⓚ [lo] [ˈsodɪəm] [mil] ⓓ [ləu] [ˈsəudiəm] [mi:l]
英文釋義 Omit salt, MSG, soy sauce, pickled, canned foods.

◆ 低鈉餐。可於訂位時預訂之特殊餐點。餐點內不加鹽、味精、醬油、醃漬品、罐頭食品等。主要為有腎臟方面疾病旅客要求之特別餐。

【M】

❶ MAAS – Meet and assist ㊎ [mit] [ænd] [əˈsɪst] ㊒ [miːt] [ænd] [əˈsist]

英文釋義 Passengers who need special assistance in the airport may ask for a MAAS badge to be identified. Usually it's for elder travellers or passengers who are not able to communicate by themselves.

◆ 乘客（通常指年長乘客或語言無法順利溝通者）於機場需要特別協助時，可要求地勤人員提供MAAS的貼紙貼在身上。

❷ Minimum connecting time ㊎ [ˈmɪnəməm] [kəˈnɛktɪŋ] [taɪm] ㊒ [ˈminiməm] [kəˈnektiŋ] [taim]

英文釋義 the smallest amount of time that is allowed to change planes at an airport.

◆ 最少轉機時間。每個機場皆會規定兩個航班間最短的轉機時間，以利轉機乘客於訂位時做為參考依據。

❸ MOML - Moslem Meal ㊎ [ˈmɑzləm] [mil] ㊒ [ˈmɔzləm] [miːl]

英文釋義 No pork, pork products gelatin and alcohol are allowed.

◆ 回教餐。乃一種宗教特別餐。所有的豬肉類製品、膠質和酒精都是禁用的。

【N】

❶ NBML – No Beef Meal ㊎ [no] [bif] [mil] ㊒ [nəu] [biːf] [miːl]

◆ 非牛肉餐。通常為不吃牛肉的亞洲旅客所準備的特別餐。

❷ Non-endorsable ㊊ [nɑn ɪn'dɔrsəbl̩] ㊒ [nɔn ɪn'dɔ:səbl]

英文釋義 a ticket which cannot be used to fly with another airline.

◆ 不可背書轉讓搭乘其他航空公司的機票。

❸ Non-revenue ㊊ [nɑn'rɛvə͵nju] ㊒ [nɔn'revinju:]

英文釋義 Passengers just pay the applicable taxes for their ticket for travel-ing. Usually the ticket is used by airline personnel.

◆ 免費票（非營收機票）。指乘客只付規定稅款、無需付票價即取得的機票，通常是航空公司從業人員才可使用的票種。

❹ Non-stop flight ㊊ [nɑn'stɑp] [flaɪt] ㊒ [nɔn'stɔp] [flait]

英文釋義 A flight that goes directly from airport A to airport B without land-ing en-route.

◆ 直飛班次。從A點至B點直飛，中間不停其他機場的航班。

❺ Non-transferable ㊊ [nɑn træns'fɜ͵əbl̩] ㊒ [nɔn træns'fə:rəbl]

英文釋義 A ticket which is specifically for just one passenger and cannot be used by anyone else.

◆ 不可轉讓的機票。此種機票僅限開票本人使用，不可轉予他人。

❻ No-shows ㊊ ['no'ʃos] ㊒ ['nəu'ʃəus]

英文釋義 Passengers either arrive late or do not arrive at all to travel on their booked flight.

◆ 未按規定時間、或根本沒有出現搭乘原預訂班機的旅客。

【O】

❶ O A G – Official Airline Guide ㊊ [ə'fɪʃəl] ['ɛr͵laɪn] [gaɪd] ㊒ [ə'fɪʃəl] ['ɛəlain] [gaid]

英文釋義 The monthly manual contains air travel information, such as airport, flight time and airlines data.

◆ 官方航班指南。每月更新的手冊,內含機場、飛行時間及各航空公司的最新資料。

❷ Offline connection KK [ˈɔflaɪn] [kəˈnɛkʃən] DJ [ˈɔːflaɪn] [kəˈnekʃən]

英文釋義 A journey where passengers travel on multiple planes using multiple airlines, checked baggage thus won't go all the way through to the final destination, but required to be picked up during the stopover and checked again with the next airline.

◆ 旅客的航程由不同航空公司之不同航班共同完成。但必須分開購票、且每個航段分開劃位及託運行李。

❸ Open-jaw KK [ˈɔpəndʒɔ] DJ [ˈəupəndʒɔː]

英文釋義 A round-trip ticket that allows the traveller to depart from city A to city B, but returning from city C to city A. For example, one may fly from Taipei to Los Angeles but return from San Francisco to Taipei.

◆ 旅客的來回航程由不同地點返回出發地。例如:可由台北飛抵洛杉磯,但從舊金山飛回台北。

【P】

❶ P.A. = Public Address KK [ˈpʌblɪk] [əˈdrɛs] DJ [ˈpʌblik] [əˈdres]

英文釋義 Public address announcement system is used to give information to passengers on board.

◆ 廣播系統。專為提供機上所有乘客與飛行航班相關的訊息。

❷ Package 🄺 ['pækɪdʒ] 🄳 ['pækidʒ]

英文釋義 Flights, hotels transportation and other services which are all bundled together and sold at a specific price to passengers.

◆ 全包式旅行。旅客從旅行社等機構以特定價格同時購得機票、飯店、交通旅遊等服務。

❸ Penalty fare 🄺 ['pɛnl̩tɪ] [fɛr] 🄳 ['penəlti] [fɛə]

英文釋義 The amount of money which a passenger has to pay in order to rearrange flights or cancel the ticket once it has been issue.

◆ 某些機票於開票時已載明，若有變更或取消，將被收取一定的金額做為罰金。

❹ Per diem 🄺 [pə'diəm] 🄳 [pə'di:əm]

英文釋義 A meal expense allowance based on the number of hours you are away from home.

◆ 航空公司給付空勤組員於服勤時的餐費零用金，以小時計價。

❺ PIC – Pilot in Command 🄺 ['paɪlət] [ɪn] [kə'mænd] 🄳 ['paɪlət] [in] [kə'mɑ:nd]

英文釋義 A captain who is assigned to be the leader of the aircrew members on duty.

◆ 統領整組空勤組員執勤的正機師。

❻ PIL - Passenger Information List 🄺 ['pæsn̩dʒɚ] [ɪnfɚ'meʃən] [lɪst] 🄳 ['pæsindʒə] [ˌinfə'meiʃən] [list]

英文釋義 This list provides information on passengers' names, seat numbers and their connecting flight information. It also shows passengers with a special request, such as wheel chair, special meal, etc..

◆ 這張資料表上會列出該航班與旅客有關的所有重要訊息。包括各艙等的乘客總數、乘客的姓名、座位號碼、轉機訊息以及特殊要求，如輪椅或特別餐等。

❼ Pitch ㉿ [pɪtʃ] ⒟ [pitʃ]

英文釋義 The distance between the front edge of one cabin seat and the front edge of the seat immediately in front when both are in an upright position.

◆ 客艙椅距。前後排客艙座位，其椅背皆豎直的狀態下，所量測的距離。

【R】

❶ Restricted to airport check-in

restricted ㉿ [rɪ'strɪktɪd] ⒟ [ris'triktid] 限制的

英文釋義 It refers to the situation that seating allocation and boarding passes can only be assigned to the passenger at the airport.

◆ 指乘客於機上的座位安排及其登機證，皆必須於機場櫃檯劃位時，才可確認取得。

❷ Runway ㉿ ['rʌnˌwe] ⒟ ['rʌnwei]

英文釋義 Defined rectangular area on a land aerodrome prepared for the landing and takeoff of aircraft (by ICAO).

◆ 機場跑道，航空器於此進行起飛及降落。

【S】

❶ Seat chart ㉿ [sit] [tʃɑrt] ⒟ [si:t] [tʃɑ:t]

英文釋義 A chart for passengers' seat arrangement with their names on it, usually used for first class or business class passengers.

◆ 座位表。載明乘客姓名及其座位號碼。通常爲便利服務頭等艙及商務艙旅客而設計使用。

❷ SFML – Seafood Meal ㉈ ['siˌfud] [mil] ㉇ ['sifuːd] [miːl]

◆ 海鮮餐。爲機上特殊餐點之一。

❸ Situated In, Ticketed In (SITI)

situate ㉈ ['sɪtʃʊˌet] ㉇ ['sitjueit]　使位（處）於

英文釋義 where you buy the ticket from the country you are leaving.

◆ 旅客的機票乃購自其出發地國家。

❹ Situated Out, Ticketed Out (SOTO)

英文釋義 where the ticket is bought from your destination country.

◆ 旅客的機票乃購自其目的地國家。

❺ Standby ㉈ ['stændˌbaɪ] ㉇ ['stændbai]

英文釋義 Passengers hold tickets that do not automatically guarantee reserved seats, instead that they are waiting for availability.

◆ 候補機位。乘客的機票無法預訂機位，必須至機場排隊候補。

❻ Station manager ㉈ ['steʃən] ['mænɪdʒɚ] ㉇ ['steiʃən] ['mænidʒə]

英文釋義 The leader of airlines representatives in the airport who is in charge of station operation.

◆ 站經理。航空公司每個航點皆會指派一站經理，統籌管理該航點的所有事務。

❼ STCR – Stretcher passenger ㉈ ['strɛtʃɚ] ['pæsn̩dʒɚ] ㉇ ['stretʃə] ['pæsindʒə]

英文釋義 If a passenger is unable to sit in the upright position in the aircraft from take-off to landing, he/she may request stretcher setup on board no later than 72 hours before departure.

◆ 擔架旅客。旅客因身體因素所需，可於起飛日至少72小時前，向航空公司申請於機上設置擔架。擔架之設置和醫療需求，皆另有特別規定。

【T】

❶ Taxiway ㊀ ['tæksɪˌwe] ㊁ ['tæksiˌwei]

英文釋義 A path in an airport used for taxiing airplanes to and from runways, ramps, hangars, terminals and other facilities.

◆ 滑行道。連結機場跑道、停機坪、維修棚、航站建築等設施的路徑。

❷ TIM - Travel information manual ㊀ ['trævl] [ˌɪnfɚ'meʃən] ['mænjʊəl] ㊁ ['trævl] [ˌinfə'meiʃən] ['mænjuəl]

英文釋義 The booklet contains current official information on travel regulations, procedures and restrictions for air travel of countries worldwide.

◆ 旅遊資訊手冊。內容包括各國官方之旅遊規定、手續及限制。

❸ Time table ㊀ [taɪm] ['tebl̩] ㊁ [taim] ['teibl]

英文釋義 The table lists the detailed flight information, including flight number, departure and arrival time, aircraft type and meal type of all flights.

◆ 班機時刻表。各家航空公司皆有免費的班機時刻表備索，裡頭載有班機號碼、班機起降時間、機型和餐型等資料。

❹ Turn –around ㊀ [tɝn] [ə'raʊnd] ㊁ [tə:n] [ə'raund]

英文釋義 Flight in which aircrew leave and return to the home base without a layover.

◆ 當天往返目的地城市和本站、無外站過夜停留的飛行任務。

❺ TWOV – Transit without visa ㊒ ['trænsɪt] [wɪ'ðaʊt] ['vizə] ㊅ ['trænsit] [wi'ðaut] ['vi:zə]

英文釋義 It refers to a transit alien traveling without a nonimmigrant visa, admitted under agreements with a transportation line, which guarantees his immediate and continuous passage to a foreign destination.

◆ 無簽證轉機旅客，此規定多見於美國機場轉機的旅客。係指依據轉機規定，外國人在未持有「非移民簽證」的情況下，經由美國任一城市轉機至第三國。

【U】

❶ UM – Unaccompanied minor ㊒ [ˌʌnə'kʌmpənɪd] ['maɪnɚ] ㊅ ['ʌnə'kʌmpənid] ['mainə]

英文釋義 Passengers aged between 5 and 12 who travel alone.

◆ 年齡介於5歲至12歲之間，獨自搭機旅行的孩童。

❷ UTC – Coordinated Universal Time ㊒ [ko'ɔrdnɪt] [ˌjunə'vɝsl̩] [taɪm] ㊅ [ko'ɔrdnɪt] [ˌju:ni'və:səl] [taim]

英文釋義 The standard time common to every place in the world, is expressed using a 24-hour clock but can be converted into a 12-hour clock (AM and PM). It reflects the mean solar time along the Earth's prime meridian.

◆ 世界標準（協調）時間。採24小時制。與格林威治標準時間同，以本初子午線做為參考基準點，原主要用於航運。上世紀始取代格林威治標準時間，全球適用。

【V】

❶ VGML – Vegetarian Meal 🔵 [ˌvɛdʒəˈtɛrɪən] [mil] 🔵 [ˌvedʒiˈtɛəriən] [miːl]

英文釋義 No meat or meat products of any type; no fish, fowl or products with lard or gelatin. Dairy products, eggs and honey are not permitted.

◆ 素食餐。所有肉類及其製品皆不可使用，蛋、乳品及蜂蜜亦不被允許使用。

【W】

❶ WCHC – Wheelchair for Cabin Seat
wheelchair 🔵 [ˈhwilˈtʃɛr] 🔵 [ˈhwiːlˈtʃɛə]　輪椅
◆ 輪椅旅客。於機上亦無法自行走動的乘客。

❷ WCHR – Wheelchair for Ramp
◆ 輪椅旅客。下機後於空橋需輪椅服務的旅客。

❸ WCHS – Wheelchair for Steps
◆ 輪椅旅客。上下樓梯行動較為不便、需要輪椅的旅客。

【Y】

❶ YP – Young passenger 🔵 [jʌŋ] [ˈpæsn̩dʒɚ] 🔵 [jʌŋ] [ˈpæsindʒə]
英文釋義 Passengers aged between 12 and 18 who travel alone.
◆ 年齡介於12歲至18歲之間，獨自搭機旅行的青少年。

Appendix　附　錄

● **ICAO phonetic (ICAO spelling alphabet)**
國際民航組織字母發音法

　　沿用「國際無線電字母發音」（International Radiotelephony Spelling Alphabets）亦即北約組織軍事上所用的「北約字母發音法」（NATO Phonetic Alp habets），每一個字母以一固定單字表示，以避免於無線電通訊聯繫時，因為有的字母只有一個音節，念起來容易混淆，導致接收方無法聽清楚整個字而誤解。所以便選擇該字母起首的兩個音節以上的英文單字，來代表這個字母。

A: Alpha	B: Bravo	C: Charlie
D: Delta	E: Echo	F: Foxtrot
G: Golf	H: Hotel	I: India
J: Juliet	K: Kilo	L: Lima
M: Mike	N: November	O: Oscar
P: Papa	Q: Quebec	R: Romeo
S: Sierra	T: Tango	U: Uniform
V: Victor	W: Whisky	X: X-Ray
Y: Yankce	Z: Zulu	

Chapter 10.　Airplane: exterior and interior
飛機外觀及客艙設備

▶ Outline: 以圖文方式介紹飛機外觀，及客艙內的各種設備和緊急逃生
用品。

▶ Learning Goals: 熟悉飛機構造，以及客艙各項設施和用品的名稱。

Fuselage means the body of an aircraft, which is combined with flight deck (cockpit), passenger cabin and cargo compartment. Flight crew members work in the cockpit to control and fly an airplane. Cockpit is a tiny space, yet contains plenty of electronic and mechanical flight instruments. Passengers are kept away from flight deck to prevent potential risk of hijacking. Cargo compartment locates under passenger cabin, which is used to stow passengers' check-in baggage and other cargoes. Passengers don't have the access to enter cargo area, either. Passenger cabin is the space where passengers and flight attendants may walk around. To provide passengers a satisfied flight experience, it is a great challenge for aircraft manufacturers and airlines to continuously upgrade the interior design of the passenger cabin.

飛機內部硬體設備共分三大部分：駕駛艙、客艙及貨艙。駕駛艙乃機師控制操作飛機之所在，空間雖小，但佈滿許多電子和機械之儀器及操控按鈕，為避免劫機的潛在風險，一般乘客無法進入駕駛艙一窺奧秘。貨艙裝載班機旅客之託運行李及其它託運貨物，位於客艙下方，乘客亦無法進入觀看。客艙則為飛行中，旅客的活動範疇。客艙內空間有限，為了在狹小移動的空間中，能盡可能地提供旅客需要的服務，持續優化客艙的空間運用，是飛機製造商及航

空公司極大的挑戰。

　　本章以圖文並呈的方式，介紹飛機外觀及内部的設備。客艙的空間，可概分為三部分：客艙、廚房、廁所。以下依序介紹飛機外觀、客艙（cabin）設備、廚房（galley）設備、廁所（lavatory）設備，第五部分則爲機上專用之緊急逃生備品介紹。

1. Airplane exterior（飛機外觀）

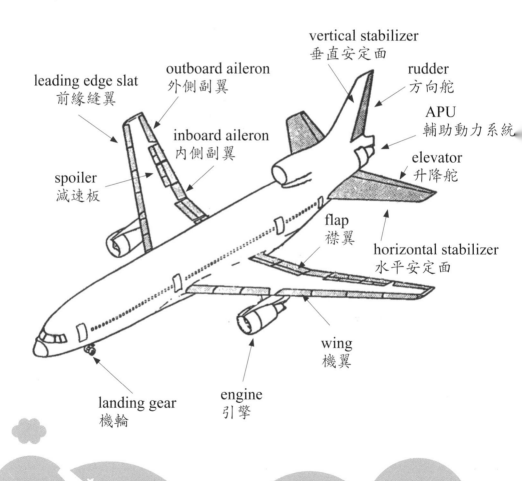

❶ aileron ㊚ [ˈeləˌrɑn] ㊛ [ˈeilərɔn]

英文釋義 Auxiliary wings, on the tail side of wings. The sideways movement of an aircraft is called rolling. Rolling is controlled by ailerons.

◆ 飛機機翼上的裝置，稱為副翼。左右對稱，靠近機身的稱為「inboard aileron」，遠端的稱為「outboard aileron」。此裝置可控制飛機機身左右轉動的動作，此運動稱為「rolling」（滾動)。

❷ APU – auxiliary power unit ㊚ [ɔgˈzɪljərɪ] [ˈpaʊɚ] [ˈjunɪt] ㊛ [ɔːgˈziljəri] [ˈpauə] [ˈjuːnit]

英文釋義 On the backend of the aircraft, supplying power mainly on ground

◆ 輔助動力系統，位於飛機尾部。飛機於地面時，在引擎發動前，除地面電源供應器（ground power unit, GPU）之外，可依靠此系統提供電力。

❸ elevator ㊚ [ˈɛləˌvetɚ] ㊛ [ˈeliveitə]

英文釋義 Locates on the back of the horizontal stabilizer. It controls the nose of an aircraft upward or downward, which is called pitching.

◆ 升降舵，位於機尾水平方向舵上，可控制飛機機頭的上下運動。此運動稱為「pitching」（俯仰）。

❹ engine ㊚ [ˈɛndʒən] ㊛ [ˈendʒin]

英文釋義 Mounted under wings (some may be on the back adjacent to vertical stabilizer or APU), producing the pounds of thrust.

◆ 引擎，位於機翼下方，某些機型亦有將引擎置於機尾的設計。可製造飛機前進的推力。

❺ flap 🅺🅺 [flæp] 🅳🅹 [flæp]

🔳英文釋義 Locates on the tail side of wings (adjacent to aileron). It increases drag and lift.

◆ 飛機機翼上的裝置，稱為襟翼。可向下(後)延展，擴大固定翼的表面積和角度，可提高升力及阻力。

❻ horizontal stabilizer 🅺🅺 ['hɑrə'zɑntl̩] ['stebl̩aɪzɚ] 🅳🅹 ['hɔri'zɔntl] ['steibilaizə]

🔳英文釋義 On the back of an aircraft. It keeps and aircraft in flight steady and level.

◆ 水平安定面，位於飛機後方，為固定裝置，可使飛機保持平穩及一定高度。

❼ landing gear 🅺🅺 ['lændɪŋ] [gɪr] 🅳🅹 ['lændɪŋ] [giə]

🔳英文釋義 The undercarriage of an aircraft to support the airplane on ground. The wheels facilitate aircraft's operation to and from hard surfaces (take-off and landing).

◆ 機輪，位於飛機下方。飛機於地面時，機輪乃支撐飛機的裝置。於地面滑行時亦靠機輪帶動飛機前進。

❽ leading edge slat 🅺🅺 ['lidɪŋ] [ɛdʒ] [slæt] 🅳🅹 ['li:dɪŋ] [edʒ] [slæt]

🔳英文釋義 It refers to the aerodynamic surfaces on the leading edge of the wings. It allows the angle of wings to be extended while deployed and increases lift and drag.

◆ 前緣縫翼，位於機翼前緣，可經由角度改變增加整片機翼的弧度，以便於飛機速度減慢時（如降落），可增加升力及阻力。

❾ rudder ⓚ [ˈrʌdɚ] ⓓ [ˈrʌdə]

英文釋義 locates on the back of the vertical stabilizer. It controls an aircraft to the right or left, which the movement is called yawing.

◆ 方向舵，位於機尾的垂直安定面上。其可控制飛機機頭的左右移動，此運動方式稱爲「yawing」（左右搖動）。

❿ spoiler ⓚ [ˈspɔɪlɚ] ⓓ [ˈspɔilə]

英文釋義 This apparatus is used to control speed and brake.

◆ 減速板，位於機翼上。此裝置的功用乃控制速度及煞車。

⓫ vertical stabilizer ⓚ [ˈvɝtɪkl̩] [ˈstebl̩aɪzɚ] ⓓ [ˈvəːtikəl] [ˈsteibilaizə]

英文釋義 Locates on the back of the aircraft and keeps an aircraft in flight steady and upright.

◆ 垂直安定面，位於飛機尾端，爲一固定裝置，可協助飛機保持穩定直線的飛行。

⓬ wing ⓚ [wɪŋ] ⓓ [wiŋ]

英文釋義 On both sides of an aircraft to create lift and serves fuel tanks.

◆ 機翼。位於飛機機身兩側，主要功能爲產生升力及放置油箱。

2. Cabin （客艙）

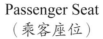

Passenger Seat
（乘客座位）

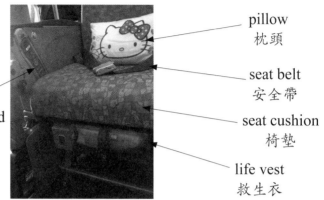

pillow
枕頭

seat belt
安全帶

seat cushion
椅墊

life vest
救生衣

Audio/Video on Demand
(AVOD) handset
（娛樂/服務控制器）

註：「娛樂／服務控制器」除機上視聽節目、電動遊戲的控制面板功
　能外，背面爲衛星電話（satellite phone）的按鍵。同時，服務鈴
　（call button）及閱讀燈（reading light）的開關鍵亦於其上。

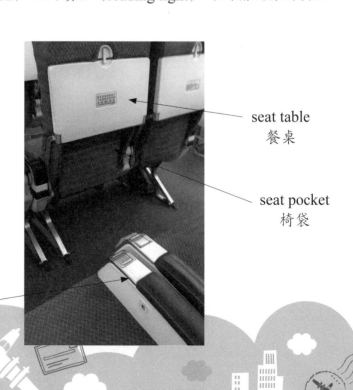

seat table
餐桌

seat pocket
椅袋

armrest
扶手

- armrest ⓚ [ˈɑrmˌrɛst] ⓓ [ˈɑːmrest]　扶手
- cushion ⓚ [ˈkʊʃən] ⓓ [ˈkʊʃən]　椅墊
- handset ⓚ [ˈhændˌsɛt] ⓓ [ˈhændˈset]　手持聽筒
- pillow ⓚ [ˈpɪlo] ⓓ [ˈpiləu]　枕頭
- pocket ⓚ [ˈpɑkɪt] ⓓ [ˈpɔkit]　口袋
- satellite ⓚ [ˈsætˌlˌaɪt] ⓓ [ˈsætəlait]　衛星

Cabin Door / Exit (A330-300)
（空中巴士A330-300機型之機艙門）

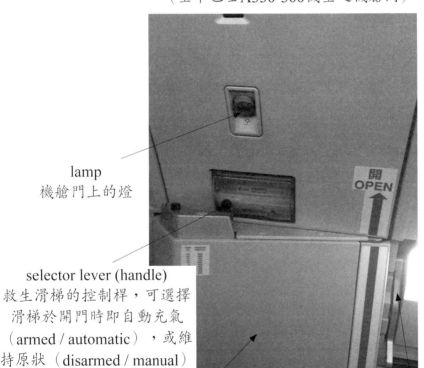

lamp
機艙門上的燈

selector lever (handle)
救生滑梯的控制桿，可選擇
滑梯於開門時即自動充氣
（armed / automatic），或維
持原狀（disarmed / manual）

door bustle/slide compartment
機門下方突出的裝置，內置
充氣前折疊平整的救生滑梯

door handle
門把（可開、關機艙門），
向上開啓、向下關閉

exit
緊急逃生出口

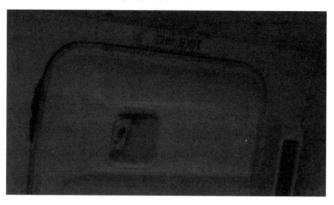

補充：客艙機門開關口訣

【開門】

1. Check to see "fasten seat belt" sign is off

   （確認「繫上安全帶」燈號已經熄滅）

2. CP announces "doors for arrival"

   （座艙長廣播"doors for arrival"）

3. Shift the selector lever to the disarmed (manual) position

   （將控制桿移至手動狀態）

4. Plug in the safety lock-out pin

   （插入安全插梢）

5. Make cross-check then report

   （與另一側空服員進行互相檢查後報告）

6. Give ground crew "OK" sign indicating that it is safe to operate the door

   （以"OK"手勢向飛機外的地勤人員表示，可以進行開門動作）

【關門】

1. Check to see that the door handle is in close position

   （檢查門把已經在關門的位置）

2. Check to see that there is no opening or anything stuck between the door and the body of the aircraft

   （檢查機門與機身間，沒有縫隙，也沒有任何雜物卡住）

3. Give ground crew "OK" sign indicating that the door has been closed properly

   （給予地勤"OK"手勢，代表門已關妥）

4. CP announces "doors for departure"

   （座艙長廣播"doors for departure"）

5. Pull out the safety lock-out pin and leave it in the safety pin container

   （拔出安全插梢並放好）

6. Shift the selector lever to the armed (automatic) position

   （將控制桿移至自動充氣的位置）

7. Make cross-check then report

   （與另一側空服員進行互相檢查後報告）

- bustle **KK** ['bʌsl̩] **DJ** ['bʌsl] 腰墊；拱起的物品
- container **KK** [kən'tenɚ] **DJ** [kən'teinə] 容器
- lamp **KK** [læmp] **DJ** [læmp] 燈
- lever **KK** ['lɛvɚ] **DJ** ['levə] 槓桿；控制桿
- selector **KK** [sə'lɛktɚ] **DJ** [si'lektə] 選擇器；分離器
- slide **KK** [slaɪd] **DJ** [slaid] 滑梯（於地面做為救生滑梯，於水面做為救生筏 "raft"）

Passenger Service Unit (PSU)
（乘客座位上方的服務系統）

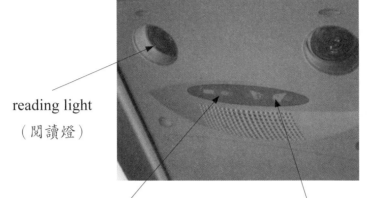

reading light
（閱讀燈）

non-smoking sign
（禁菸燈號）

fasten seat belt sign
（繫上安全帶燈號）

Overhead compartment / bin/cabinet
（頭頂置物櫃）

pull-down
（下拉式）

pivot
（上掀式）

seat locator sign
（座位號碼）

Stowage
（小型貯物櫃）

latch
（門閂，用以固定櫃子的門）

CA seat (double)
（空服員雙人座椅）

Interphone handset
（機內對講機/話筒）

 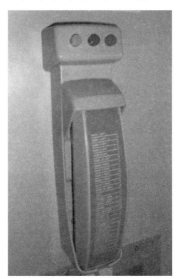

- bin ᴋᴋ [bɪn] ᴅᴊ [bin]　箱子；倉
- cabinet ᴋᴋ ['kæbənɪt] ᴅᴊ ['kæbinit]　櫥；櫃

- interphone handset ⓚ ['ɪntəˌfon] ['hændˌsɛt] ⓓ ['ɪntəˌfəun] ['hænd'set]
  對講機

- latch ⓚ [lætʃ] ⓓ [lætʃ]　門閂

- pivot ⓚ ['pɪvət] ⓓ ['pivət]　樞軸

- unit ⓚ ['junɪt] ⓓ ['juːnit]　單位；單元

3. Galley (廚房)

tea / coffee maker
（煮茶 / 咖啡機）

oven
（烤箱）

control panel
（控制面板）

stowage
（貯物櫃）

container
（手提鐵箱）

curtain
（窗簾）

meal cart
（餐車）

meal tray
（餐盤）

- cart ᴋᴋ [kɑrt] ᴅᴊ [kɑ:t]　手推車
- curtain ᴋᴋ ['kɝtn̩] ᴅᴊ ['kə:tn]　窗簾
- galley ᴋᴋ ['gælɪ] ᴅᴊ ['gæli]　廚房
- oven ᴋᴋ ['ʌvən] ᴅᴊ ['ʌvən]　烤箱
- panel ᴋᴋ ['pænl̩] ᴅᴊ ['pænəl　控制板
- stowage ᴋᴋ ['stoɪdʒ] ᴅᴊ ['stəuidʒ]　貯物櫃
- tray ᴋᴋ [tre] ᴅᴊ [trei]　盤

4. Lavatory（廁所）

door latch
（門栓）

No smoking sign
（廁所內禁菸標誌）

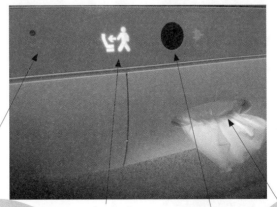

廁所內叫人鈴
（attendant call button）　　提醒回座燈號
（return to seat sign）　　插座
（socket）　　面紙
（facial tissue）

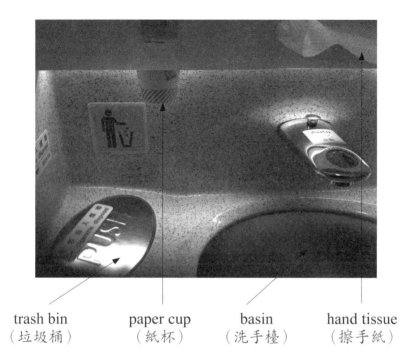

trash bin	paper cup	basin	hand tissue
（垃圾桶）	（紙杯）	（洗手檯）	（擦手紙）

smoke detector
（煙霧偵測器）

 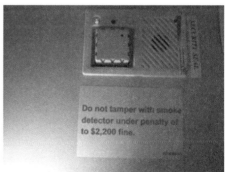

diaper changing table
（尿布檯）

flush button
（沖水按鍵）

- basin ⓀⓀ ['besn̩] ⒹⒿ ['beisn] 洗手檯
- detector ⓀⓀ [dɪ'tɛktɚ] ⒹⒿ [di'tektə] 偵測器
- diaper ⓀⓀ ['daɪəpɚ] ⒹⒿ ['daɪəpə] 尿布
- facial ⓀⓀ ['feʃəl] ⒹⒿ ['feiʃəl] 臉部的
- flush ⓀⓀ [flʌʃ] ⒹⒿ [flʌʃ] 沖洗
- socket ⓀⓀ ['sɑkɪt] ⒹⒿ ['sɔkit] 插座
- tissue ⓀⓀ ['tɪʃʊ] ⒹⒿ ['tiʃu] 紙巾
- trash ⓀⓀ [træʃ] ⒹⒿ [træʃ] 垃圾

5. 緊急逃生備品

doctor kit
（醫療箱）

first aid kit
（急救包）

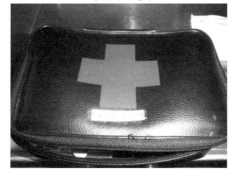

water extinguisher
（水滅火器）

halon extinguisher
（泡沫滅火器）

smoke hood
（防煙面罩）

megaphone
（擴音器）

oxygen mask
（氧氣面罩）

life vest
（救生衣）

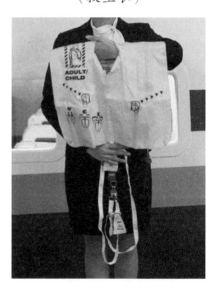

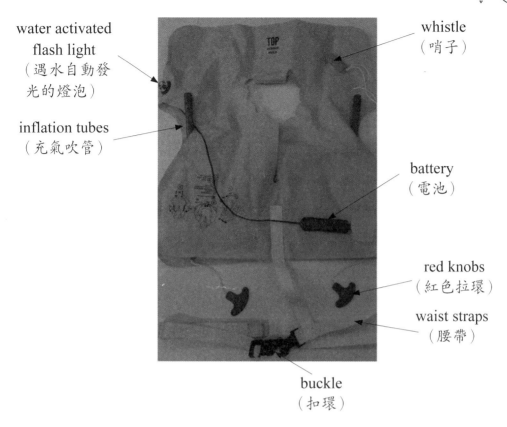

water activated
flash light
（遇水自動發
光的燈泡）

whistle
（哨子）

inflation tubes
（充氣吹管）

battery
（電池）

red knobs
（紅色拉環）

waist straps
（腰帶）

buckle
（扣環）

- buckle ⓚⓚ ['bʌkl̩] ⓓⓙ ['bʌkl̩]　扣環
- extinguisher ⓚⓚ [ɪk'stɪŋgwɪʃəʳ] ⓓⓙ [iks'tiŋgwiʃə]　滅火器
- hood ⓚⓚ [hʊd] ⓓⓙ [hud]　兜帽
- knob ⓚⓚ [nɑb] ⓓⓙ [nɔb]　瘤；球型把手
- megaphone ⓚⓚ ['mɛgə͵fon] ⓓⓙ ['mɛgəfəun]　擴音器
- whistle ⓚⓚ ['hwɪsl̩] ⓓⓙ ['hwisl̩]　哨子

Chapter 11.　Public address-I

▶ Outline: 整理自旅客登機至下機前之客艙服務相關廣播詞，可據此對
客艙服務內容及流程更加熟稔。此章內容亦為空服員面試之必考項
目。

▶ Learning Goals: 熟讀廣播詞，並能流利誦出每段內容。

【Greeting passengers（地面歡迎詞）】

❶ avoid ⓀⓀ [ə'vɔɪd] ⒹⒿ [ə'vɔid]　避免；躲開 (v.)

英文釋義 To prevent something from happening

同義詞 keep away from

❷ properly ⓀⓀ ['prɑpəlɪ] ⒹⒿ ['prɔpəli]　正確地；適當地 (adv.)

英文釋義 Behave in the right manner

同義字 appropriately; suitably

廣　播　▶　🎵11-1

Good morning/ afternoon/ evening

　　Ladies and gentlemen, welcome aboard airline flight flight number
to destination . For your comfort and safety, please place your carry-on baggage in the overhead compartment or under the seat in front of you. Please
be careful that your baggage is properly stowed in the overhead compartment to avoid dropping when opened. Please let us know if you need assistance. Thank you.

譯　文　▶

各位貴賓，早安／午安／晚安：

　　歡迎搭乘　公司名稱　航空　班機號碼　前往　目的地　。為

了您的舒適及安全，請將您的手提行李，放在頭頂的置物櫃中，或是您前方的座位下。在您打開頭頂置物櫃時，請務必小心，以免行李掉落。如果需要任何協助，請通知我們，謝謝。

【Emergency exit seating（緊急出口座位）】

❶ duration ㏍ [djʊˈreʃən] ㎗ [djuˈreiʃən] 持續時間 (n.)

英文釋義 The length of time that something continues or exists

同義字 period; time

❷ function ㏍ [ˈfʌŋkʃən] ㎗ [ˈfʌŋkʃən] 功能；作用 (n.)

英文釋義 An action performed by something or someone that produces a result

同義字 action; role

❸ navigation ㏍ [ˌnævəˈgeʃən] ㎗ [ˌnæviˈgeiʃən] 航行（空、海)、導航 (n.)

英文釋義 Travel by vessels; The act of plotting a route and directing a ship, aircraft, or car, etc.

同義字 steering

❹ notify ㏍ [ˈnotəˌfaɪ] ㎗ [ˈnəutifai] 通知 (v.)

英文釋義 To let someone know about something

同義字 inform; tell

❺ perform ㏍ [pəˈfɔrm] ㎗ [pəˈfɔːm] 執行；表演 (v.)

英文釋義 To carry out an action or a piece of work; to put on any kind of show

同義字 act; execute

❻ remote KK [rɪˈmot] DJ [riˈməut]　遙遠的；遠端的 (a.)

英文釋義 situated at some distance away

同義字 apart; far-off

廣　播　▶　♪11-2

Ladies and gentlemen,

If you are seated next to an emergency exit, please read carefully the special instructions card located by your seat. If you do not wish to perform the functions described in the event of an emergency, please ask a flight attendant to reseat you.

At this time, we request that all mobile phones, radios and remote controlled toys be turned off for the full duration of the flight, as these items might interfere with the navigational and communication equipment on this aircraft. We request that all other electronic devices be turned off until we fly above 10,000 feet. We will notify you when it is safe to use such devices. Thank you.

譯　文　▶

各位貴賓：

如果您的座位是在緊急出口旁的位置，請您仔細閱讀座位旁的「緊急逃生出口座位須知卡」。若您無意願在緊急狀況發生時，協助執行須知卡上所載事項，請告知空服員為您換位。

同時，請您於全程飛行中，勿使用手機通訊、無線電及遙控玩具，這些裝備可能對導航及通訊儀器造成干擾。其它電子產品在飛機抵達一萬英呎的高度後，我們將另行廣播告知可以使用的時間。謝謝。

【Safety demonstration（安全示範）】

❶ automatically ⓀⓀ [ˌɔtə'mætɪkḷlɪ] Ⓓ Ⓙ [ˌɔ:tə'mætɪkəli] 自動地（adv.）

英文釋義 To move or start something independently or without thinking

同義字 naturally; voluntarily

❷ demonstration ⓀⓀ [ˌdɛmən'streʃən] Ⓓ Ⓙ [ˌdemən'streiʃən] 示範 (v.)

英文釋義 a proof or example of something

同義字 display; show

❸ destroy ⓀⓀ [dɪ'strɔɪ] Ⓓ Ⓙ [dis'trɔɪ] 破壞；毀壞 (v.)

英文釋義 To tear down something or cause it to end

同義字 ruin; demolish

❹ inflation ⓀⓀ [ɪn'fleʃən] Ⓓ Ⓙ [in'fleiʃən] 充氣；擴張 (n.)

英文釋義 being filled with air

同義字 swelling; expansion

❺ knob ⓀⓀ [nɑb] Ⓓ Ⓙ [nɔb] 圓形鈕；球型突出物 (n.)

英文釋義 It is a projecting part (usually rounded) which forms the handle of a door or drawer.

同義字 button; node

❻ release ⓀⓀ [rɪ'lis] Ⓓ Ⓙ [ri'li:s] 鬆開；釋放 (v.)

英文釋義 To allow being free from something

同義字 loose; liberate

❼ strap ⓀⓀ [stræp] Ⓓ Ⓙ [stræp] 帶子 (n.)

英文釋義 A long narrow strip of flexible material such as leather

同義字 belt

❽ tighten ⟨KK⟩ ['taɪtn̩] ⟨DJ⟩ ['taitn̩]   綁緊 (v.)

（英文釋義）To make something become firmer or less flexible

（同義字）fasten; secure

❾ undo ⟨KK⟩ [ʌn'du] ⟨DJ⟩ ['ʌn'du:]   打開；脫去 (v.)

（英文釋義）To release or reverse something to its previous state

（同義字）unlock; unfasten

廣 播 11-3

Ladies and gentlemen,

     Please direct your attention to the safety demonstration on the screen nearest to you. Please let us know if you have any question. Thank you.

- Please keep your seat belt fastened while seated. To release, simply undo the buckle.
- If cabin pressure changes suddenly, oxygen masks will automatically appear above your head. Place the mask over your mouth and nose, and breathe normally.
- Put on your mask before assisting children.
- This plane has ___number___ exits. All are clearly marked with instructions.
- A life vest is stowed under your seat. First pull it over your head. Pull the waist straps to the front and tighten. Pull red knobs for automatic inflation. For manual inflation, blow into the tubes at either side. Inflate your vest when you get to the emergency exit.
- To ensure safety, the use of personal telephones is prohibited at all times. Other electronic devices are prohibited only during take-off and landing.
- The law also prohibits destroying any smoke detector in the rest room.

- Keep hand luggage clear of the aisles and exits. During take-off and landing, be sure your seat back and table are in their fully upright positions.
- Please observe the "FASTEN SEAT BELT" and "NO SMOKING" signs. Please refer to the safety information card for detailed information. Thank you.

譯文

各位貴賓：

　　我們即將開始爲您示範機上安全須知。有關本飛機各項安全設備及使用方法，請您注意前方螢幕上的示範，若是有任何疑問，請隨時詢問空服人員。

．使用安全帶時，將扣環扣好繫緊，扣把向外一撥，即可鬆開。

．氧氣罩在您上方，機艙失壓時，會自動落下。拉下面罩，罩住口、鼻，調整鬆緊帶，正常呼吸。

．如果有小孩隨行，請先行使用氧氣面罩再照顧小孩。

．本機艙共有 ＿數字＿ 個緊急出口，使用方法及位置均有標示。

．救生衣在您座位下，使用時由頭上套下，腰帶拉至前方扣好、拉緊，用力拉下紅色拉環即可充氣，無法自動充氣時，請吹前面兩條管子。

．到緊急出口前，才將救生衣充氣。

．爲了飛航安全，禁用無線電話機，起飛及降落時，禁止使用電子產品。

．依法規定，不得損毀化妝室內的煙霧偵測器。

．手提行李請勿阻礙通道及出口，起飛和降落時，請豎直椅背、收好桌子。

．請遵守繫緊安全帶和禁菸燈號，有關安全救生事項，請參閱安全須知卡。

【Ready for take-off（預備起飛）】

廣 播 ♪11-4

Ladies and Gentlemen,

　　We are ready for take-off. Please make sure again that your seat belt is fastened. Thank you.

譯 文

各位貴賓：

　　我們現在即將起飛，請再次確認您的安全帶是否繫緊。謝謝您的合作。

【Cabin crew introduction（介紹組員）】

❶ throughout **KK** [θru'aʊt] **DJ** [θru:'aut]　遍布 (prep.)；始終 (adv.)

英文釋義 In or during the entire time or part of something.

同義字 during; through

廣 播 ♪11-5

Ladies and gentlemen,

　　Your flight is under the command of Captain _____, I am the chief purser _____ , in addition, we have _____ cabin attendants who will be available throughout the flight to serve you. Thank you.

譯 文

各位貴賓：

　　今天班機的機長是 _____。我是座艙長 _____。此外，我們共有 _____ 位空服人員於機上為您服務。謝謝。

【Service introduction（介紹服務）】

❶ appreciate ㋖ [əˈpriʃɪˌet] ㋛ [əˈpriːʃieit]　感激；欣賞 (v.)

英文釋義 To place a high estimate on someone or something

同義字 cherish; value

❷ cruise ㋖ [kruz] ㋛ [kruːz]　巡航；以最省燃料的速度航行 (v.) (n.)

英文釋義 To go or travel; to fly, drive or sail at a constant speed that permits maximum operating efficiency

同義字 sail

廣 播　♪11-6

Ladies and Gentlemen,

　　Upon reaching our cruising altitude, we will be serving you a beverage and meal. A wide selection of duty free items and a movie presentation are also available. Our in-flight magazine may help you with more detailed information. If you have any question, please contact our cabin attendants. Please be noticed that this is a non-smoking flight, we appreciate your cooperation in not smoking on this flight. Thank you.

譯 文

各位貴賓：

　　當飛機到達預定高度後，我們將供應飲料及餐點，機上也有免稅物品的銷售服務及電影欣賞，相關的資料，請您參閱機上雜誌。如果您有任何疑問，請隨時詢問空服人員。同時本班機施行全面禁菸，請勿在機上任何地方吸菸，謝謝您的合作。

【Form distribution（分發入境表格）】

❶ distribute ⓚⓚ [dɪ'strɪbjʊt] ⓓⓙ [di'stribjut] 分發；派送 (v.)

英文釋義 To hand out something or spread something around

同義字 deliver; allocate

廣 播 ▷ ♪11-7

Ladies and Gentlemen,

In a few minutes, we are going to distribute the forms to you. If you have any question, please contact your cabin attendants. Thank you.

譯 文 ▷

各位貴賓：

再過幾分鐘，我們將分發入境表格。填寫時若有任何問題，請告知空服人員，謝謝。

【Seat belt sign off （安全帶燈號熄滅）】

廣 播 ▷ ♪11-8

Ladies and Gentlemen,

The captain has turned off the fasten seat belt sign, however, we recommend that you keep your seat belt fastened while seated, thank you.

譯 文 ▷

各位貴賓：

機長已經將繫緊安全帶的燈號熄滅了，為了您的安全，當您在座時請仍將安全帶繫好，謝謝您的合作。

【Duty free sales（販賣免稅品）】

❶ featured ⓚ ['fitʃəd] ⓓ ['fiːtʃəd] 特色的；做為號召的（adj.）

英文釋義 Something given highlighted, displayed, advertised, or presented as a special attraction

同義字 highlighted

廣 播 ▷ ♪11-9

Ladies and gentlemen,

The cabin attendants are now providing you with our in-flight duty free sales. You can find a listing of our featured items in our in-flight magazine. Please let us know if you want to make a purchase during the flight. Thank you.

譯 文 ▷

各位貴賓：

空服員即將為您進行免稅品的銷售服務。您可以從機內雜誌上瀏覽我們的特色商品。如果您有意購買，請告知空服人員，謝謝。

【Turbulence（亂流）】

❶ turbulence ⓚ ['tɝbjələns] ⓓ ['təːbjuləns] 亂流 (n.)

英文釋義 Air moves in an unstable manner

同義詞 bumpy air

廣 播 ▷ ♪11-10

Ladies and Gentlemen,

We are expecting to pass some turbulence. Please return to your seat and fasten seat belt. Thank you for your cooperation.

譯 文

各位貴賓：

　　我們將通過一段不穩定的氣流，請回到您的座位並繫上安全帶，謝謝您的合作。

【Descending（下降）】

廣 播 11-11

Ladies and gentlemen,

　　We will start descending in _____ minutes and will be landing in _____ at _____ local time. Please make sure that all landing forms have been filled out completely. To prevent the interference with aircraft navigation, please do not use any electronic equipment from now on. Please return to your seat and fasten your seat belt. Thank you.

譯 文

各位貴賓：

　　再過 _____ 分鐘，我們即將開始下降。預計在當地時間 _____ _____ 點 _____ 分降落於 _____ 機場。請確認您已填妥入境表格。為避免飛機導航設備遭受干擾，從現在起，請勿使用任何電子用品。請回到您的座位，繫上安全帶。謝謝。

【Landing（降落）】

廣 播 11-12

Ladies and gentlemen,

　　We have just landed at _____ international airport in _city_ . For

your own safety, please remain seated with your seat belt fastened until the aircraft has come to a complete stop and the "fasten seat belt" sign has been turned off. We would like to take this opportunity to thank you for flying with airline . We hope that you have enjoyed the flight and we are looking forward to serving you again in the near future. Thank you.

譯 文

各位貴賓：

我們已經降落在 城市名   機場名 機場。為了您的安全，在飛機完全停妥，繫上安全帶燈號尚未熄滅以前，請您留在座位上並繫好安全帶。在此感謝您搭乘 航空公司 航空班機，希望您對我們的服務感到滿意。期待在不久的將來能再次為您服務。謝謝。

【Crew change（更換組員）】

❶ behalf 〔KK〕 [bɪ'hæf] 〔DJ〕 [bɪ'hɑ:f]　代表；利益 (n.)

〔英文釋義〕 In place of or for someone or something

〔同義字〕 interest

❷ pleasant 〔KK〕 ['plɛzənt] 〔DJ〕 ['pleznt]　歡愉的；舒適的 (adj.)

〔英文釋義〕 The sensation of being given pleasure or enjoyment

〔同義字〕 enjoyable; delightful

廣 播　♪11-13

Ladies and Gentlemen,

There will be a crew change here. On behalf of the captain and all the crew, we hope that you have enjoyed the flight with us and wish you another pleasant flight. Thank you.

譯 文 ▷

各位貴賓：

　　我們將在此地更換飛行組員，希望您滿意本組為您所做的服務，並祝您旅途愉快，謝謝。

【Disembarkation（下機）】

❶ forward ㏍ ['fɔrwəd] ⅅ ['fɔ:wəd]　向前的 (adj.) (adv.)

　英文釋義 Toward the front

　同義字 advance

❷ remind ㏍ [rɪ'maɪnd] ⅅ [ri'maind]　提醒 (v.)

　英文釋義 Cause to think or remember

　同義字 recall

廣 播 ▷　♪11-14

Ladies and Gentlemen,

　　You may disembark from the forward door now. May we remind you to take all your belongings with you while deplane. Thank you.

譯 文 ▷

各位貴賓：

　　現在請由前方機門順序下機，下機時，請記得攜帶您的隨身行李，謝謝。

Chapter 12.　Public address-II　機上廣播―II

▶ Outline: 列舉班機遭遇特殊狀況時所做的廣播詞；以及飛往各國時，
應其國家要求所做的特殊廣播。

▶ Learning Goals: 熟讀廣播詞，暸解各國之特殊規定。

Ⓐ Announcements for irregular or emergency situations 異常或緊急狀況廣播

【Delay departure （飛機於地面延誤起飛）】

❶ congestion ᴋᴋ [kən'dʒɛstʃən] ᴅᴊ [kən'dʒɛstʃən]　壅塞 (n.)

英文釋義 A condition of overcrowded with people or vehicles or else

同義字 jam

• air traffic congestion　空中交通擁擠

❷ technical ᴋᴋ ['tɛknɪkl̩] ᴅᴊ ['teknikəl]　技術的；工藝的 (adj.)

英文釋義 Tasks or issues relating to mathematical, engineering, scientific or
computer-related duties.

同義字 mechanical

廣 播 ▷ ♪12-1

Ladies and Gentlemen,

　　We are expecting a limited delay due to (1) operational reasons

(2) a holding by Air Traffic Control

(3) traffic congestion

(4) ground handling

(5) weather conditions

(6) technical reasons

We'll be on the ground for another _____ minutes. We apologize for any inconvenience and thank you for your patience.

譯 文 ▷

各位貴賓：

　　由於　(1)航務作業　(2)航路管制　(3) 空中交通擁擠

　　　　　(4)地面作業　(5)天氣惡劣　(6)機務作業

　　我們將再等待 _____ 分鐘才能啟程，耽誤您許多寶貴時間，請您多多原諒。謝謝您的耐心與合作。

【Abort taxing（終止滑行）】

❶ maintenance ⓀⓀ ['mentənəns] ⒹⒿ ['meintinəns]　維修；保養 (n.)

　英文釋義 Activities required to provide support or upkeep to something's original condition as long as possible

　同義字 preservation; service

廣 播 ▷　♪12-2

Ladies and Gentlemen,

　　Due to technical problem, our Captain has decided to return to the ramp area for maintenance check. We apologize for any inconvenience and thank you for your patience and understanding.

譯 文 ▷

各位貴賓：

　　儀表版指示有不正常狀況，為了安全起見，機長決定滑回停機坪檢查，帶來不便之處，請您多多原諒，感謝您的耐心與諒解。

【Quick-return flight（返航）】

❶ further KK ['fɝðɚ] DJ ['fə:ðə]　更遠的；更進一步的 (adj.) (adv.)

英文釋義 It means more distant in degree, time, or space

同義字 farther; advance

廣　播　▶　🎵12-3

Ladies and Gentlemen,

　　Due to (1)technical problem　(2)security reason

　　　　　(3)weather conditions　(4)a seriously sick passenger on board

our captain has decided to return to the _____ airport, you will be

informed of further information as soon as possible. We apologize for any

inconvenience and thank you for your patience and understanding.

譯　文　▶

各位貴賓：

　　由於　(1)技術困難（機件故障）　(2)安全理由

　　　　　(3)天氣不好　(4)機上有急病旅客

　　機長已經決定返回 _____ 機場，若有進一步消息，我們將盡

快通知各位，帶來不便之處，請您多多原諒，感謝您的耐心與諒解。

【Shortage of landing form（入境表格不足）】

❶ shortage KK ['ʃɔrtɪdʒ] DJ ['ʃɔ:tɪdʒ]　短缺 (n.)

英文釋義 The quantity of supply is not sufficient

同義字 lack; deficiency

廣播 🎵12-4

Ladies and Gentlemen,

Due to a shortage of the landing forms, please obtain the necessary forms after disembarkation. We apologize for any inconvenience caused. Thank you.

譯文

各位貴賓：

由於機內入境表格不足，請各位旅客下機後拿取表格；帶來不便之處，請您多多原諒。謝謝。

【To put duty-free sales on hold（暫停免稅品服務）】

❶ encounter KK [ɪnˈkaʊntɚ] DJ [inˈkauntə] 發生；遭遇 (v.)

英文釋義 To experience some difficulty or meet someone without expectation

同義字 come across; confront

廣播 🎵12-5

Ladies and Gentlemen,

As we are encountering some turbulence, we will close our duty free sales for a moment. We apologize for any inconvenience this may cause you. Thank you.

譯文

各位貴賓：

由於氣流不穩定，為了安全起見，我們必須暫停免稅品的銷售服務，如有帶來不便之處，請您多多原諒。謝謝。

【To cancel duty-free sales（取消免稅品販賣）】

廣　播 ▷ 🎵12-6

Ladies and Gentlemen,

　　Due to a short flying time, we are unable to provide duty free sales on board today. We apologize for the inconvenience and thank you for your understanding.

譯　文 ▷

各位貴賓：

　　由於飛行時間過短，我們無法提供免稅品銷售服務，帶來不便之處，請您多多原諒。

【Count passenger number（地面清點乘客人數）】

廣　播 ▷ 🎵12-7

Ladies and Gentlemen, may we have your attention,

　　Our ground staff has requested that we count the number of passengers on our flight. Please remain in your seats while we are making this check. Thank you.

譯　文 ▷

各位貴賓，請注意：

　　因應地勤工作人員要求，我們需要清點乘客人數，請您暫時不要離開座位，謝謝您的合作。

【Special announcement for holidays （特別節日致意）】

❶ meanwhile 🄺🄺 ['mɪn,hwaɪl] 🄳🄹 ['miːnˈhwaɪl]　其時；其間 (adv.) (n.)

英文釋義 During or in the intervening time

同義字 in the meantime

廣 播 ▶ 🎵12-8

Ladies and Gentlemen,

   Airline takes great pleasure to send our best regards to you and your family during this special time of the year. We wish you a very happy holiday . Meanwhile, our cabin attendants wish to present you with a gift that we hope will add to the spirit of the holiday .

譯 文 ▶

各位貴賓：

   謹代表　 航空公司 　及全體組員在此　 節日 　期間，敬祝各位 　 節日 　愉快／萬事如意。我們準備了一份特別的禮物送您，希望更能為您增添節慶的氣氛。

【Service survey（旅客意見調查）】

❶ frank KK [fræŋk] DJ [fræŋk]　坦白的；真誠的 (adj.)

英文釋義 To act or express thoughts without inhibition or subterfuge

同義字 open; straightforward

廣 播 ▶ 🎵12-9

Ladies and Gentlemen,

   We are conducting a survey to see how we can improve our service. We would appreciate it if you could take a few minutes to fill out the survey (in the seat pocket in front of you). We welcome your frank opinion of our service. Thank you.

譯 文

各位貴賓：

　　為了提高我們的服務水準，我們在各位座位前方的口袋中有一份調查問卷，請您提供寶貴的意見，並將此問卷交給空服人員，以作為我們改進的參考，謝謝。

【Lost and found（失物招領）】

廣 播 🎵12-10

Ladies and Gentlemen,

　　We have just found a /an ___item___ in ___location___. If you have lost it, please contact the cabin attendants.

譯 文

各位貴賓，請注意：

　　我們在 ___地點___ 撿到一個 ___物品___ ，若有旅客遺失，請與空服員聯絡，謝謝。

【Stand-by for parking（等候停靠停機坪）】

❶ queue **KK** [kju] **DJ** [kju:]　排隊；人或車輛的長列 (v.) (n.)

　英文釋義 To line up; A line of people or vehicles

　同義字 align; line

❷ rush **KK** [rʌʃ] **DJ** [rʌʃ]　衝；闖；忙碌的 (v.) (n.) (adj.)

　英文釋義 Go doing something in a very quick manner

　同義字 hasten; hurry

廣 播 ▷ 🎵12-11

Ladies and Gentlemen,

At this moment, the airport is operating its rush hour. We are still in a queue for parking at the terminal. We apologize for this inconvenience and thank you for your patience.

譯 文 ▷

各位貴賓：

目前正值機場的交通尖峰時段，我們仍在依序等待進入停機坪，帶來不便之處，請您多多包涵，並謝謝您的耐心等候。

【For transit passenger（轉機）】

❶ aware [ə'wɛr] [ə'wɛə]   知道的；察覺的 (adj.)

　英文釋義 To know about something

　同義字 knowing; conscious

廣 播 ▷ 🎵12-12

Ladies and Gentlemen,

Our passenger service agents are aware that some passengers have connecting flights and will be on hand to assist you when you disembark. Please contact our agents after disembark. Thank you.

譯 文 ▷

各位貴賓：

如果您在此地轉機，請您下機後與我們的地勤人員聯絡，他們會很樂意協助您辦理轉機手續，謝謝。

【Claim for duty-free items（領取免稅品）】

廣 播 ▶ 🎵12-13

Ladies and Gentlemen,

If you have not claimed duty-free items at the boarding gate which you purchased at the airport shops, please contact your cabin attendants. Thank you.

譯 文 ▶

各位貴賓：

如果您還沒有在登機門前，領取您所購買的免稅物品，請您儘快與空服人員聯絡。謝謝。

【Defer disembarkation（暫緩下機）】

❶ authority ㊎ [ə'θɔrətɪ] ㊐ [ə'θɔ:riti]　職權；當局 (n.)

英文釋義 The power or right to direct or control someone or something ; A public organization that is entitled to control an area or certain activities

同義字 power; government

廣 播 ▶ 🎵12-14

Ladies and Gentlemen,

Due to congestion in the Immigration area at the airport, we are advised by the airport authorities to ask passengers to remain on board until conditions have been improved. We apologize for any inconvenience which may cause you. Thank you.

譯 文

各位貴賓：

　　由於機場的證照及海關查驗處人潮擁擠，機場單位要求所有旅客在機上稍候，等機場的通關人潮漸少後再陸續下機，帶來不便之處，請您多多原諒，謝謝。

【Asking for medical aid on board（尋求醫護人員協助）】

❶ stomachache 〔KK〕['stʌmək͵ek] 〔DJ〕['stʌməkeik]　胃痛；腹痛 (n.)

　英文釋義 Feeling pain in the stomach or abdominal region

❷ urgently 〔KK〕['ɝdʒəntlɪ] 〔DJ〕['əːdʒəntli]　緊急的；急切的 (adv.)

　英文釋義 It means that something requires immediate attention or action

　同義字 instantly; eagerly

廣 播　🎵12-15

Ladies and Gentlemen,

　　We have encountered a situation that one passenger in economy class is having a serious stomachache. We urgently need some medical aid. If you are a doctor or nurse, please kindly contact your cabin attendants. Thank you very much for your assistance.

譯 文

各位貴賓：

　　目前機上有一位經濟艙的旅客感到腹部劇痛不適，急需專業的醫療協助。如果您是醫生或護士，請您告知空服人員，非常感謝您的協助。

【Refueling（飛機加油）】

❶ refuel ⓀⓀ [ri'fjuəl] ⒹⒿ [ri:'fju:əl] 加油；補給燃料 (v.)

英文釋義 To fill up the tank with fuel

廣 播 ▶ 🎵12-16

Ladies and Gentlemen,

　　Due to refueling, for your own safety, please remain seated, and release your seat belt. Refrain from smoking and using matches, cigarette lighters or any electronic devices. Thank you for your cooperation.

譯 文 ▶

各位貴賓：

　　由於飛機正在加油，為了安全，請留在座位，鬆開安全帶，不要吸菸，也不可以使用火柴、打火機及其他電器用品，謝謝您的合作。

【Bomb threat（爆裂物威脅）】

❶ evacuate ⓀⓀ [ɪ'vækjʊ'et] ⒹⒿ [i'vækjueit] 撤離 (v.)

英文釋義 To remove someone from danger

同義字 remove; withdraw

❷ explosive ⓀⓀ [ɪk'splosɪv] ⒹⒿ [iks'pləusiv] 爆炸性的；爆裂物 (adj.) (n.)

英文釋義 A substance which may cause explosion

同義字 bomb

❸ threat ⓀⓀ [θrɛt] ⒹⒿ [θret] 威脅 (n.)

英文釋義 Indicating an intention or determination to elicit a negative response

同義字 warning; intimidation

廣 播 ▶ ♪12-17

Ladies and Gentlemen,

　　We have just been informed of an explosive threat on board the airplane. Please remain calm and stay seated with your seat belt fastened until the aircraft has come to a complete stop. Please remove all of the sharp objects and leave them in the seat pocket in front of you. Your carry-on luggage has also to be left on board. Cabin crew will guide you to evacuate the plane through the emergency doors. Please follow their instructions. Thank you for your cooperation.

譯 文 ▷

各位貴賓：

　　我們方才接到通知，機上有疑似爆裂物。請您保持冷靜，在飛機尚未完全停妥前，留在座位上並繫好安全帶。同時請您移除身上所有的尖銳物品，放置在前方的椅袋內。您的手提行李必須留在機上。空服員會引導您從緊急出口撤離飛機，請遵循他們的指引。謝謝您的合作。

【Encountering clear turbulence（遭遇晴空亂流）】

❶ panic ⓀⓀ [pænɪk] ⒹⒿ ['pænik]　恐慌；驚慌 (v.) (n.) (adj.)

英文釋義 To become filled with fear and anxiety suddenly

同義字 frighten; fear

❷ securely ⓀⓀ [sɪ'kjʊrlɪ] ⒹⒿ [si'kjuəli]　安全地；牢固地（adv.）

英文釋義 Free from danger or risk of loss; Put something in place that it will not fall or become loose

同義字 safely; firmly

廣播 ▶ 🎵12-18

Ladies and Gentlemen,

We have just passed through clear turbulence. We apologize for any panic caused by such an unexpected situation. Please make sure that your seatbelt is securely fastened. If you need any help or medical care, please inform your cabin attendants. We will provide you with the immediate assistance. Thank you for the cooperation.

譯文 ▶

各位貴賓：

我們方才遭遇晴空亂流，很抱歉因此無法預期的狀況造成您的驚恐。請確認您的安全帶已經繫緊。如果您需要任何協助或醫療照護，請通知空服員，我們會立即為您處理。謝謝您的合作。

【Emergency landing（緊急迫降）】

❶ brace ㊐ [bres] ㊐ [breis]　支架；使做好準備 (n.) (v.)

英文釋義 Something used to hold parts together or in place; Prepare for the forthcoming event

同義字 support; reinforce

◆ brace position 防撞安全姿勢（緊急狀況時，在飛機即將觸地或水面前，以此姿勢保護頭部和身體）

❷ proper ㊐ ['prɑpɚ] ㊐ ['prɔpə]　適當的；適合的 (adj.)

英文釋義 Someone or something is in a correct or decorous manner

同義字 appropriate; suitable

廣 播 12-19

Ladies and gentlemen,

In consideration of all people on board leaving the plane, please follow flight attendants' instruction. Now put your seat in an upright position and tighten your seatbelt as securely as possible. Flight attendants will guide you to the proper exits and give you the instruction for the evacuation.

When you hear the command "brace, brace, brace", please bend over and put your hands above your head. After impact, once you get evacuation instruction, get out of the plane via the assigned exits.

譯 文

各位貴賓：

為使所有的人能順利離機，請遵照空服員的指示行動。現在請您豎直椅背，盡可能地將安全帶繫緊。空服員會在降落後指示您逃生出口的位置。當您聽到「brace, brace, brace」的口令時，請彎下腰，並將雙手置於頭部上方。在飛機觸地後，當您聽見緊急逃生的指令，請從指定的逃生門撤離。

B Announcements for different countries 各國廣播

【Taiwan（台灣）】- I

❶ chilling ㉿ ['tʃɪlɪŋ] ⑁ ['tʃilin]　發冷

　diarrhea ㉿ [ˌdaɪə'rɪə] ⑁ [ˌdaɪə'riːə]　腹瀉

　fever ㉿ ['fivə'] ⑁ ['fiːvə]　發熱

　lymph node ㉿ [lɪmf nod] ⑁ [limf nəud]　淋巴結

　vomit ㉿ ['vɑmɪt] ⑁ ['vɔmit]　嘔吐

❷ enlargement ㉿ [ɪn'lɑrdʒmənt] ⑁ [in'lɑːdʒmənt]　擴大；增訂 (n.)
　英文釋義 The expansion of an item's size
　同義字 increase; spread

❸ executive ㉿ [ɪg'zɛkjʊtɪv] ⑁ [ig'zekjutiv]　執行的；執行者 (adj.) (n.)
　英文釋義 Person or group appointed and given the responsibility and author-
　　　ity to manage the affairs of an organization and make decisions
　同義字 administrative; governor
　• Department of Health of the Executive Yuan　行政院衛生署

❹ symptom ㉿ ['sɪmptəm] ⑁ ['simptəm]　症狀；癥候 (n.)
　英文釋義 Signs of disease or physical disturbance observed by the patient

廣播　12-20

Ladies and gentlemen,

　In a few minutes, we are going to distribute the forms to you. If you have any questions, please contact your cabin attendants. In addition, according to the regulations from the Department of Health of the Executive

Yuan, if you have the symptoms of chilling and fever, enlargement of lymph nodes, vomiting or diarrhea, or related symptoms, please contact the Airport Quarantine officer. Thank you for your cooperation.

譯 文

各位貴賓：

　　再過幾分鐘，我們將分發入境表格，如果您有任何疑問，請告知空服員。此外，根據行政院衛生署的規定，如果您有發冷發燒、淋巴結腫大、嘔吐腹瀉或其他症狀，請與聯繫機場檢疫人員，謝謝您的合作。

【Taiwan（台灣）】- II

❶ illegal ㎏ [ɪˈligl̩] ⒟ [iˈliːgəl]　不合法的 (adj.)

英文釋義 The act is against to the law

同義字 unlawful; criminal

❷ importation ㎏ [ˌɪmporˈteʃən] ⒟ [ˌimpɔːˈteiʃən]　進口 (n.)

英文釋義 To bring something from a foreign country

反義字 exportation

❸ mandatory ㎏ [ˈmændəˌtorɪ] ⒟ [ˈmændətəri]　命令的；代理者 (adj.) (n.)

英文釋義 Something is compulsory and authoritatively ordered

同義字 obligatory

❹ offense ㎏ [əˈfɛns] ⒟ [əˈfɛns]　犯罪；進攻 (n.)

英文釋義 It refers to a violation or breaking of a social or moral rule

同義字 crime; violation

❺ trafficking ⓚ ['træfɪkɪŋ] ⓓ ['træfikɪŋ] 非法交易 (n.)
英文釋義 Illegal transaction of people or drugs

廣 播 ▶ 🎵12-21

Ladies and gentlemen,

　　According to the regulations of the Republic of China government, we must make the following announcement: The trafficking and importation of illegal drugs is a serious offense and the mandatory penalty for such is: "death". Thank you for your attention.

譯 文 ▶

各位貴賓：

　　根據中華民國政府的規定，我們必須於機上廣播：非法販賣毒品、攜帶毒品入境是嚴重的犯罪行為，將可處以死刑。請您務必注意。

【U.S.A（美國）】

❶ accurately ⓚ ['ækjərɪtlɪ] ⓓ ['ækjuritli] 正確地；精準的 (adv.)
英文釋義 The situation is free from error or defect
同義字 correctly; precisely

❷ agriculture ⓚ ['ægrɪ'kʌltʃɚ] ⓓ ['ægrikʌltʃə] 農業；農耕 (n.)
英文釋義 It refers to the science, art or practice concerned with cultivating land to produce crops.
同義字 cultivation

❸ declare ⓚ [dɪ'klɛr] ⓓ [di'klɛə] 宣告；聲明 (v.)
英文釋義 To say or state something officially or publicly
同義字 announce; proclaim

❹ equivalent 🆺 [ɪˈkwɪvələnt] 🆍 [iˈkwivələnt]　相等的；相同的 (adj.)

英文釋義 Two things are equal in value, measure, force or other manners

同義字 equal; same

❺ marketable 🆺 [ˈmɑrkɪtəbḷ] 🆍 [ˈmɑːkitəbəl]　可銷售的 (adj.)

英文釋義 It refers to a measure of the ability of a security to be sold or bought

同義字 merchantable; salable

廣　播 ▶ 🎵12-22

Ladies and gentlemen,

All arriving passengers or heads of families must complete a U.S. Declaration. All questions must be answered accurately and completely. Passengers carrying fruits, vegetables, meats, plants, seeds or related agricultural products are reminded to declare those items. If you take out or bring into the United States more than 10,000 U.S. dollars or its equivalent in foreign currency or marketable securities, you are also required to declare with Customs. Thank you.

譯　文 ▷

各位貴賓：

　　所有入境旅客或一家之主必須填寫美國海關申報單。所有問題必須詳實地填答。乘客若攜帶水果、蔬菜、肉類、植物、種子或其他農產品，都必須向海關申報。如果您攜帶超過一萬美元、等值外幣及有價證券進出美國，也必須向海關申報，謝謝。

【Australia / New Zealand （澳洲 / 紐西蘭）】- I

❶ Amnesty Bins ㎞ ['æm͵nɛstɪ] [bɪnz] ㏪ ['æmnesti] [binz]　免疫箱 (n.)
amnesty　赦免 (n.) (v.)

英文釋義 To grant a general pardon granted by a government, especially for political offenses.

◆ 機場檢疫單位為防止旅客將未經過檢疫的食品攜入該國，通常會在入境大廳中設置好幾處的檢疫箱，供旅客棄置規定不可攜帶入境的食物。

❷ concourse ㎞ ['kɑnkors] ㏪ ['kɔŋkɔ:s]　匯合；廣場 (n.)

英文釋義 It refers to a large space or room in a public building, such as railway station or airport terminal.

同義字 congregation

廣 播　🎵12-23

Ladies and gentlemen,

　　Due to the Quarantine regulations, all aircraft food must be left on board. Those passengers who carry food must declare it at Customs or dispose of it in the "Amnesty Bins" in the arrival concourse. Thank you.

譯 文

各位貴賓：

　　根據檢疫規定，所有飛機上的食物必須留在機上。若您攜帶食物，必須向海關申報，或丟置於入境大廳的檢疫箱中。謝謝。

【Australia / New Zealand（澳洲 / 紐西蘭）】- II

❶ administer ㎞ [əd'mɪnəstɚ] ㏪ [əd'ministə]　掌管；管理 (v.)

英文釋義 To manage something or bring something into use or operation

同義字 direct; govern

❷ conform ㏍ [kən'fɔrm] ㏌ [kən'fɔːm] 遵守；遵照 (v.)

英文釋義 To obey the rules or behave in a manner that it agreed by most people

同義字 comply; follow

❸ contact lenses ㏍ ['kɑntækt] ['lɛnzəz] 隱形眼鏡

❹ specifically ㏍ [spɪ'sɪfɪklˌlɪ] ㏌ [spi'sifikəli] 特別地；明確地 (adv.)

英文釋義 Things are in particular or with distinct characteristics

同義字 particularly; explicitly

❺ spray ㏍ [spre] ㏌ [sprei] 噴灑；噴霧 (v.) (n.)

英文釋義 To discharge liquid from a pressurized container

同義字 splash; mist

廣 播 ▶ 🎵12-24

Ladies and Gentlemen,

To conform with local Agriculture and Health requirements, the cabin will now be sprayed. We are using a non-toxic spray which is recommended specifically for this purpose by the World Health Organization to spray this cabin. Please remain seated and keep the aisles clear while the spray is being administered. If you wear contact lenses, we suggest you to close your eyes or cover your nose and mouth to avoid feeling uncomfortable. Thank you!

譯 文

各位貴賓：

　　為了遵守當地政府農業與健康規定，現在客艙內將開始噴灑消毒劑。我們所用的消毒劑是世界衛生組織所建議的，對人體無害。當機內開始噴灑時，請留在座位並保持走道暢通。如果您戴隱形眼鏡，我們建議您閉上眼睛，或遮掩口鼻以減低不適，謝謝。

【Parama（巴拿馬）】

❶ Bureau KK [ˈbjʊro] DJ [ˈbjuərəu] 　事務處；連絡處 (n.)

英文釋義 A government department or an independent administrative unit

同義字 office; division

廣 播　🎵12-25

Ladies and Gentlemen,

　　To comply with the request of the local Bureau of Customs and to speed your entry into the country, we suggest that you please complete your immigration and customs declaration forms before disembarkation. Thank you for your cooperation.

譯 文

各位貴賓：

　　根據巴拿馬海關當局要求，請於下機前填妥您的入境表格及海關申報單，以利通關作業，謝謝您的合作。

Chapter 13.　In-flight health care　　機上保健須知

▶ Outline: 概述一般人於機上的基本保健，以及身體有些疾病的乘客，如何於客艙環境中減少不適的方式。

▶ Learning Goals: 熟悉客艙的特殊環境中，減少身體不適的英文表達方式。

Ⓐ Basic Vocabulary　基礎必備單字

❶ acute 🅚 [əˈkjut] 🅓 [əˈkjuːt]　嚴重的；尖銳的；敏銳的 (adj.)

英文釋義 Applying to describe severe disease or extremely clear sensitivity

同義字 sharp; keen

❷ adaption 🅚 [əˈdæpʃən] 🅓 [əˈdæpʃən]　適應；改編 (n.)

英文釋義 Making change in order to be suitable to a different situation

同義字 adjustment; modification

❸ affordable 🅚 [əˈfɔrdəbl̩] 🅓 [əˈfɔːdəbl]　負擔得起的 (adj.)

英文釋義 Things are within one's financial means

同義字 inexpensive; approachable

❹ asthma 🅚 [ˈæzmə] 🅓 [ˈæsmə]　氣喘 (n.)

英文釋義 A chronic inflammatory disease of the airways, which can make breathing difficult

❺ capacity 🅚 [kəˈpæsətɪ] 🅓 [kəˈpæsiti]　容量；能力 (n.)

英文釋義 The space or ability to receive or contain

同義字 volume; capability

❻ certificate 🅚 [səˈtɪfəkɪt] 🅓 [səˈtifikit]　證明書；執照 (n.)

英文釋義 A document, which is an official proof to serve as evidence or written testimony

同義字 warrant; license

❼ circulation KK ['sɝkjə'leʃən] DJ ['sə:kju'leiʃən]　循環；運行 (n.)

英文釋義 The movement of air, water, blood etc., through the different parts of something

同義字 rotation; distribution

❽ clot KK [klɑt] DJ [klɔt]　凝塊 (n.) (v.)

英文釋義 An almost solid piece of something (A blood clot is a thickened mass in the blood formed by tiny substances called platelets)

同義字 curdle; clog

❾ consequence KK ['kɑnsə'kwɛns] DJ ['kɔnsikwəns]　後果；結果 (n.)

英文釋義 A natural result of something you do; The effect or outcome of something occurring earlier

同義字 effect; result

❿ constantly KK ['kɑnstəntlɪ] DJ ['kɔnstəntli]　不斷地；時常地 (adv.)

英文釋義 Things stay in the same manner without being changing in nature, value, or extent for a long time

同義字 always; continually

⓫ contagious KK [kən'tedʒəs] DJ [kən'teidʒəs]　感染性的；接觸傳染的 (adj.)

英文釋義 Describing the diseases which are capable of being transmitted by bodily contact with an infected person or object

同義字 infectious

⑫ contamination KK [kən,tæmə'neʃən] DJ [kən,tæmi'neiʃən] 污染（物）；髒污 (n.)

英文釋義 Making something (material, physical body, natural environment, workplace, and so on) impure or unsuitable by contact with something unclean

同義字 contagion; pollution

⑬ disorder KK [dɪs'ɔrdə] DJ [dis'ɔ:də] 混亂；無秩序 (n.) (v.)

英文釋義 Lack of order or regular arrangement. It can be used to describe physical environment or one's physical or mental condition.

同義字 chaos; mess

⑭ disruption KK [dɪs'rʌpʃən] DJ [dis'rʌpʃən] 分裂；瓦解 (n.)

英文釋義 To interrupt or impede the progress of ongoing event

同義字 interruption; disturbance

⑮ dysfunction KK [dɪs'fʌŋkʃən] DJ [dis'fʌŋkʃən] 器官功能不良（障礙）(n.)

英文釋義 An abnormality or impairment in a part of the body

同義字 functional disorder

⑯ exacerbate KK [ɪg'zæsə'bet] DJ [eks'æsə:beit] 使惡化；使加重 (v.)

英文釋義 To increase the severity or bitterness of the situation or condition

同義字 worsen; aggravate

⑰ exposure KK [ɪk'spoʒə] DJ [iks'pəuʒə] 曝曬；曝露 (n.)

英文釋義 It refers to a state or condition of being unprotected and open to damage or risk.

同義字 disclosure; display

⓲ fluid KK [ˈfluɪd] DJ [ˈfluːid]　流動的；液體 (adj.) (n.)

英文釋義 Being capable of flowing freely like water; A substance like liquid, gas or plasmas

同義字 flowing; liquid

⓳ humidity KK [hjuˈmɪdətɪ] DJ [hjuːˈmiditi]　濕度；濕氣 (n.)

英文釋義 It refers to the density of water vapor per unit volume of air

同義字 humidness; moistness

⓴ infectious KK [ɪnˈfɛkʃəs] DJ [inˈfekʃəs]　有傳染力的；具傳染性的 (adj.)

英文釋義 Being capable of passing a disease to someone else by pathogenic microorganism or agent

同義字 contagious

㉑ inhaler KK [ɪnˈhelɚ] DJ [inˈheilə]　吸入器；人工呼吸器 (n.)

英文釋義 It is a device that gets medicine directly into a person's lungs

同義字 inhalator

㉒ malaise KK [mæˈlez] DJ [mæˈleiz]　不舒服；心神抑鬱 (n.)

英文釋義 A feeling of general discomfort or uneasiness, either mentally or physically

同義字 discomfort; distress

㉓ malignancy KK [məˈlɪgnənsɪ] DJ [məˈlignənsi]　惡意；惡性腫瘤 (n.)

英文釋義 Feeling or showing ill will or hatred; Cancerous tumor

同義字 ill-will; cancer

㉔ moderate ⓀⓀ ['mɑdərɪt] ⒹⒹ ['mɔdərɪt]　適度的；溫和的；普通的 (adj.)

英文釋義 Something is within reasonable limit, not extreme, excessive, or intense

同義字 mild; gentle

㉕ pacifier ⓀⓀ ['pæsəˌfaɪə] ⒹⒹ ['pæsifaɪə]　撫慰者；橡膠奶嘴 (n.)

英文釋義 Something may calm people down; A rubber or plastic device for a baby to suck or bite on

同義字 comforter; conciliator

㉖ phlebitis ⓀⓀ [flɪ'baɪtɪs] ⒹⒹ [fli'baitis]　靜脈炎（醫）(n.)

英文釋義 A medical condition which occurs when a blood clot blocks one or more of veins, usually in legs.

同義字 thrombophlebitis

㉗ physiologically ⓀⓀ [ˌfɪzɪə'lɑdʒɪkəlɪ] ⒹⒹ [ˌfiziə'lɔdʒikəli]　生理上的 (adv.)

英文釋義 Things are of or relating to physiological processes

㉘ potential ⓀⓀ [pə'tɛnʃəl] ⒹⒹ [pə'tenʃəl]　潛在的；可能的 (adj.) (n.)

英文釋義 Things are with the power or being capable of happening

同義字 probable; possible

㉙ practitioner ⓀⓀ [præk'tɪʃənə] ⒹⒹ [præk'tiʃənə]　執業者（多指醫生、律師）(n.)

英文釋義 A person engaged in the practice of a profession, usually refers to doctor or lawyer

同義字 physician; attorney

㉚ precaution KK [prɪ'kɔʃən] DJ [pri'kɔːʃən]　預防措施；警惕；謹慎 (n.)

英文釋義 An action taken beforehand to prevent possible danger, failure, or injury

同義字 preparation; protection

㉛ prolonged KK [prə'lɔŋd] DJ [prə'lɔŋd]　延長的；拖延的 (adj.)

英文釋義 To lengthen out in time or make longer in spatial extent

同義字 lengthy; extended

㉜ reject KK [rɪ'dʒɛkt] DJ [ri'dʒɛkt]　拒絕；否定；抵制 (v.)

英文釋義 Refuse to take, have or recognize

同義字 decline; refuse

㉝ subsequently KK ['sʌbsɪˌkwɛntlɪ] DJ ['sʌbsikwəntli]　隨後；接著 (adv.)

英文釋義 To occur or come immediately later or after

同義字 thereafter; afterwards

㉞ trauma KK ['trɔmə] DJ ['trɔːmə]　創傷；傷口 (n.)

英文釋義 A body wound produced by sudden physical injury; An emotional or mental response to a terrible event

同義字 injury; wound

Ⓑ Contents 內文

The volume of air traffic has constantly risen in recent years. Since the modern commercial aircraft offers rapid, convenient and safe transportation, the number of long distance flights has greatly increased. With the increment of passenger capacity of long distance aircraft, there are relatively larger numbers of travellers aboard a single aircraft than before. When air travel has become affordable and accessible to all sectors of the population, it is easily forgotten that an unfamiliar and physiologically unusual environment like passenger cabin may exacerbate the pre-existing conditions or develop an acute medical problem for ill passengers. Staying for long hours inside a narrow and motion cabin, jetlag, low oxygen and humidity may also cause discomfort to healthy and mobile passengers.

　　近年來航空運輸的總量不斷向上成長。由於現代商用客機足以提供快速便捷又安全的運輸方式，長途飛行班次的數量亦可見明顯增加。隨著大型飛機的容量持續擴增，與過去相比，每架飛機可搭載的旅客人數越來越多。當搭機旅行的可及性提高，機票價格也越來越親民後，人們很容易忽略了一個事實，那就是：飛機客艙是一個一般人既不熟悉、且與人體生理結構不甚協調的環境。而這種環境對於本身已有某些病徵的乘客而言，可能會加大不適的感受，甚至造成一些急性醫療問題的發生。即使對健康且行動無虞的乘客來說，長時間處於狹窄又不停移動的空間裡，時差、氧氣濃度低和溼度不足等狀況，也可能會產生不適的感覺。

Most airlines provide special assistance upon request by passengers with medical needs or their medical practitioners prior to the commencement of the flight. In addition to the effect of the condition upon the sick passengers, it has to be taken into account regarding the effect of potential effect on other passengers or aircrew members. Meanwhile, it is an International Health Regulation that an individual should not fly during the infectious stage of a contagious disease.

　　如果本人或醫師於航程開始之前提出申請，多數航空公司會提供

旅客特殊的醫療協助需求。除了身體有狀況的旅客需要注意飛行可能產生的影響之外，其它旅客或空勤組員，也應該小心飛行可能帶來的潛在影響。同時，國際衛生法規明文規定，若患傳染性疾病的人，不能於仍具感染可能性的階段搭乘飛機。

The following conditions are commonly observed onboard an aircraft which passengers must be aware of the potential risk and pay attention to the related subjects.

以下狀況常可見於飛行途中，所有乘客皆應注意其可能導致的潛在風險，且小心相關事項。

❶ Common signs/ symptoms and the prevention for all passengers
所有乘客皆應注意的常見徵狀及其避免方法

• If you feel uncomfortable in ears or sinuses during take-off and descending, try to swallow, chew or widely open your mouth to promote better airflow. If your babies have such problems, provide them with drinks or a pacifier to promote better airflow and relieve discomfort.

起飛及下降時，如果覺得耳朵和鼻腔於不舒服，試著吞嚥口水、咀嚼或張大嘴，如此可以幫助空氣進出耳鼻。如果嬰兒出現以上的不適狀況，可以餵嬰兒喝水，或給予奶嘴吸吮，如此可通暢耳鼻內的空氣流動，減低不適感。

• Avoid taking a plane within 24 hours after diving.

潛水後24小時內避免搭機。

• If you have an airsick problem, make reservation for seats near the wings.

如果你會暈機，盡量要求機翼附近的位置。

• Try not to take heavy food, alcohol and caffeine drinks while onboard, because these substances may cause your body to lose fluid.

飛行中，盡量不攝取重口味的食物、酒精和咖啡因飲料，因為這些物質可能造成體內水分的流失。

• Frequently drink water and juice.
多喝水或果汁。

• Try to do easy exercise in the seat before standing up from waking. It is for preventing feeling dizzy when standing up suddenly.
睡醒時，試著在起身前做些輕鬆的運動。這樣可以避免突然站起來時，感覺頭暈。

• Patients suffered from contagious diseases are strongly recommended not to take any plane, since a cabin is a public area where contamination is possible.
患有傳染性疾病的人，強烈建議勿搭飛機。因為客艙是個公共區域，可能形成污染。

• Use rich moisturizer often to protect your skin from getting dry.
經常塗抹較油的乳液，可以保護皮膚不容易乾燥。

❷ **Advice for pregnant women　給孕婦的建議**

Most of airlines refuse to carry women in the latter stages of pregnancy, typically after 32 weeks. Although pregnancy is not in a "medical condition", it is considered risky to the mother and baby if delivery occurs in flight. Pregnant women are recommended to always check the immigration regulations of the destination before departure, in order to make sure that they will not be rejected by the immigration. In addition, airlines may require medical certificate if the pregnancy is after 28 weeks to confirm the estimated date of delivery. Passengers are reminded that health travel insurance in the latter stages of pregnancy can be difficult to obtain.

多數航空公司會拒載懷孕後期的孕婦，通常是32周以後的孕婦不能搭機旅行。雖然懷孕不是「病症」，但萬一於機上分娩，對於母親和胎兒皆有風險。建議孕婦應該於出發前，事先確認目的地國家的入境法規，以免因為預產期接近而被拒絕入境。此外，航空公司可能要求，懷孕超過28周的孕婦出具醫療證明，確認預訂的生產日期。提醒乘客，懷孕後期將較難取得保險公司出售的旅遊平安保險。

❸ Asthma and chest diseases　氣喘及胸腔疾病

• Asthmatic passengers should keep inhaler in the hand baggage and avoid causes of occurrence during flight.

氣喘患者應將吸入器置於手提行李內，且於飛行途中，避免可能產生氣喘的因素。

• Passengers with chest diseases should keep in mind that heart attack occurs twice as often onboard an aircraft than on the ground. If you recently have suffered from a heart attack, please do not take air travel.

有胸腔病史的旅客必須牢記，於飛行中發生心臟病的機率，是於地面上的兩倍。如果最近心臟病曾經發作，建議您不要搭機旅行。

❹ Deep Vein Thrombosis (DVT)　深層靜脈栓塞

It should be noticed that the potential risk for the development of traveller's thrombosis, particularly on long haul flights, could cause serious problems. Prolonged leg immobility will usually affect blood circulation in the lower part of body, and subsequently forms blood clot in the deep veins within legs.

必須提醒旅客，尤其是搭乘長途班機者，血管栓塞的產生，極可能產生嚴重的問題。長時間靜止不動，通常會造成下肢血液循環不良，進而於腳部的靜脈中，形成血塊。

The warning signs of DVT include (1) redness and swelling of the skin, (2) pain and tenderness in the leg muscles. It is possible to cause breathing difficulties if the blood clot moves to the lung. Limited consequences may occur to healthy passengers, yet it is dangerous to those passengers who suffered from heart disease, certain types of malignancy, phlebitis, clotting disorders, trauma, and the ones who have recently received venous surgery on legs.

深層靜脈栓塞的警示症狀包括：1. 皮膚紅腫2. 腳部肌肉疼痛無力。當血塊流入肺部時，有可能造成呼吸困難。對於一般身體健康的旅客而言，影響不大。但就原有心臟方面疾病、罹患某些惡性腫瘤、靜脈炎、凝血功能不全、外傷或近期曾接受腳部靜脈手術的旅客來說，則可能會有危險。

To effectively reduce the potential risks for those passengers, it is recommended to follow the instructions below:

為了有效降低這些潛在風險，以下的建議事項提供參考：

• seek medical advice and take appropriate precautions before the flight
  飛行前應諮詢專業醫療建議或採取適當的預防措施。

• drink sufficient water and juice frequently on board
  於機上不斷補充充足的開水或果汁。

• no smoking, alcohol and caffeine drinks on board
  機上勿抽菸、喝酒及飲用含咖啡因的飲料。

- wear loose clothes in the cabin

  穿著寬鬆的衣服。

- stretch arms and legs every couple of hours while seating, and walk around the cabin whenever it is possible

  就座時，每隔一段時間便伸展手臂和雙腿。盡可能於方便時，在機艙內走動。

❺ Diabetes Mellitus　糖尿病

Passengers with diabetes mellitus can usually travel without difficulty and medical clearance, as long as they can administer their own medication. However, it is important that they are aware of problems caused by time zone changes, and recommended to take medication according to the time of the departure place. Also, the following suggestions are for passengers with diabetes to proceed prior to the commencement of the flight:

糖尿病患者若能自主處理其醫療所需事項，便可如一般乘客搭機旅行，無需出具醫療證明。但患者必須注意其飛行區域和目的地的時區變更，建議服藥的時間，仍以出發地的時區為準。以下建議提供糖尿病患者旅客於出發前的參考。

- Order special diets while making reservation.

  訂位時即告知需用糖尿病特別餐。

- Put the medication in the hand luggage.

  將藥品置於手提行李內。

- Always bring a written medical record of health conditions.

  隨身攜帶病歷資料。

❻ Jet lag

Jet lag describes the symptoms caused by the disruption of the body's internal clock, when flying crossing multiple time zones. It may lead to daytime sleepiness or sleepless at night, indigestion, general malaise and physical or mental dysfunction. The above symptoms may gradually wear off with the adaptions of one's body to the new time zone. According to the World Health Organization, although jet lag cannot be prevented, there are some ways to moderate the discomfort:

所謂時差症係指身體由於飛經不同時區,造成生理時鐘產生混亂的一些症狀。時差症可能產生的現象包含:白天嗜睡、夜晚失眠、消化不良、心緒不寧以及身心的功能失調。當生理時鐘逐漸適應了新的時區後,這些症狀便會慢慢消失。根據世界衛生組織的說法,雖然時差症無法避免,但某些作法可以減緩其產生的不適:

- Get sufficient rest time before the flight. Try to sleep during the medium or long-haul flights.

  飛行前充分休息。中長程航班上,盡可能試著睡覺。

- Take light meal and consume limited alcohol / caffeine on board.

  在機上吃些清淡的食物,減少攝取酒精和咖啡因的飲料。

- "Anchor sleep" (a minimum block of 4-hour sleep during the local night at destination) is essential to allow the body's internal clock to adapt to the new time zone.

  「固定睡眠」,係指於目的地的夜晚,最少應有四小時的固定睡眠,此能有效促使身體的生理時鐘盡快適應新的時區。

- Exercise during the daytime may help promote a good night sleep.

  白天運動將有助於夜晚睡個好覺。

- Sufficient time exposure to bright sunlight will usually help adapt to the new time zone.

  充足地陽光照射將可幫助身體盡快適應新的時區作息。

- Seek specialist travel medicine advice may help find an effective coping strategy.

  尋求專業人員提供旅行的醫藥建議，試著找出有效的對策。

❼ **General reminders for all passengers　給予所有乘客的提醒**

Traveling by air is not a natural activity for humans. However, it can be safe and enjoyable if you have basic understanding regarding the features of passenger cabin, making good medical consultation and necessary precautions before a flight. The followings are some general reminders for all passengers before departure.

搭機旅行並非人類出於本能的活動。但只要對於客艙有一定的基本了解、飛行前諮詢專業醫療建議、做足事前預防措施，搭機旅行可以既安全又愉快的。以下便是提供所有旅客於起飛前可注意的事項。

- Be sure that you do not have any immune system problem.

  確定自己沒有任何免疫系統的問題。

- Wear loose and comfortable clothes, and prevent from wearing contact lenses.

  穿著寬鬆舒適的服裝，避免配戴隱形眼鏡。

- If you have any concern, consult the doctor about your health condition, and inform the airline of your problems while making a reservation.

  如果覺得擔心，請醫生檢查您的身體狀況，並於訂位時，告知航空公司有關健康狀況的問題。

- Always have the medication in the hand luggage.

  永遠將您的藥品放置於手提行李中。

Chapter 14.　Miscellaneous information

其他搭機須知

▶ Outline: 整理其他重要搭機訊息。包含緊急逃生出口座位須知、安全須知卡資訊、手提行李禁帶物品、危險品分類及注意事項。

▶ Learning Goals: 熟悉以上各項訊息之相關英文專業用語及其規範。

Ⓐ Emergency exit row seating　緊急逃生出口座位須知

A. **Vocabulary**　單字

❶ activate 🅚 [ˈæktəˌvet] 🅓 [ˈæktiˌveit]　使活化；使生動 (v.)

英文釋義 To start something or make it active

同義字 awaken; trigger

❷ assess 🅚 [əˈsɛs] 🅓 [əˈses]　評價；估價 (v.)

英文釋義 To make an judgment or estimate the value of something

同義字 judge; evaluate

❸ assure 🅚 [əˈʃʊr] 🅓 [əˈʃuə]　向……保證 (v.)

英文釋義 To state something in a definite and positive way

同義字 ensure; guarantee

❹ category 🅚 [ˈkætəˌgorɪ] 🅓 [ˈkætigəri]　種類；範疇 (n.)

英文釋義 It refers to any general or comprehensive division

同義字 classification; type

❺ convey 🅚 [kənˈve] 🅓 [kənˈvei]　傳達；運送 (v.)

英文釋義 To communicate something to someone; To carry something from one place to another

同義字 communicate; deliver

❻ deployment KK [dɪˈplɔɪmənt] DJ [diˈplɔimənt]　佈署；調度 (n.)

英文釋義 To come into the position where is ready for use

同義字 arrangement; placement slide deployment　係指用於緊急逃生之救生梯／救生筏已充氣

❼ designate KK [ˈdɛzɪɡˌnet] DJ [ˈdezigneit]　委任；標出 (v.)　指定的 (adj.)

英文釋義 To select or name for a duty; To point out

同義字 appoint; mark

❽ dexterity KK [dɛksˈtɛrətɪ] DJ [deksˈteriti]　靈巧；熟練 (n.)

英文釋義 The ability to skillfully use one's hands

同義字 proficiency; cleverness

❾ impede KK [ɪmˈpid] DJ [imˈpiːd]　妨礙；阻止 (v.)

英文釋義 To delay or make difficult for something to happen

同義字 hinder; block

❿ lean KK [lin] DJ [liːn]　傾斜；靠 (v.) (n.)

英文釋義 To incline in posture, feeling, opinion or action

同義字 incline; slope

⓫ mechanism KK [ˈmɛkəˌnɪzəm] DJ [ˈmekənizəm]　機制；機械裝置 (n.)

英文釋義 A process or system that is applied to produce a particular result; A piece of machinery

同義字 appliance; means

⑫ orally 🅚🅚 ['orəlɪ] 🅓🅙 ['ɔ:rəli]　口頭地；口述地 (adv.)

〔英文釋義〕 To express one's thoughts by speaking

〔同義字〕 verbally; vocally

⑬ recognize 🅚🅚 ['rɛkəgˌnaɪz] 🅓🅙 ['rekəgnaiz]　認出；承認 (v.)

〔英文釋義〕 To identify something that has been perceived before

〔同義字〕 acknowledge; identify

⑭ stabilize 🅚🅚 ['stebḷˌaɪz] 🅓🅙 ['steibilaiz]　使平衡；使穩固 (v.)

〔英文釋義〕 To make something firm or steadfast

〔同義字〕 secure; balance

⑮ visual capacity 🅚🅚 ['vɪʒuəl] [kə'pæsətɪ] 🅓🅙 ['vizjuəl] [kə'pæsətɪ]　視力

aural capacity 🅚🅚 ['ɔrəl] [kə'pæsətɪ] 🅓🅙 ['ɔ:rəl] [kə'pæsətɪ]　聽力

B. **Contents**　內文

　　According to the regulation and to assure cabin safety, the exit row seat cannot be designated to the passengers who fall into the following categories:

　　根據規定及爲維護客艙安全，下列乘客不可就座緊急逃生出口旁的座位。

❶ Pregnant mothers, seriously ill, or lacks sufficient mobility, strength or dexterity in both arms/hands or legs.

孕婦、重病乘客、雙臂／雙手／雙腿缺乏足夠力量及靈巧活動力的乘客。

❷ Less than 12 years old.

12歲以下乘客。

❸ Lacks the ability to read or understand instructions related to emergency evacuation provided in printed or graphic form or the ability to convey information orally to other passengers.

缺乏足夠能力閱讀或理解緊急逃生卡上之文字或圖片訊息，或無法有效口述相關訊息予其他乘客。

❹ Blind or lacks sufficient visual capacity.

盲胞或視障旅客。

❺ Deaf or lacks sufficient aural capacity.

耳聾或聽障旅客。

❻ Has the responsibility of carrying small children.

有幼童隨行的旅客。

❼ Deportees or their escorts; or traveling with pets.

被強制遣返的旅客及其押解人員；帶寵物上機的旅客。

If you have been assigned an exit row seat, you will be asked to perform the following acts:

如果您的位子是在緊急逃生出口旁，必要時將請您協助執行以下事項：

❶ Be able to locate the emergency exit

能夠確認緊急逃生出口的位置。

❷ Be able to recognize the emergency exit opening mechanism and the operation instructions

能夠理解緊急逃生門的開門及操作方式。

❸ Be able to read Chinese or English well enough to understand these instructions, follow hand signals and oral directions given by crewmembers

能夠充分理解中文或英文的操作指示，且可依循空服員口頭或手勢的引導。

❹ Be able to stow or secure the over-wing emergency exit door so that it will not impede use of the exit

有能力將機翼上方的緊急逃生門取下後，放置在不會阻礙出口的地方。

❺ Be able to activate the slide, and stabilize the slide after deployment to assist others in getting off the slide

可以啟動緊急逃生滑梯，並在滑梯充氣後將其固定以協助其他乘客滑下逃生。

❻ Be able to assess, select, and follow a safe path away from the emergency exit and aircraft. Be willing to help other passengers away from the plane. If you cannot or do not wish to be responsible for these procedures, or would likc to bc scated on other seats, please contact our representatives to be reseated.

能夠評估、選擇並找到安全離開緊急逃生門及飛機的路線，且願意協助其他人自飛機撤離。如果您沒有意願執行這些工作，或希望更換座位，請與服務人員聯繫為您換位。

Ⓑ Safety information card 安全須知卡

A. **Vocabulary** 單字

❶ don 🄺🄺 [dɑn] 🄳🄹 [dɔn] 穿上 (v.)

英文釋義 The action of putting on a dress or hat

同義字 put on; wear

❷ escape 🄺🄺 [ə'skep] 🄳🄹 [is'keip] 逃脫；避免 (v.)

英文釋義 To slip or get away from a situation

同義字 evade; avoid

❸ infant 🄺🄺 ['ɪnfənt] 🄳🄹 ['infənt] 嬰兒 (n.)

英文釋義 A child in the first period of life

同義字 baby

❹ inflate 🄺🄺 [ɪn'flet] 🄳🄹 [in'fleit] 使充氣；膨脹 (v.)

英文釋義 To make an item become larger by filling it with air or gas

同義字 swell; expand

❺ obstruction 🄺🄺 [əb'strʌkʃən] 🄳🄹 [əb'strʌkʃən] 妨礙；阻礙（物）(n.)

英文釋義 Something that blocks the way to make the movement difficult

同義字 obstacle; hurdle

❻ placard 🄺🄺 ['plækɑrd] 🄳🄹 ['plækɑ:d] 公告；標語牌 (n.) (v.)

英文釋義 A small card to post information

同義字 notice; poster

B. **Contents**

• Please comply with the safety instructions including signs, placards, and instructions given by crewmembers.

請遵守所有安全指示，包括燈號、標示及空服員的指示。

- All electronic devices are not allowed to use during take-off and landing.
  起飛及降落期間，禁用所有電子產品。

- No smoking in this aircraft.
  機上全程禁菸。

- Keep seat belt fastened while seated.
  就座時，請繫好安全帶。

- Put on oxygen mask before assisting children.
  先戴上氧氣面罩再協助孩童。

- Taking brace position when instructed.
  聽到指示時，採取安全防撞姿勢。

- Infant life vest is provided by flight attendant.
  嬰兒的救生衣由空服員另外提供。

- Donning instructions of life vest for children: Pass the straps between the legs and secure in front.
  兒童著救生衣的方式：將腰帶從兩腿間穿過，在前方固定。

- During an evacuation, follow escape-path markings to emergency exits.
  緊急逃生時，遵循地板指示燈的方向至逃生出口。

- No baggage and shoes are allowed during an evacuation.
  緊急逃生時，不可攜帶行李，並需脫鞋。

- Do not open doors or windows, in case of smoke, fire or obstruction outside the aircraft.

窗外有煙、火、或障礙物時，切勿打開門或窗。

- Pull handle if slide/raft does not automatically inflate.

  如果逃生梯／救生筏沒有自動充氣，請拉手動充氣握把。

C. **In-flight safety instruction card　安全須知卡圖例- I**

安全須知卡圖例- II

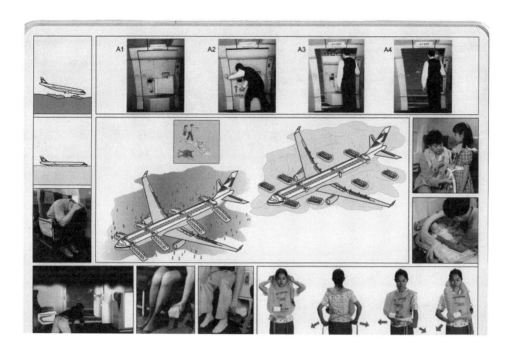

Ⓒ Hand baggage restrictions　手提行李禁帶物品

A. **Vocabulary**　單字

❶ broad ᴋᴋ [brɔd] ᴅᴊ [brɔːd]　寬闊的；寬廣 (adj.) (adv.)

　英文釋義 Measure from side to side or large in expanse

　同義字 expansive; general

❷ confiscate ᴋᴋ ['kɑnfɪs'ket] ᴅᴊ ['kɔnfiskeit]　沒收；充公 (v.)

　英文釋義 To take something away from someone by legal order

　同義字 seize; expropriate

❸ consistency ⓚⓚ [kənˈsɪstənsɪ] ⓓⓙ [kənˈsistənsi]　濃度；一致性 (n.)

英文釋義 A degree of firmness or density; Firmness of material substance

同義字 density; harmony

❹ exemption ⓚⓚ [ɪgˈzɛmpʃən] ⓓⓙ [igˈzempʃən]　免除 (n.)

英文釋義 Someone is free from an obligation, a duty, or a liability

同義字 exoneration; exception

❺ transparent ⓚⓚ [trænsˈpɛrənt] ⓓⓙ [trænsˈperənt]　透明的；清澈的 (adj.)

英文釋義 Something is clear and easy to see through

同義字 see-through; clear

❻ visible ⓚⓚ [ˈvɪzəbl] ⓓⓙ [ˈvizəbl]　可看見的；明白的 (adj.)

英文釋義 Something is perceptible to the eye

同義字 seeable; observable

B. **Contents**　內文

The following information contains the broad messages for the air passengers' hand-baggage restrictions at UK airports, Canada airports, U.S.A airports and EU airports.

以下資訊包含英國、加拿大、美國境內機場及歐盟對航空旅客手提行李物品之規定概要。

❶ **UK airports**（英國機場）

• Hand luggage allowances　手提行李限制

Check with your airline regarding how many and what size bags you can take on the plane with you.

向航空公司諮詢手提行李的件數及尺寸限制。

- Taking liquids through security　攜帶液體通過安檢

There are restrictions on the amount of liquids you can take in your hand luggage. If possible, pack liquids in your hold baggage (luggage that you check in).

手提行李對於液體的分量有所限制，建議您盡可能將液體置於託運行李內。

Liquids include　液體包含以下幾種：

- all drinks, including water　所有飲料，包括水。
- liquid or semi-liquid foods, e.g. soup, jam, honey and syrups
  液狀或半液狀的食物，例如湯品、果醬、蜂蜜、楓糖漿。
- cosmetics and toiletries, including creams, lotions, oils, perfumes, mascara and lip gloss
  化妝品及衛浴用品，包含乳液、化妝水、油、香水、睫毛/眉毛膏、護唇膏。
- sprays, including shaving foam, hairspray and spray deodorants
  噴霧劑，包含刮鬍膏、頭髮定型液、除臭噴霧。
- pastes, including toothpaste
  膏狀物，包含牙膏。
- gels, including hair and shower gel
  膠狀物，包含洗髮乳及沐浴乳。
- contact lens solution
  隱形眼鏡藥水。
- any other solutions and items of similar consistency
  其他藥水類或相等黏稠度的物品。

- If you do take liquids in your hand luggage

  如果您攜帶任何液體上機

  - containers must hold no more than 100ml

    容器容量不能超過一百毫升。

  - containers should be in a single, transparent, resealable plastic bag, which holds no more than a litre and measures approximately 20cm x 20cm

    容器必須裝進一只透明且可以重複使用的夾鏈袋內，一只夾鏈袋內不能放入超過一公升的液體，夾鏈袋大小約為20平方公分。

  - contents must fit comfortably inside the bag so it can be sealed

    夾鏈袋內的內容物必須可以輕易地完全置入袋內且密封。

  - the bag must not be knotted or tied at the top

    夾鏈袋頂端不能打結或綁起來。

  - you're limited to 1 plastic bag per person

    每個人僅能攜帶一只夾鏈袋。

  - you must show the bag at the airport security point

    在行李檢查時，要主動出示夾鏈袋。

- Liquids in containers larger than 100ml generally can't go through security even if the container is only part full. However, there are some exemptions.

  超過一百毫升的容器一般而言不能通過安檢，即使瓶內溶液並未裝滿。然而以下為例外狀況：

  You can take liquid containers larger than 100ml through security if they

如果你攜帶的容器容量超過一百毫升，但符合以下情況，則可通過安檢：

- are for essential medical purposes

  因為某些必要的醫療目的。

- are for special dietary requirements

  因為某些特殊的飲食需求。

- contain baby food or baby milk

  內含嬰兒食品或嬰兒牛奶。

You can also take liquids bought at an airport or on a plane (e.g. duty free) through security if

如果符合以下狀況，您也可以攜帶在機場或飛機上所購買的液體

- the items are sealed inside a security bag when you buy them

  購買時，物品是封存在一個密閉袋子中的。

- the receipt for the items is sealed in the security bag and visible

  收據亦置於密封的袋子內且清楚可見。

• You must not open the security bag until you reach your final destination. Airport staff may need to open the items to screen the liquid at the security point.

在抵達目的地前，您不能打開密封的袋子，機場安檢人員可能會在行李檢查處，要求打開物品掃描檢查。

• Liquid restrictions outside the EU

非歐盟國家之液體載運限制

Countries outside the EU might have different rules on carrying liquids as a transit or transfer passenger. You should check these rules with the relevant airlines and airports before travelling.

非歐盟國家對於中途停靠或轉機的旅客，於其攜帶液體物上機之規定可能有所不同。出發前建議您先行詢問機場或搭乘的航空公司。

Airport security staff won't let anything through that they consider dangerous - even if it's normally allowed in hand luggage.

機場安檢人員不會放行任何他們認為可能造成危險的物品，即使一般情況下，這些物品被允許做為手提行李。

- Lighters

  打火機

You can only carry 1 lighter on board. You should put it inside a resealable plastic bag (like the ones used for liquids), which you must keep on you throughout the flight. You can't:

您只能攜帶一只打火機，而且必須放入可重複使用的夾鏈袋內，同液體處理方式。且打火機必須隨身攜帶，不允許下列情事：

- put it in your hold luggage

  放在託運行李內。

- put it in your hand luggage after screening

  通過安檢後放入手提行李中。

❷ **Canada airports**（加拿大機場）

- Liquids gels and aerosols are permitted in carry-on baggage on the following conditions

  液體和凝膠在符合以下規定時，可置於手提行李內：

- They are in containers of 100 ml/ 100g (3.4 oz.) or less (Containers over 100 ml/ 100g (3.4 oz.) will be confiscated from carry-on baggage at the security checkpoint.)

裝進等同一百毫升或容量更小的容器內。超過一百毫升的容器於安檢處將會被沒收。

- The containers are placed in one (1) clear, closed and resealable plastic bag no larger than 1 litre (1 quart) (One reasonable plastic bag per passenger is permitted.)

容器必須放入一個透明、密封、可重複使用、不超過一公升的夾鏈袋內，每人僅可攜帶一只塑膠袋。

• Lithium metal or alloy cells and batteries

鋰或鋰合金電池芯及電池:

- Consumer electronic devices containing accepted lithium metal cells or batteries

消費性電子產品內含鋰合金電池芯或電池。

- Spare lithium metal cells or batteries (in reasonable quantities)

合理數量的備用鋰合金電池芯或電池。

- Batteries must be individually protected to prevent short circuits

電池必須單顆分開保存以避免短路。

• Lighters　打火機

- Only one of the following items, intended for individual use, is permitted when it is when carried on one's person（e.g. in pocket or purse)

以下三種打火機，只能擇一攜帶，數量一只，個人使用，且隨身攜帶，置於口袋或錢包裡。

One (1) Bic-type butane lighter, OR（一個Bic型丁烷打火機。）

One (1) USB lighter, OR（USB 充電打火機。）

One (1) book of matches（一盒火柴。）

- Dry ice　乾冰
  - Is properly vented to allow for the release of carbon dioxide gas

    經適當包裝，有缺口可供使二氧化碳氣體排出。
  - Is in good condition and free of any damage

    物品狀態佳，沒有任何破損。
  - Must not exceed 2.5 kg (5 lbs) in weight (total weight of 2.5 kg is for carry-on baggage and checked baggage combined per passenger)

    託運行李加手提行李的乾冰總重量不能超過2.5公斤 / 5 磅。

- Other prohibited or restricted items as hand-luggage　其他手提行李禁帶物品
  - Air purifiers and ionizers（空氣淨化器及負離子空氣淨化器。）
  - Avalanche rescue equipment （雪崩 / 山崩的救難器材。）
  - Compressed gas, cylinders（壓縮氣體及鋼瓶。）
  - Defense/incapacitating sprays（用於防禦或使對方失能的噴霧。）
  - Fuel-powered equipment（以汽油為動能的裝備。）
  - Paint（油漆、塗料。）

❸ U.S.A. airports (Rules for liquid carried on board)

（美國機場關於攜帶上機的液體相關規定）

　　The US Transportation Security Administration (TSA) regularly updates and publishes guidelines on security requirements for international US flights. There are prohibitions on bringing in certain items, and restrictions on the liquids that may be carried on board. Guidelines on liquids are expressed in the 3-1-1 rule for carry-ons: each passenger may only carry on liquids in maximum bottle sizes of 3.4 ounce (100ml) all contained in one single clear, plastic, zip-top bag of one-quart (about 1 litre) capacity. Larger quantities of liquids must be declared. Medications, baby formula and food, and breast milk may be carried on board in larger quantities but must be declared and examined.

美國運輸安全管理局,皆定時更新發佈有關美國國際航線保安規定的手冊。禁止攜帶某些物品進入美國,對於攜帶上機的液體亦有相關限制。手提行李中的液體規定遵循3-1-1原則:每位旅客只能攜帶一瓶不超過3.4盎司(100毫升)的液體;必須放入一個透明的塑膠夾鏈袋內,夾鏈袋的容量不超過1夸脱(約1公升)。超出這個規定的液體必須申報。醫療物品、嬰兒奶水及食物和母奶可以攜帶超出這規定的容量上機,但必須先申報且經過檢查。

❹ **EU (Rules for liquid carried on board)**

(歐盟國家攜帶液體上機的規定)

To protect passengers against the threat of liquid explosives, the European Union (EU) security rules restrict the amount of liquids that can be taken through security checkpoints. This applies to all passengers departing from airports in the EU regardless of the destination. This means that, at security checkpoints, both passengers and hand luggage must be checked for liquids in addition to other prohibited articles.

為保護乘客免於液體爆裂物的威脅,歐盟安檢條例限制可通過機場安檢的液體容量。此項規定適用於所有自歐盟國機場起飛的旅客,無論其目的地何在。也就是說,在機場安檢區內,無論乘客本身或其手提行李,除一般違禁品外,所攜帶的液體亦需經過檢測。

- Liquids may be carried in luggage that is checked in to the hold
  液體可置於託運行李內。

- Medicines and dietary requirements, including baby foods, for use during the trip may be carried in hand luggage. Proof may be requested.

藥物或因飲食規定於機上必須使用的液體，包括嬰兒食品可置於手提行李內，但必須取得證明。

- Liquids such as drinks and perfumes may be bought either in an EU airport shop when located beyond the security check or on board an aircraft operated by an EU airline

飲料、香水等液體可於歐盟各國機場內、安檢線外的免稅店購買，或購於歐盟各國班機上。

Note: If liquids are sold in a special sealed bag, do not open it before being screened, otherwise the contents may be confiscated at the checkpoint. (If transferring at an EU airport, do not open the bag before screening at the airport of transfer, or at the last one if there is to be more than one transfer).

註記：如果液體買進時，是置於一特殊的密封袋內，在經過檢查前，請勿打開，否則安檢員於行李檢查處可將內容物沒收。於歐盟國機場轉機的旅客，於通過最後轉機地的行李檢查以前，請勿打開密封袋。

Ⓓ Dangerous goods classifications 危險品分類

A. **Vocabulary** 單字

❶ criteria ㊚ [kraɪˈtɪrɪə] ㊙ [kraiˈtiəriə] 準則；尺度（複數形）(n.)

英文釋義 A standard or principle to evaluate or test something

同義字 criterions (criterion) 標準；尺度（單數形）

❷ imply ㊚ [ɪmˈplaɪ] ㊙ [imˈplai] 暗示；意味 (v.)

英文釋義 To indicate or express something without being explicitly stated

同義字 suggest; denote

❸ specialist KK [ˈspɛʃəlɪst] DJ [ˈspeʃəlist]　專家 (n.)

英文釋義 An individual who has special knowledge and skill relating to a particular profession or area of study

同義字 expert; authority

B. **Contents**　內文

Dangerous goods are divided into 9 classes, reflecting the type of risk involved. The order of the 9 classes is merely for convenience and does not imply a relative degree of danger. In other words, the Class 1 is not necessarily more dangerous than Class 2 or 3, etc. The danger classed used in the IATA regulations are defined by UN (United Nations).

危險品依其不同種類共分九類。此九類區分概以方便辨識為原則，而非依其危險程度劃分。換言之，第一類危險品並非較第二或第三類危險品具更高的危險程度，依此類推。國際航空運輸協會所使用的危險品分類乃根據聯合國危險品定義而制定。

There are specific criteria used to determine whether an article or substance belongs to that class or division. These criteria are technically detailed and classification of an item requires specialist knowledge of the criteria.

危險品的分類方式有其一定標準。這些標準要求嚴格仔細，必須具備專業知識才可司職分類工作。

The 9 classes are as follows（九類危險品列於下方）

(1)Class 1 Explosives.（爆裂物）

(2)Class 2 Gascs.（瓦斯／可燃氣）

(3)Class 3 Flammable liquids.（可燃液體）

(4)Class 4 flammable solids.（可燃固體）

(5)Class 5 Oxidizing substances and Organic Peroxides.（氧化物／有機過氧化物）

(6)Class 6 Toxic and infectious substances.（有毒或傳染性物質）

(7)Class 7 Radioactive Material.（放射性物質）

(8)Class 8 Corrosive.（腐蝕性物質）

(9)Class 9 Miscellaneous dangerous goods.（其他種類危險品）

Part III　Preparing for Airline Employment Opportunities

航空業求職面試

 Chapter 15.　Resume / Autobiography 撰寫履歷自傳

 Chapter 16.　Interview　　　　　面試須知

Chapter 15.　Resume / Autobiography

▶ Outline: 針對航空業的工作特性及求才標準,提供撰寫英文履歷自傳
之建議,並以若干航空公司之履歷格式做爲範本以供參考。

▶ Learning Goals: 運用範本及提供之參考寫法,完成自己的英文履歷
自傳。

　　航空地勤職務的要求,大多與一般公司相似,依照工作性質要求
相關科系、專業能力或證照。而客艙組員因工作地點與工作性質較爲
特殊,航空公司對於其外在條件、身體健康狀況、人格特質及年齡等
等,多數會以較嚴格的標準甄選。以下列舉cabin crew(客艙組員)的
基本條件要求,每家航空公司要求條件雖略有不同,但均包含以下幾
項:

Ⓐ Basic qualifications　基本條件

❶ academic degree ㋗ [ˌækəˈdɛmɪk] [dɪˈgri] ㋖ [ˌækəˈdemik] [diˈgri:]
學歷

• 國內航空公司多要求大專以上學歷;外籍航空公司某些具高中學歷即可
報考。

　- 學歷

　　high school diploma(高中畢業)

　　bachelor(大學學士)

　　master(碩士)

　　doctor(博士)

❷ physical condition ⓚⓚ ['fɪzɪkl̩] [kən'dɪʃən] ⓓⓙ ['fizikəl] [kən'diʃən]
身體條件

- 包括外型條件，如身高、體重、手臂長度等（特別是客艙組員）；以及身體健康狀況。

- Medical check　體檢項目
    - Height　身高
    - Weight　體重
    - Arm length　臂長: e.g. minimum arm reach of 212 cms on tip toes
      墊腳尖後伸直手臂，最少應有212公分高
    - Eyesight　視力
    - Hearing　聽力
    - Blood pressure　血壓
    - Blood and Urine　血液、尿液
    - Electrocardiography, ECG or EKG　心電圖
    - Ultrasound　超音波
    - Thalassemia　地中海型貧血
    - Hepatitis B　B型肝炎
    - Contagious disease　傳染性疾病
    - Scoliosis　脊椎側彎

❸ Age ⓚⓚ [edʒ] ⓓⓙ [eidʒ]　年齡

- Minimum age of 18, usually up to 32　各家要求不同，多落在此區間
  （18～32歲）

Ⓑ Position requirements 職務要求

❶ Language skill / proficiency 語言能力

proficiency ⓚ [prə'fɪʃənsɪ] ⓓ [prə'fiʃənsi] 精通程度;熟練度

- spoken / reading / written 要求應徵者自行填寫 口說 / 閱讀 / 書寫的程度
- tick mark as appropriate 要求應徵者依據程度勾選適當的選項

❷ Personal skills and attributes 人際關係技巧 / 個人特質

attribute ⓚ ['ætrə‚bjut] ⓓ ['ætribju:t] 特性;特質

- strong communication skills 出色溝通技巧
- confidence in dealing with a variety of people 有自信能與各式各樣的人協調相處
- great team working skills 優秀的團隊工作技巧
- respect for the contributions of teammates 敬重團隊成員的貢獻
- unwavering customer service target 堅持顧客服務的理念
- competence in handling challenging situations 處理困難情況的能力
- remain calm under pressure and in emergency situations 於緊急狀況壓力下仍能保持冷靜
- the capability to work speedy and efficiently with time constraints 在時間壓力下能迅速有效率地工作
- the ability to cope with diverse situations calmly and quickly 能夠冷靜快速地處理各種不同狀況
- the capacity to work in a confined space 適應於密閉空間中工作
- flexibility in working unsocial hours on any day of the year 願意在非正常作息的時間工作

• passion for aviation and travel　對航空業及旅行充滿熱情

❸ **Preferred characteristics for airline employees**　航空從業人員較適特質

characteristic ⓀⓀ [ˌkærəktəˈrɪstɪk] ⓄⒿ [ˌkæriktəˈristik]　特色 / 特性

employee ⓀⓀ [ˌɛmplɔɪˈi] ⓄⒿ [ˌemplɔiˈi:]　從業人員 / 員工

• active ⓀⓀ [ˈæktɪv] ⓄⒿ [ˈæktiv]　積極的；活潑的

• adaptable ⓀⓀ [əˈdæptəbļ] ⓄⒿ [əˈdæptəbl]　適應力強的

• amiable ⓀⓀ [ˈemɪəbļ] ⓄⒿ [ˈeimjəbl]　友善的；厚道的

• calm ⓀⓀ [kɑm] ⓄⒿ [kɑ:m]　冷靜的

• caring ⓀⓀ [ˈkɛrɪŋ] ⓄⒿ [ˈkɛərɪŋ]　貼心的

• competent ⓀⓀ [ˈkɑmpətənt] ⓄⒿ [ˈkɔmpitənt]　稱職的；有能力的

• confident ⓀⓀ [ˈkɑnfədənt] ⓄⒿ [ˈkɔnfidənt]　有自信的

• considerate ⓀⓀ [kənˈsɪdərɪt] ⓄⒿ [kənˈsidərit]　體貼的；周到的

• decisive ⓀⓀ [dɪˈsaɪsɪv] ⓄⒿ [diˈsaisiv]　果斷的；堅決的

• dedicated ⓀⓀ [ˈdɛdəˌketɪd] ⓄⒿ [ˈdediˌkeitid]　專注的；全力奉獻的

• dependable ⓀⓀ [dɪˈpɛndəbļ] ⓄⒿ [diˈpendəbl]　值得依靠的

• diligent ⓀⓀ [ˈdɪlədʒənt] ⓄⒿ [ˈdilidʒənt]　勤奮的

• discreet ⓀⓀ [dɪˈskrit] ⓄⒿ [diˈskri:t]　謹慎的；考慮周到的

• easygoing ⓀⓀ [ˈizɪˈgoɪŋ] ⓄⒿ [ˈi:ziˌgəuiŋ]　平易近人的

• efficient ⓀⓀ [ɪˈfɪʃənt] ⓄⒿ [iˈfiʃənt]　有效率的

• energetic ⓀⓀ [ˌɛnəˈdʒɛtɪk] ⓄⒿ [ˌenəˈdʒetik]　活力充沛的

• enthusiastic ⓀⓀ [ɪnˌθjuzɪˈæstɪk] ⓄⒿ [inˌθju:ziˈæstik]　熱心的；熱情的

• flexible ⓀⓀ [ˈflɛksəbļ] ⓄⒿ [ˈfleksəbl]　可靈活變通的；有彈性的

• friendly ⓀⓀ [ˈfrɛndlɪ] ⓄⒿ [ˈfrendli]　友善的

• generous ⓀⓀ [ˈdʒɛnərəs] ⓄⒿ [ˈdʒenərəs]　大方的

- gregarious ㏍ [grɪˈgɛrɪəs] ⓓ [greˈgɛərɪəs] 合群的
- honest ㏍ [ˈɑnɪst] ⓓ [ˈɔnist] 誠實的
- humorous ㏍ [ˈhjumərəs] ⓓ [ˈhjuːmərəs] 幽默的
- innovative ㏍ [ˈɪnoˌvetɪv] ⓓ [ˈinəuveitiv] 創新的；不拘泥的
- interesting ㏍ [ˈɪntərɪstɪŋ] ⓓ [ˈintəristiŋ] 風趣的
- kind ㏍ [kaɪnd] ⓓ [kaind] 仁慈的；善良的
- lawful ㏍ [ˈlɔfəl] ⓓ [ˈlɔːfəl] 守法的
- open-minded ㏍ [ˈopənˈmaɪndɪd] ⓓ [ˈəupənˈmaindid] 心胸寬闊的； 能納諫的
- organized ㏍ [ˈɔrgənˌaɪzd] ⓓ [ˈɔːgənaizd] 有條理的；有組織性的
- outgoing ㏍ [ˈaʊtˌgoɪŋ] ⓓ [ˈautˌgəuiŋ] 外向的
- patient ㏍ [ˈpeʃənt] ⓓ [ˈpeiʃənt] 有耐性的
- people-oriented ㏍ [ˈpiplˈɑrɪentɪd] ⓓ [ˈpiːplˈɔːrientid] 以人為本的； 尊重人的
- pleasant ㏍ [ˈplɛzənt] ⓓ [ˈpleznt] 討喜的；令人愉悅的
- polite ㏍ [pəˈlaɪt]] ⓓ [pəˈlait] 有禮貌的；客氣的
- positive ㏍ [ˈpɑzətɪv] ⓓ [ˈpɔzitiv] 正向的
- prudent ㏍ [ˈprudn̩t] ⓓ [ˈpruːdənt] 謹慎的
- punctual ㏍ [ˈpʌŋktʃʊəl] ⓓ [ˈpʌŋktjuəl] 準時的
- reliable ㏍ [rɪˈlaɪəbl̩] ⓓ [riˈlaiəbl] 值得依賴的
- resourceful ㏍ [rɪˈsorsfəl] ⓓ [riˈsɔːsfəl] 足智多謀的
- responsible ㏍ [rɪˈspɑnsəbl̩] ⓓ [riˈspɔnsəbl] 負責任的
- socialized ㏍ [ˈsoʃəˈlaɪzd] ⓓ [ˈsəuʃəlaizd] 懂交際的
- sweet ㏍ [swit] ⓓ [swiːt] 親切的；溫柔的
- thoughtful ㏍ [ˈθɔtfəl] ⓓ [ˈθɔːtfəl] 體貼的

- trustworthy ㉖ ['trʌst,wɜ·ðɪ] ㉑ ['trʌst,wɔ:ði]　值得信賴的
- vigilant ㉖ ['vɪdʒələnt] ㉑ ['vidʒilənt]　警覺的
- vigorous ㉖ ['vɪgərəs] ㉑ ['vigərəs]　精力旺盛的

Resume samples　履歷範本

❶ Required information on resume　履歷常見欄位說明

A. Personal Data / Details　個人資料

- name　姓名
  - first name / given name　名
  - surname / family name / last name　姓
  - full name　全名
  - alias　別名
  - name in Chinese characters (if applicable)　如有中文姓名，請以中文書寫
- birthday / date of birth　生日
- contact information　聯絡資料
  - permanent address / residential address　戶籍地址；永久地址
  - local address / mailing address / present address / contact address / postal address　目前居住地址
  - email address　電子信箱
  - cell phone number / cellular phone number / mobile phone number / hand phone number　手機號碼
  - house phone number　家用電話
- nationality / native province and city　國籍 / 出生地

- ID number / social security number / passport number　身分證號碼 / 社會安全號碼 / 護照號碼
- gender / sex　性別
  - male　男性
  - female　女性
- marital status　婚姻狀況
  - married　已婚
  - divorced　離婚
  - separated　分居
  - single　單身
- height / weight　身高 / 體重
- eyesight　視力
- religion　宗教
  - Buddhism　佛教
  - Taoism　道教
  - Christian　基督教
  - Catholicism　天主教
  - Judaism　猶太教
  - Islam　回教
  - Hinduism　印度教

B. Position Information　職務資料

- position applied for　應徵職務
- salary requirement / expected　期望薪資
- Yes / No questions　簡答「是」或「否」的問題：某些此類問題（以下標註*者），公司會要求應徵者寫下細節（details）加以說明。

- Are you willing to relocate? 你願意遷居嗎？

- Will you accept temporary or part-time employment? 你接受暫時或兼職的工作嗎？

- Can you swim? 你會游泳嗎？

- * Do you hold dual Nationality? 你有雙重國籍嗎？

- Have you ever filed an application with ___公司名___ ? / Have you made any previous applications to ___公司名___ ? / Have you ever applied on any previous occasions for employment in any capacity with ___公司名___ ? 你應徵過 ___公司名___ 的工作嗎？

- *Have you previously employed by ___該公司名___ ? 你曾在 ___公司名___ 公司工作過嗎？

- *Any friends / relatives working with ___該公司名___ ? 是否有朋友或家人於 ___公司___ 工作呢？

- *Have you lived and worked overseas previously? 你曾經在海外居住或工作過嗎？

- Have you dealt with the general public in your previous jobs? 你先前的工作需要與大眾接觸嗎？

- *Have you ever been charged with any offence or convicted by any court or detained by the authorities under the provisions of law in any country? 你曾經於任何國家，因為任何犯罪事例遭到拘留、起訴或判決有罪嗎？

- *Have you signed a promissory note or an acknowledgement of indebtedness for which the amount pledged has not already been fully repaid? 你是否仍有任何簽署的本票或經確認的債務尚未全數償還？

- Do you have any involvement in any business undertaking? 你目前

仍參與經營任何公司嗎？

- *Have you suffered from any mental illness or any physical illness or disability for which you have received medical treatment (e.g. diabetes, tuberculosis, epilepsy, asthma, etc.)　你曾因爲任何精神上或身體上的疾病而接受治療嗎？如：糖尿病、肺結核、癲癇、氣喘等

- Do you have a birthmark, tattoo or any visible mark on the areas between your elbow and finger tips, and from your knees to the ankles? 你的身上，從手肘到手指、從膝蓋到腳踝，是否有任何胎記、紋身或看得見的疤痕？

- *Will you receive a satisfactory reference from your current and all previous employers?　你的現任和所有前雇主，都會肯定你的工作表現嗎？

- *Have you ever been suspended, discharged, or asked to resign by an employer?　你曾被雇主要求停職、免職或辭職嗎？

• commencement date　可以正式報到上班的日期

C. Education and Special training　教育及特殊訓練

• name of school / college / university　學校 / 學院 / 大學名稱

• major / minor　主修 / 副修

• grade / form / course /subject　級別 / 種類 / 課程 / 學科

• degree received / degree studying for / degree obtained / results achieved　取得的學位

• years attended (from month / year to month / year)　就讀期間：通常要求寫下入學及畢業的年、月

• grade point average　平均成績

• scholarship / award　獎學金 / 授予獎勵

- extra-curricular activity　課外活動
- certificate　證書
- professional qualification　專業資格認證

D. Employment Record / Employment History / Job History / Previous Working Experience　工作經歷

- name of company / employer　公司名稱
- employers – start with present / most recent　公司：從現職 / 最近任職的公司寫起
- employers – start with your first job　公司：從第一家任職的公司寫起
- position held / job title and duties　職務名稱 / 負責工作
- period with company (from month / year to month / year)　工作期間
- last drawn salary　最後薪資
- reason for leaving　離職原因

E. Language proficiency　語言能力

Candidates with multilingual skills are preferred. （應徵航空業職務，若能擁有多種足以溝通無礙的語言能力，較具優勢）

- spoken / reading / written　口語 / 閱讀 / 書寫
- standard　程度
  - fluent　流利
  - good　佳
  - satisfactory　良好
  - average　普通
  - fair　普通
  - conversational　一般口語會話程度

- little　尙懂
- poor　不好
- none　完全不會

F. Supplement Information　補充資料：公司制式履歷上的填寫說明或其他要求

- Instructions
  - Please ensure that you provide accurate information. It will become part of your staff record if your application is successful. Complete all parts of this form. If an item is not applicable, write N/A. Incomplete applications will NOT be processed.

    請確認你所提供的資料均屬實，若你進入本公司任職，這些資料將成爲你的員工檔案。請勿漏填任何題項，不適用的問題，可以N/A表示。填寫不全的履歷將不被採用。

  - To assist us in giving your application the fullest consideration, you are asked to complete this form in as much as possible. The information will be treated with the utmost confidence and no reference will be taken up without your prior permission.

    爲使你的求職申請取得最充分的機會，請務必盡可能地完整填寫這份履歷表。履歷表上的資料會被完善保管，沒有你的授權，資料不會提供他人使用。

- Declaration
  - I hereby declare that the information given is correct to the best of my knowledge and belief, and that I have not withheld any information which might reasonably be calculated to adversely affect my suitability for employment. I further declare that I have/have not

been previously been employed by ___公司名___ .

我宣誓於此提供的所有訊息，就我所知所信皆屬實，我亦無刻意隱藏任何對我不利或不適任的資料。此外，我亦宣告於此之前從未在 ___公司名___ 任職過。

- I declare that to the best of my knowledge, the information I have provided is true and correct. I understand that if I am selected and if any information declared herein is subsequently found to be false or misleading it will lead to my dismissal.

我宣誓我已盡其所能地提供確實及正確的資料。我瞭解若我通過甄選，但所填寫的資料中，被發現有任何不實或誤導的內容，則我的資格將被取消。

• Character Referees

- Give particulars of 2 referees (other than relatives). They should be responsible persons who know you well and at least one should be well acquainted with you in your private life. Names of distinguished persons must not be given unless they know you well and have agreed to be your referees. Testimonials from these referees should not be sent. ___公司名___ will write to them if necessary.

請提供兩位除親屬外的推薦人。推薦人必須是足以自負言行之責、且真正瞭解你的人，而其中至少一人必須非常熟悉你的私人生活。你所提供的人選必須對你有足夠瞭解且同意成為你的推薦人。請勿寄送推薦函，如有需要，公司會與其聯繫。

❷ Sample 1 – Airlines Cabin Crew Application Form (I)

NAME: SEX: F M
PRESENT ADDRESS:
TEL. NO. HOME: WORK:

PERMANENT ADDRESS(if different from above)
TEL. NO. HOME: WORK:

NAME IN CHINESE CHARACTERS(If applicable)

IMPORTANT

Please ensure that you provide accurate information. It will become part of your staff record if your application is successful. Complete all parts of this form. If an item is not applicable, write N/A. Incomplete applications will NOT be processed.

DATE OF BIRTH _____

PLACE OF BIRTH _____

NATIONALITY _____

ID/PASSPORT NO. _____

MARITAL STATUS: SINGLE   MARRIED

SEPERATED   DIVORCE

ATTACH

PASSPORT

PHOTO

HERE

EDUCATION (Start with present or most recent)

NAME OF SCHOOL/COLLEGE/UNIVERSITY	GRADE/ FORM/ COURSE	YEARS ATTENDED FROM: TO:

EMPLOYMENT RECORD (Start with your present or most recent employment)

COMPANY NAME	DATE JOINED	DATE LEFT	JOB TITLE	REASON FOR LEAVING	SALARY

LANGUAGES:SPOKEN AND READING ABILITY

LANGUAGE	SPOKEN		READING		
	FLUENT	LITTLE	GOOD	LITTLE	NONE
English					

HEIGHT, WEIGHT, EYESIGHT AND HEALTH

HEIGHT:_____cm (CHK:) **WEIGHT:**____kg (CHK:)

EYESIGHT:□ GOOD   □ SPECTACLES DEGREE/POWER:

□ NEED EYEWEAR □ CONTACTS _____

HOW MANY DAYS OF WORK/SCHOOL HAVE
YOU MISSED THROUGH ILLNESS IN THE PAST YEAR?_____

DO YOU HAVE(OR HAVE YOU EVER HAD)
ANY SERIOUS ILLNESS? □ NO   YES:_____

HAVE YOU ANY SCARS, BIRTHMARKS
OR TATTOOS THAT WOULD BE VISIBLE
IF WEARING THE UNIFORM ? □ NO   YES:_____

FAMILY PARTICULARS

FATHER'S NAME: _____

OCCUPATION: _____

ADDRESS: _____

TEL. NO: _____

MOTHER'S NAME: _____

OCCUPATION: _____

ADDRESS: _____

TEL. NO: _____

NO. OF BROTHERS: _____   NO. OF SISTERS: _____

HUSBAND'S/ WIFE'S NAME: _____

OCCUPATION: _____

ADDRESS: _____

TEL. NO: _____

NO.OF   CHILDREN:

ADDITIONAL INFORMATION

Please explain why you would like to become a member of A
Airlines Cabin Crew. List any other information, such as any special
skills, training service industry or travel experience which you may
have that would support your application:

_____

_____

_____

_____

_____

_____

_____

_____

_____

_____

_____

_____

_____

COMMENCEMENT DATE
IF SELECTED, WHAT IS THE EARLIEST DATE THAT YOU WOULD BE ABLE TO START WORK?

ATTACHMENTS

**PLEASE ATTACH TO THIS APPLICATION THE ITEMS LISTED
BELOW. NOTE THAT THESE ARE NOT RETURNABLE.**

- □ ONE PASSPORT-SIZE PHOTOGRAPH
- □ ONE FULL-LENGTH(5") PHOTOGRAPH
- □ PHOTOCOPY OF ID CARD/PASSPORT
- □ PHOTOCOPY OF BIRTH CERTIFICATE
- □ PHOTOCOPIES OF SCHOOL/COLLEGE CERTIFICATES
- □ EMPLOYMENT TASTIMONIALS OR REFERNCE LETTERS

_____

HOW DID YOU KNOW ABOUT THIS VACANCY?
- □ PRESS AD-NAME OF PAPER/MAGAZINE:
- □ TV
- □ RADIO
- □ CAREER TALKS
- □ WALK-IN ENQUIRIES
- □ TELEPHONE ENQUIRIES
- □ INTERNAL CIRCULARS
- □ FRIENDS

OTHER DETAILS AND DECLARATION

HAVE YOU MADE ANY PREVIOUS APPLICATIONS TO CATHAY PACIFIC?
□NO IF YES, DATE/DETAILS:
_____
_____

ANY FRIENDS/RELATIVES WORKING WITH CATHAY PACIFIC?   □NO
IF YES, NAME: POSITION:
_____
_____

**Have you ever been arrested, indicted or summoned into a court as a defendant in
any Civil or Criminal proceedings or convicted, fined or imprisoned or placed on
probation, or have you ever been ordered to deposit bail or collateral for any
violation of any Law, Police Regulation or Ordinance? □NO   □YES**

IF YES, GIVE DETAILS:
_____
_____

DECLARATION
**I DECLARE THAT TO THE BEST OF MY KNOWLEDGE, THE INFORMATION I HAVE
PROVIDED IS TRUE AND CORRECT. I UNDERSTAND THAT IF I AM SELECTED AND IF
ANY INFORMATION DECLARED HEREIN IS SUBSEQUENTLY FOUND TO BE FALSE
OR MISLEADING IT WILL LEAD TO MY DISMISSAL.**

SIGNED: **DATE:**

❸ Sample 2 –Airlines Cabin Crew Application Form (II)

Passport
Photograph

Full Name _____

Present Address _____ Permanent Address(if different)

_____

_____

_____

Tel No. _____ Fax No. _____ Tel No. _____ Fax No. _____

E-mail address: _____ Date Available

Date of Birth _____ Place of Birth _____

Marital Status: Married ☐ Divorced ☐ Separated ☐ Single ☐

Religion _____ Nationality at Birth _____

Present Nationality: _____ Do you hold dual Nationality Yes☐ No☐

If Yes, Please Specify _____

Provide details of passport you intend to use

LANGUAGES

Languages	Spoken		Written	
	Fluent	Average	Fluent	Average

Height in CMS _____ Weight in KGS _____

Do you wear: Glasses Yes ☐ No ☐ Contact Len Yes☐ No☐
If yes, give correction factor: Left _____ Right _____

Provide details of any illness: _____
Can You Swim: Yes☐ NO☐

EDUCATION QUALIFICATIONS

Dates		Name and Address of School/University	Subjects	Results Achieved
From	To			

EMPLOYMENT   RECORD

Name	Relationship	Department	Title

DETAILS   OF   RELATIVES

Dates		Name of Company	Position Held	Salary	
From	To			Starting	Final

CURRENTLY   IN   DNATA/EMIRATES   EMPLOYMENT

Have you been interviewed by __B Airlines__ previously for Cabin Crew:
If Yes, _____ when _____

Applicant's Declaration

I hereby declare that the information given is correct to the best of my
knowledge and belief, and that I have not withheld any information which
might reasonably be calculated to adversely affect my suitability for
employment. I further declare that I have/have not been previously been
employed by _B   Airlines_.

Signature _____ Date _____

❹ Sample 3 – regular English resume sample (I)
一般英文履歷範本格式-I

Name
Address
Cell No.
Email address

EDUCATION & TRAINING

- Degree of _____, School name, City / State or Province or Country   Period
- Degree of _____, School name, City / State or Province or Country   Period
- Certificate of _____, Institution Name, City / State or Province or Country   Period
- Training Course, Institution Name, City / State or Province or Country   Period

EXPERIENCE

- Job Title, Company Name, City / State or Province or Country   Period
  - Duty 1
  - Duty 2
  - Duty 3
- Job Title, Company Name, City / State or Province or Country   Period
  - Duty 1
  - Duty 2
  - Duty 3

COMPUTER SKILLS:
Provide details and certificates if any

LANGUAGE SKILLS:
- Language 1: level
- Language 2: level
- Language 3: level

Reference available upon request.

❺ Sample 4 – regular English resume sample (II)

一般英文履歷範本格式-Ⅱ

Name

Address　/　Contact Number

Email Address

Job Title

Brief statement / Job objective

（應徵工作職稱，簡述自己的求職動機和條件）

TECHNICAL SKILLS

- If any
- If any
- If any

LANGUAGE SKILLS

- Language 1　　Spoken:　　　　Reading:　　　　Written:
- Language 2　　Spoken:　　　　Reading:　　　　Written:

WORK EXPERIENCE

Company　Name　　　　　Title　　　Location　　　　　Working Period
- Duty description
    - details
    - details

Company　Name　　　　　Title　　　Location　　　　　Working Period
- Duty description
    - details
    - details

INTERN & PART-TIME EXPERIENCE

Company　Name　　　　　Title　　　Location　　　　　Working Period

Company　Name　　　　　Title　　　Location　　　　　Working Period

EDUCATION

Degree　：　Department, School　　　　Status　　　　Time Period

　　　　　　　　　　　　　　　　　　　　　　　　　GPA

Degree　：　Department, School　　　　Status　　　　Time Period

　　　　　　　　　　　　　　　　　　　　　　　　　GPA

Autobiography samples　自傳範本

　　自傳篇幅不需太長，一頁A4紙即可。對即將踏出校園的畢業生而言，沒有「豐功偉業」的事蹟十分正常，不必為了擴充篇幅而絞盡腦汁，只需將每個段落的重點清楚呈現即可。但最好於每個段落中，都能製造一個清楚的記憶點，所以，盡量以「實例」取代空泛堆砌的形容詞。自傳的內容，可以適時加入旁人對你的看法和觀察，以達到平衡報導的效果。

❶ Outlines　自傳大綱

- Paragraph 1 - Basic information　個人基本資料
  - ➢ greetings　問候語
  - ➢ name / family members / birthday place / birth order　姓名／家庭成員／出生地／排行
  - ➢ the story of growth　成長的故事
  - ➢ educational background　畢業學校／科系
  - ➢ hobbies or specialties　興趣或專長
- Paragraph 2 - Motivation　應聘動機
  - ➢ Why are you interested in this industry (position)?　為何想從事這份行業／工作？
  - ➢ Why are you interested in this company?　為何想進入這家公司工作？
  - ➢ What do you know about this position?　你對這份工作的了解
- Paragraph 3 - Your advantages　個人優勢
  - ➢ your personalities　你的個性
  - ➢ your achievement　你的成就

➤ your extra-curricular activities　你的課外活動

➤ your working or intern experience　你的工作或實習經驗

➤ your language or professional skills　你的語言或專業能力

➤ provide actual examples　舉出實例

- Paragraph 4 - Conclusion　結論

➤ emphasize your qualifications　強調你的資格和能力

➤ express your passion　展現你的熱情

➤ share your vision　分享你的願景

❷ **Sample 1 – autobiography sample for flight attendant position 應徵空服員自傳範例**

The advertisement for cabin crew recruitment on Airlines Website has interested me greatly. Here I am to pursue my dream work and hopefully you will consider me for the position. I was born and brought up in city / country . We are a family of number : my title , my title , ... , and me. I received a bachelor's degree (or master's degree) in department title / subject from school name in June. I love singing and travel. Traveling around the world to expand my horizons has always been one of my life goals.

　　航空公司名 於網頁上的空服員招募廣告十分吸引我，所以我決定應徵這份夢寐以求的工作，希望貴公司能加以考慮。我出生成長於 地名 ，一家 數字 口，分別是我的　　　　、　　　　、　　　　　……和我。今年六月畢業於 學校名 　系所名稱 系（所），喜歡唱歌和旅行。環遊世界增廣見聞一直是我的目標之一。

　　Airlines is well-known for its professionalism and continuous improvement. Your great cabin service has received numerous prizes worldwide. The well-established structure, good reputation and competitive benefits have all made Airlines the best company to work for. Being a flight attendant is my dream. It is not only because it can provide me the opportunities to experience diverse exoticism, but also train me to upgrade myself in several ways. Surrounded by people from all over the world, offering satisfied service and protecting them from any potential risk are definitely challenging. I am ready to accept this challenge.

航空公司名 以其專業性和不斷進步的努力知名於世。客艙服務更是榮獲全球許多獎項的肯定。組織體系健全、公司聲譽佳以及具有競爭力的福利制度，都讓貴公司成為許多人求職的首選。成為空服員是我的夢想，不只因為空服員可以讓我體驗不同國度的經歷，這份工作更能鞭策我不斷向上提升。當你置身於全球各色各樣的人種之間，提供令人滿意的服務和保護旅客避免潛在的風險絕對是件極具挑戰的工作，我自認已準備好接受這個挑戰。

I am an easygoing and thoughtful person, who enjoy making friends and helping others. To fulfill my dream, I continuously improve my English and interpersonal skills. I have taken the TOEIC test and scored number . During the summer vacations, I took internship programs twice in company to practice customer service and face-to-face communication skills. By always wearing smile and listening to customers' demands with patience, I have received positive comments from the managers and many customers. It encourages me to devote more efforts to enhancing my service skills. I am confident that I can apply my service experience and skills to provide passengers satisfactory service on board.

我的個性平易近人又十分體貼，而且喜歡交朋友，更樂於助人。為了完成夢想，我不斷提升自己的語言能力和處理人際關係的技巧。

多益測驗我已取得 <u>分數</u> 分的分數，亦利用暑假期間至 <u>公司名</u> 實習，實際練習顧客服務和面對面溝通技巧。因為我總是面帶微笑，充滿耐心地聆聽顧客的需求，無論是主管或顧客，都給了我正面的評價，這也讓我更願意努力地提升自己的服務技巧。我有信心，可以將我的服務經驗及技巧，運用在客艙的工作之中，提供讓旅客滿意的服務。

Working on board an aircraft requires great physical fitness and energy, as well as good manner and passion. Growing up in a supportive family, I have no fear to express myself and undertake responsibility. I sincerely assure you of my enthusiasm and proficiency as being a qualified candidate. Your decision will be highly appreciated if you would grant me an interview to state my thoughts and vision. Thank you very much.

　　機上工作需要健康的身體和充沛的活力，還有良好的禮節及工作熱忱。在一個家人間彼此支持鼓勵的家庭中長大，我從不害怕表達自己和承擔責任。真誠地向您保證，我的熱忱和能力，一定可以勝任空服員的工作。衷心希望您能讓我有機會參加面試，當面陳述我的理念和願景。非常感謝您。

- advertisement ㏍ [ˌædvɚ'taɪzmənt] ㄉㄐ [əd'vəːtismənt]　廣告
- recruitment ㏍ [rɪ'krutmənt] ㄉㄐ [ri'kruːtmənt]　招募
- pursue ㏍ [pə'su] ㄉㄐ [pə'suː]　追求；從事
- horizon ㏍ [hə'raɪzn̩] ㄉㄐ [hə'raizn]　地平線；眼界
- professionalism ㏍ [prə'fɛʃənl̩ˌɪzəm] ㄉㄐ [prə'feʃənəlizəm]　專業度
- competitive ㏍ [kəm'pɛtətɪv] ㄉㄐ [kəm'petitiv]　競爭的；有競爭力的
- benefit ㏍ ['bɛnəfɪt] ㄉㄐ ['benifit]　福利
- exoticism ㏍ [ɛg'zɑtəsɪzəm] ㄉㄐ [ɛg'zɔtisizəm]　異國情調

- challenging KK ['tʃælɪndʒɪŋ] DJ ['tʃælɪndʒɪŋ] 具挑戰性的
- fulfill KK [fʊl'fɪl] DJ [ful'fɪl] 實現；實行
- internship KK ['ɪntɜ·n'ʃɪp] DJ ['intə:nʃip] 實習
- demand KK [dɪ'mænd] DJ [di'mɑ:nd] 要求
- encourage KK [ɪn'kɜ·ɪdʒ] DJ [in'kʌridʒ] 鼓勵
- devote KK [dɪ'vot] DJ [di'vəut] 貢獻；投入
- physical KK ['fɪzɪkl] DJ ['fizikəl] 身體的
- passion KK ['pæʃən] DJ ['pæʃən] 熱情
- enthusiasm KK [ɪn'θjuzɪˌæzəm] DJ [in'θju:ziæzəm] 熱忱
- grant KK [grænt] DJ [grɑ:nt] 同意；准予

❸ Sample 2 – autobiography sample (II)

I come from city / country , where I grew up with many lovely people and made numerous unforgettable memories. Being the youngest one in the family, I love surrounding myself with families, relatives and friends. What I enjoy most is to have fun with people and make them laugh.

我的故鄉是 地名 ，我在那兒成長，那裡有許多可愛的人和我無數難忘的回憶。身為家中的老么，我最喜歡和家人親友共聚一堂，讓大家開開心心、充滿歡笑地在聚在一起，是我最享受的事。

I earned a bachelor's degree in department title / subject . When I was in school, I always maintained a good balance between classroom and extra-curricular activities. My favorite subject is Organizational Behavior. When I applied some related concepts to improve teamwork and obtained positive feedback, it boosted my confidence. I am certain that I am a good team play-er. This is why I am motivated to apply for the position of airport ground

staff with enthusiasm.

　　我已取得大學學士學位，我的主修是 系名 。就學期間，我一直能夠兼顧課業和課外活動。我最喜歡的課程是組織行為，每當我運用課堂所學，讓大家的團隊合作表現能夠更好，因而得到正向的回應，我的自信心便又向上提升。我確定我是一個具有良好團隊精神的人，這是我積極進取，希望爭取成為地勤的動機。

　　Airlines has successfully gained a reputation of reliability and satisfied customer service. I have longed for the chance to be one of your ground crew members since I was 15, and traveled abroad alone for the first time. The caring ground staff helped me with check-in procedures and my overweight baggage patiently. The one who escorted me to the boarding gate thoroughly explained the Immigration and Customs processes. His company took my anxiety away and filled my heart with warmth. I wish to return the favor by becoming a competent and considerate ground staff to help others.

　　航空公司名 成功地以其可靠度和顧客服務滿意度贏得良好聲譽。從我15歲，自己第一次一個人出國開始，我便一直渴望能夠成為貴公司的地勤人員。當時，不但劃位櫃檯的地勤親切貼心地幫助我處理行李過重的問題，陪我前往登機門的地勤，更是十分詳盡地為我解說證照和海關的檢驗程序，讓我忐忑不安的心情，能夠平靜下來，而且心中充滿的溫暖。一直希望有一天，我也能成為既有專業能力，又善解人意的地勤人員，將這份溫暖，帶給其他旅客。

　　I am fluent in Mandarin, Taiwanese, English and know some Japanese. It is my sincere hope that you may take my application into consideration, and offer me the opportunity to have an interview with you. I may not be the best candidate on the list. Nevertheless, I assure you that I will not fail your decision. Thank you very much for your time and consideration.

　　我能流利地以國語、台語和英文溝通，也懂一些日文。眞誠地希望您能考慮給予我面試的機會。也許在眾多的應徵者中，我並非最優秀的那一位，但我向您保證，我一定不會讓您失望的。謝謝您撥冗考慮我的申請。

- concept ㊚ ['kɑnsɛpt] ㊛ ['kɔnsept]　觀念；概念
- feedback ㊚ ['fid,bæk] ㊛ ['fi:dbæk]　回應
- boost ㊚ [bust] ㊛ [bu:st]　提高；促進
- motivate ㊚ ['motə,vet] ㊛ ['məuti,veit]　刺激；激發
- thoroughly ㊚ ['θɝolɪ] ㊛ ['θʌrəli]　詳細地
- anxiety ㊚ [æŋ'zaɪətɪ] ㊛ [æŋ'zaiəti]　焦慮；掛念
- nevertheless ㊚ [,nɛvɚðə'lɛs] ㊛ [,nevəðə'les]　然而

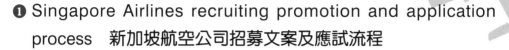

Appendix　附　錄

❶ Singapore Airlines recruiting promotion and application process　新加坡航空公司招募文案及應試流程

• Career development　職涯發展

Singapore Airlines believes in helping all employees achieve their full potential. Throughout your career with us, you will be offered an extensive array of learning and development opportunities to enhance your professional and personal competencies.

新航有信心能幫助所有員工淋漓盡致地發揮個人潛能。在新航任職，你將可獲得最多最大的學習和發展機會，提升你的專業與個人職能。

Upon joining us, you will embark on an enriching on-boarding experience ranging from customised orientation programmes, site visits and attachments for exposure to our business and the airline industry, as well as our other general management and leadership programmes.

一加入新航，你便可獲得量身打造的新訓機會，實地觀察瞭解新航事業體與航空產業的發展，並且學習一般管理和領導的課程。

You will also be assigned a mentor in your first year, to help you adjust to working life and adapt to the culture of Singapore Airlines. At each stage of your career with Singapore Airlines, you will interact with peers and senior management from across the organisation and across the globe through your involvement in various committees and task forces. There will also be opportunities for overseas duty travel.

同時，新進員工的第一年，將有一位指導員從旁協助你適應工作和融入公司文化。在新航工作的每一個階段，依據不同的職務，你會與跨組織及全球各地的同儕和資深管理人員互相切磋，且也有海外出差旅行的機會。

Singapore Airlines is committed to developing our employees into true airline professionals. The diverse nature of our business provides varied scope for development. With our job rotation scheme, you can look forward to job postings within your field of specialisation or across functional areas.

新航承諾可使員工成為航空業真正的專業人才。新航事業體的多樣性，足以提供各種不同領域的發展。我們的內部輪調制度，讓你有機會於自己的專業或橫跨其他領域獲得發展。

After some years of experience, you can also apply, if you are so inclined, to be part of the Overseas Managers Scheme. You may eventually become one of the Airline's General Managers overseas. You will be responsible for all aspects of the Airline's business interests at overseas offices, which include sales and marketing, HR, management, finance and government relations.

擁有幾年的工作經驗後，如果有意願，你也可以申請海外管理職的工作。你有機會成為新航駐海外各站的站經理，負責該站的所有航空相關事務，包括業務與行銷、人力 資源、管理、財務及維護與當地政府的關係。

- Application process　申請程序

Please visit our recruitment portal for the list of available positions and to submit your application online. Shortlisted candidates are required to complete our selection tests.

請流覽我們的人員招募首頁，以瞭解開缺的職務，同時請於線上繳交你的申請單。通過文件審核的應徵者，必須完成一連串的招募考試項目。

1. Written test (essay and précis)　筆試：文章和摘要
2. Psychometric assessment (critical thinking appraisal, numerical test and abstract test)

   心理測驗，包括：明辨性思考評量（邏輯推理）、數值測驗、抽象推理測試等

The recruitment process includes　招募流程包含：

- Application　申請
- Processing　處理申請文件
- 1st round of interview　第一輪面試
- Written tests　筆試
- Final interview　最後階段面試
- Medical/other checks　體檢及其他檢查
- Offer　取得工作

❷ **Start an exciting career in aviation: Cathay Pacific Airways 國泰航空招募訊息**

• About Cathay Pacific　關於國泰

At Cathay Pacific, we've been letting our passion fly for over 65 years.

國泰航空，我們已經以熱情飛過了65個年頭。

Our airline was founded in 1946 as a small Hong Kong based freight and passenger carrier. Today, we stand proud as Hong Kong's home airline, and as one of the best in the world. Our 135 wide-bodied passenger and cargo aircraft fly to 174 destinations in 41 countries and territories.

我們的公司，於1946年以小小的香港做爲總部開始客貨運的承載工作。今天，我們驕傲地成爲香港的航空公司代表，也是全球最佳航空公司之一。我們的135架廣體客、貨機飛越全世界41國，174個航點。

Despite our global growth, we've remained deeply committed to our home base. Significant investments have been made in our fleet and operations to help transform Hong Kong into a world-leading global transportation hub. These include catering, aircraft maintenance and ground handling companies, as well as the new Cathay Pacific Cargo Terminal and Cathay Pacific City, our corporate headquarters located at Hong Kong International Airport.

雖然我們朝向全球的版圖發展，但我們仍持續深耕孕育我們的基地總部。大量投資擴充機隊及營運據點，我們努力使香港成爲全球重要的指標性轉運站。這些投資包括空廚、機務維修、地勤運務公司，以及全新的國泰貨運航站和國泰城。我們的總公司座落於香港國際機場。

We have also invested heavily in passenger and cargo services to expand our network across Asia. The Cathay Pacific Group is the proud parent company of Dragonair, which operates 39 passenger aircraft serving 45 throughout the Asia Pacific region. It is also the majority shareholder in Air Hong Kong, Hong Kong's only all-cargo carrier, and a part owner of Air China, the leading provider of passenger and cargo services in Mainland China.

我們同時大量投資於擴充乘客及貨運於亞洲區的服務據點。讓國泰航空引以爲傲的子公司-港龍航空，於亞洲地區以39架客機經營45條航線。國泰也是香港唯一一家全貨運航空公司-香港華民航空的最大股東；此外，國泰亦是中國航空的經營者之一，而中國航空目前於中國大陸的航空市場上，扮演客貨航空服務領頭羊的角色。

As we look to the future, our vision is simple – to become the world's best airline. Being the best means always striving to excel in everything we do. It means putting safety first, maintaining a world-class fleet, and consistently delivering service that's straight from the heart. With the commitment and passion of our global family, it's a goal we believe we can achieve.

放眼未來，我們的目標很簡單：成爲全球最佳航空公司。所謂的「最佳」，代表我們所做的每一件事，都必須不斷努力超越、追求極致。也就是說，我們要以安全爲首要顧念，維持世界一流的機隊，持續提供「從心出發」的服務。有了我們寰宇一家團隊的承諾和熱情，我們相信成爲世界第一是可以達成的目標。

- Working at Cathay Pacific　任職國泰航空

As one of the world's leading airlines, we're able to offer you unique opportunities to let your passion for travel and aviation fly.

身爲全球航空公司先驅之一，國泰可以提供你獨一無二的機會，讓你對旅行及航空的熱情展翅翱翔。

The lifestyle on offer to our global family is second-to-none. With generous travel discounts and flexible rosters available in many business areas, as part of our team you can experience diverse cultures, expand your horizons and explore the world.

國泰提供你寰宇一家的最佳生活型態。大方的旅遊折扣和多種領域的工作機會，身為國泰一員的你，可以親自感受不同的文化，更能拓展你的視野和探索這個世界。

No matter where you are based, you'll be immersed in a friendly and supportive environment that thrives on teamwork. Our people are like family. Each team works together to overcome obstacles and share a great sense of achievement and pride in delivering common goals: delivering an unbeatable customer experience and a high standard of safety, products and services.

無論你的工作地點何在，你一定能身處充滿友善及支持的團隊氣氛中。國泰員工彼此間就像家人一般，每位團隊成員一起努力克服障礙，分享達成共同目標的成就與榮耀。我們的共同目標就是：提供顧客高規格的安全與產品，以及無與倫比的服務體驗。

Our vision to become the world's best airline wouldn't be achievable without the commitment of our people, and so we work hard to ensure that they stay fulfilled by offering a great range of learning experiences and development opportunities. When you start a career with us, you'll be supported to develop a broad skill-set and explore your potential in a number of different roles and business areas. You'll start a career that could really take you anywhere.

沒有所有員工的承諾，我們便不可能達成世界最佳航空公司的願景。所以我們致力於提供所有員工多樣的學習經驗及寬廣的發展機會。當你成為我們的一員後，你一定可以從各種不同的角色及事業體中，發展多樣技能和探索你的潛能。在國泰，你將展開一種可以真的帶你走向任何地方的職業。

- Entry roles　入行初階工作

If you've always dreamed of working in aviation, an entry-level role at Cathay Pacific will get your career off to a flying start.

如果你一直夢想能進航空業，國泰航空提供你的初階工作就是你職涯起飛的最好開端。

As one of the world's biggest and best airlines, we're able to offer graduates a range of training programs, internships and other entry-level opportunities that are second-to-none. With us you can expect high quality on-the-job and classroom based training as soon as you start, as well as mentoring from people who are the best in their field.

身為全球最大最好的航空公司之一，我們有能力提供大學畢業的你，多種獨一無二的訓練課程、實習機會以及入門的初階職務。成為我們的一員，你可以立即接受高品質的課堂及在職訓練，同時有業界最佳人才從旁指導。

Our entry-level opportunities are designed to enable you to explore your interests and expand your horizons. This means that the role you begin with won't be your last. We'll provide you with ongoing opportunities to develop your skill set as well as the support you need to progress your career in whichever direction you would like to go.

我們提供的入門初階工作，可以讓你探索自己的興趣所在以及拓展視野。這代表了你不會永遠只停留在同樣的職位上。我們將持續提供機會，幫助你不斷提升職能，使你能依自己設定的目標前進。

Explore our training programmes and internships via the links below and discover just how far an entry-level career with Cathay Pacific can take you.

經由以下職務的連結，尋找國泰航空所提供訓練計畫和實習機會，去發掘國泰航空的入門初階工作能帶你走多遠！

- Management Trainees　儲備幹部
- IT Graduate Trainees　資訊科技訓練生
- Engineering Trainees　維修工程師訓練生
- Customer Service Officer　客服人員
- Internships　實習計畫
- Flight Attendants　空服員
- Cadet Pilots　培訓機師

• The Recruitment Process　應徵流程

If you are short-listed for an office-based role, you may be invited to participate in a two-stage selection process involving a preliminary and second stage interview.

如果你通過內勤人員的初步篩選，你可能會應邀參加兩階段的遴選過程，包括初步及第二階段的面試。

- Interviews

During the preliminary interview, you can expect to be asked both behavioural and biographical questions. Behavioural questions require you to speak about how you have previously performed in specific workplace situations, and what the end result was. Biographical questions require you to discuss your CV and employment history, outlining your achievements and career path.

面試：

第一階段面試時，你會被詢問一些個人經歷及行為相關的問題。行為相關問題會需要你陳述過往職場上的表現，以及處理特定狀況的結果。經歷部分會與你討論履歷表上的一些問題以及你的職涯歷程，提供面試官有關你的職涯概略藍圖。

If you are invited to a second stage interview, there may be a chance that you will be asked to present ideas around a pre-set topic and to complete aptitude tests that assess relevant skills such as verbal and numerical reasoning.

如果你有機會參加第二階段的面試，你可能會被要求針對一個預設的主題提供自己的看法和見解。也可能需要完成性向能力測驗，藉以評量如口語表達和數字推理等的相關能力。

- Assessment Centres

Depending on the role you have applied for, you may be asked to attend an assessment centre so that we are able to better measure your competencies in specific areas. This process is particularly common for entry into trainee or internship programmes.

評量中心法：

依據你所申請的職務，你可能必須參加某些特定領域的能力測試。這個流程於應試實習計畫或訓練生工作時，是常使用的。

Each assessment centre is customised for specific roles so that we can accurately assess your relevant competencies. Examples of assessment exercises include group discussions, fact-finding exercises, role-plays, aptitude tests, psychometric tests, and presentations. Assessment centres may take up to a full day, although a half-day is most common.

每一種評量皆會為特定的工作量身打造測驗方式，以便我們能正確地衡量你在工作上的相關職能。評量方式包括團體討論、找尋真相演練、角色扮演、性向測驗、心理測驗以及簡報。評量中心法的施作可能需要一整天的時間，但通常歷時半天可以完成。

Chapter 16. Interview　　　　　面試須知

▶ Outline: 整理面試的注意事項，並提供英文面試的Q & A範例。

▶ Learning Goals: 熟練英文面試的題目及回答方式，再依個人特質整理量身打造的英文面試錦囊。

　　面試是成為航空業第一線從業人員的最重要關卡。準備面試應把握 "Know your enemy and know yourself, and you can fight a hundred battles without disaster." （知己知彼、百戰百勝）的原則。詳細收集應徵公司的資料，了解其組織文化、管理模式和對員工的要求及期許。不同的公司應有其對應的策略和方針。

Ⓐ Tips　密技

- Psychological construction (mental preparation)　心理建設

  持續和自己對話，隨時將以下的想法思之再三，直到自己能夠全然接受並深信不疑。

  - I might not be the best one, but I am definitely the right one for this position.

    我可能不是最優秀的，可是我一定是最適任的人。

  - It is normal to be nervous. Everyone does.

    覺得緊張很稀鬆平常，大家都一樣。

  - I can't wait to share my views with interviewers.

    我等不及和面試官分享我的看法了。

  - I will work on my best and enjoy the whole recruiting process.

    我會盡全力準備，並且享受整個過程。

- Practice your voice　練習聲音控制

  發音部位、發音方式、氣息收放以及咬字，在在影響口語表達和聲音表情，清朗柔和的聲音，絕對可以為面試加分。

  - Be aware of diverse voice emotions　能夠覺察不同的聲音表情。
  - Record your own voice　錄下自己練習時的聲音。
  - Articulation practice　發音部位的練習。

- Practice answering technique　練習答題技巧

  Q & A的答案，務必以具體例子取代形容詞的堆砌。舉例而言，形容本身的性格時，舉出自己的興趣、參加過的社團或擔任的職務，即可具體化呈現一個人的個性，較之以大量但空泛的形容詞進行描述，效果更好。

  此外，百密中難免一疏，某些問題，無論是因為事前未曾準備或臨場緊張，一時沒有答案，都應該坦然面對這種狀況，不必太過驚慌失措。可以提問方式代替回答，向主考官求教，展現積極學習的態度。

  航空面試大多是以「多對多」的形式進行。除了主試官之外，應該適時和試場內的所有人產生互動。注意其它應徵者的回答，以眼神或微笑等肢體語言予以肯定。

  - Provide the applicable examples to replace abstract description
    形容自己時，以具體事例取代抽象的描述。

  - Ask the right questions when you do not have the good answers
    不知如何作答時，不妨提出一些適當的問題，化被動為主動。

  - Interact with everyone in the room
    與現場所有人產生互動。

Ⓑ Dos & Don'ts 守則

- Always wear smile 保持微笑
- Make eye contact 以眼神交流
- Keep calm and be polite 保持冷靜，注意禮貌
- Last-minute grooming check 上場前，服裝儀容最後確認無誤

  Don't wear a suit with the tag still on it.

  不要穿上沒有撕掉標籤的套裝:面試服應該提早準備好，且不定時穿上，於穿衣鏡前整理檢查，一來讓自己熟悉這套服裝，二來避免臨時發生狀況。

- Don't show up at the last minute. 不要最後一分鐘才出現，給自己約15分鐘緩衝和整理服裝儀容的時間。
- Don't talk loudly in the restroom. 切勿在化妝室大聲談話，主考官可能就在你身邊。
- Don't overuse body language. 切勿使用過多的肢體語言。

Ⓒ Sample Q & A 範例問題及解答

　　面試問題百千萬種，考前的準備工作不可能完全命中。但要有效率地化繁為簡，可以將題目大致歸類為以下五類。

　　以列舉「題目(Q) / 建議回答方向或答案(A)」的方式呈現，將建議的回應視為例句，各人可依據本身的英語口說能力加以增刪。英文口說能力未臻流利者，建議盡量以直述句及簡單句應對，以避免因緊張而辭不達意。

❶ Personal basic information 個人資料基本問題

Q Would you please briefly introduce yourself?

能否請你簡短地自我介紹？

Q Tell me / us something about yourself, please.

請你談談你自己。

A: Greeting 打招呼

Good morning/afternoon. My name is _____.

（早安 / 午安，我叫 _____ 。）

註.中文姓名直述，英文姓名先道名後說姓。

A: Age 年齡

I am number years old.

（我今年 _____ 歲。）

I was born in month , year .

（我出生於西元 _____ 年 _____ 月。）

A: Hometown 家鄉

I am / come from city/ county .

（我是 _____ 人。）

A: Degree & Major 學位及主修

I graduated from school name , majoring in subject .

（我從 _____ 畢業，主修 _____ 。）

A: About family 家庭相關訊息

➢ There are number people in my family. I am the _____ child.

（我家有 _____ 人，我排行第 _____ 。）

- eldest 老大

- second / third 老二 / 老三

- youngest 老么

- only　獨子／獨女

➤ I grew up in a/an _____ environment.

（我在 _____ 的環境長大。）

- supportive　支持的

- difficult　艱困的

- open　開放的

- traditional　傳統的

➤ My family is quite well-off.　我的家境不錯。

I was born to a middle-class family.　我的家境小康。

I grew up in a below-average-income household.　我的家境清寒。

A: My hobbies　我的興趣

I like / enjoy _____ very much.

I am interested in _____ .

My favorite hobbies are _____ , _____ , _____ .

（我的興趣是： _____ 、 _____ 、 _____ ……）

- travel / sightseeing　旅遊／觀光

- taking exercise / sports　運動

> basketball（籃球），volleyball（排球），badminton（羽毛球），golf（高爾夫球），football（橄欖球），soccer（足球），baseball（棒球），tennis（網球），bowling（保齡球）

> swimming（游泳），scuba-diving（潛水），surfing（衝浪），rowing（划船），white water rafting（泛舟），river trekking（溯溪）

> jogging（慢跑），marathon（馬拉松），hiking（健行），mountain climbing（登山），rock climbing（攀岩），biking（騎自行

車）, dancing（舞蹈）, aerobics（有氧運動）, yoga（瑜珈）

- singing（唱歌）, reading（閱讀）, watching TV / movie（看電視 / 電影）, art（藝術）, listen to music（聽音樂）, painting（畫 圖）, shopping（逛街）, chitchat（聊天）

A: My personality　我的個性

I am a/an _____ person.

My personality is _____.

I would describe myself as a/an _____ person.

I can be described as a/an _____ person.

（我是一個 _____ 的人）

註：Refer to chapter 15 : Preferred characteristics for airline employees
（可參考第15章，航空從業人員較適特質列舉之形容詞。）

A: My strong and weak points　我的優缺點

- I am honest, diligent and humorous. However, I tend to trust people easily and sometimes am overly sympathetic.

  我誠實、努力而且有幽默感，但我太容易相信別人，而且有時候會婦人之仁。

- I have an open mind to appreciate individual personal traits, thus I can make friends easily. Yet I don't know how to refuse people. It becomes an issue sometimes.

  我可以心胸開放地去欣賞每個人的不同特質，所以很容易交到朋友。但我不太懂得如何拒絕別人，有時候這會造成一些小問題。

• sympathetic KK [ˌsɪmpəˈθɛtɪk] DJ [ˌsimpəˈθetik]　有同情心的

A: My motivation to apply for this position　我應徵這份工作的動機

- I love travel and enjoy interacting with others.

  我熱愛旅行，喜歡和別人互動。

- I have been dreaming of working in the airline industry since I was little.

  我從小就夢想能在航空業服務。

- Being a/an position is both fun and challenging.

  成為 工作職稱 既有趣又很有挑戰性。

- It is the best way for me to reach out and open the doors to the world.

  對我來說，這是我朝世界走出去，也讓世界走入我生命的最好方法。

- This is my dream job. I can earn decent salary to take care of my parents, and make friends from all over the world.

  這是我夢寐以求的工作。既能有不錯的薪水奉養父母，也可以和全世界的人交朋友。

❷ Personal advantage and plan　個人優勢及計劃

Q What is your greatest strength?

你最大的長處是甚麼？

Why are you better than other candidates?

為什麼你比其它的應徵者更好？

What makes you the best candidate?

是甚麼讓你成為這裡最好的應徵者？

Why should we hire you?

我們為甚麼要僱用你呢？

Why should I choose you over others?

爲什麼我該選你，而非其它人？

A: Personality　個性

- I am a very open-minded and easy-going person. I can undoubtedly team up with diverse range of people.

  我是個心胸寬闊的人，毫無疑問地，我可以和各種不同的人一起合作。

- I am an independent person and never do things by halves. I assure you of my determination to exceed your expectation, and I always keep my promise.

  我的個性獨立，做事從不半途而廢。我向您保證，我有決心做到超乎您預期的表現，而且我從不食言。

- I am generous in giving help. Making people happy and smile always brings me great joy.

  我樂於助人。讓別人快樂和微笑，總能帶給我莫大喜悅。

- I am a self-motivated person who enjoy taking on challenges. It helps enhance my self-learning ability. I have no problem to either working independently or engaging in teamwork.

  我是個可以自我激勵，主動行事的人，而且樂於接受挑戰。這樣的性格使得我能夠無礙地自主學習。對我而言，獨立工作或團隊合作都是沒有問題的。

• determination ㋘ [dɪˌtɝməˈneʃən]　㋒ [diˌtəːmiˈneiʃən]　果斷；堅定

A: Expertise　專長

- I am good at oral expression. I often represented my class for the speech contest and won the first or second place.

我的口語表達能力很好。以前常代表班上參加演講比賽，總是拿到第一或第二名。

- I am proficient in the Abacus computer reservation system. I have already obtained the certificate.

  我能熟練地使用Abacus 電腦訂位系統，我已經取得證照了。

- During the school days, I was often elected as the class leader or club president. I enjoy serving others and cherish the precious chance to practice the leadership skills. I am sure that I can fully apply my leadership skills to improve the overall team performance.

  就學期間，我常被推選爲班代或社長。我喜歡爲他人服務，也很珍惜能夠練習領導統御技能的寶貴機會。我確信可以好好發揮自己領導統御的能力，提升團隊的整體表現。

- I am skilled in accounting / finances / computer programming / computer software /engineering / marketing. I take full responsibility for my learning and always maintain good academic standing.

  我擅長會計／財政／程式設計／電腦軟體／工程／行銷，我對自己的學習成果完全負責，總是能在班上名列前茅。

• contest ⓀⓀ ['kɑntɛst] ⒹⒿ ['kɔntest]　比賽

• proficient ⓀⓀ [prə'fɪʃənt] ⒹⒿ [prə'fɪʃənt]　熟練的

• elect ⓀⓀ [ɪ'lɛkt] ⒹⒿ [i'lekt]　推派；選舉

• precious ⓀⓀ ['prɛʃəs] ⒹⒿ ['preʃəs]　珍貴的

A: Language ability　語言能力

- I can communicate with others in Mandarin, Taiwanese and English without any problems.

  我能以國語、台語、英語和旁人溝通無礙。

- I took the TOEIC test and scored 750 one year ago. In addition, I recently passed the Japanese Language Proficiency Test at N4 level.

  一年前我參加多益考試，成績為750分。此外，最近我剛通過N4的日文檢定考試。

- I have constantly worked on improving my English speaking skills. I am confident that I have no trouble communicating in English.

  我一直持續地加強英文口說能力，我有自信，可以使用英文溝通沒有問題。

A: Interpersonal skill 人際關係能力

- I can adapt myself to new environment fast and take the initiative in making friends.

  我可以很快地適應新環境，同時主動認識結交朋友。

- I love to compliment my friends and teammates on their performance.

  我樂於讚美朋友和夥伴的表現。

- I often play the role as a coordinator among friends, because they trust my judgment, and know that I always play fair.

  在朋友之間，我常扮演協調者的角色，因為他們信任我的判斷，也知道我一向處事公正。

- My friends usually describe me as a "jokesmith". I enjoy bringing lots of laughter into other people's lives.

  我的朋友總說我是個「開心果」。我喜歡為他人的生命帶來許多歡笑。

- I am a good listener and decent secret keeper. That's why all of my friends would love to have a heart-to-heart chat with me.

我是個很好的聽眾，也擅於保守秘密，所以我的朋友們都喜歡找我談心。

- compliment ㏍ ['kɑmpləmənt] ㏅ ['kɔmplimənt]　讚美；恭維
- coordinator ㏍ [ko'ɔrdn'etɚ] ㏅ [kəu'ɔ:dineitə]　協調者

A: Experience　經驗

- I took part-time jobs in an international chain fast-food restaurant during winter and summer vacations to enhance my service skills. I often impressed the customers by memorizing their preferences.

  寒暑假時，我會去一家國際連鎖速食餐廳打工，藉此提升我的服務技巧。我常讓顧客留下深刻的印象，因爲我會記住他們的偏好。

- I had an internship with airline during the summer vacation in 2012. I was assigned to Kaohsiung International Airport. Working as a gate agent, I found that it was both exciting and challenging. In addition, I had better work out regularly, since it is not uncommon that I have to run with passengers to catch flights.

  2012年的暑假，我到 航空公司 實習，我被分派到高雄國際航空站在登機門工作時，我發現這份工作非常刺激、很有挑戰性。而且，我最好養成固定運動的習慣，因爲經常要和乘客一起跑百米趕搭飛機。

- When I was in school, I regularly participated in extra-curricular activities. It is clear to me that I benefit from those activities greatly. I learned about time management and prioritizing tasks when one thing led to another. Getting involved in social activities also helped me learn how to act appropriately in diverse situations and build solid relationship skills.

就學期間，我固定參加一些課外活動。我很清楚，這些課外活動對我助益甚大。當太多事情接踵而來時，我學會了時間管理以及判斷輕重緩急。參與社交活動，也幫助我學習面對不同狀況時，如何正確地應對，同時，建立牢靠的關係處理技巧。

- impress **KK** [ɪm'prɛs] **DJ** [im'pres]　使……印象深刻；令……感動
- preference **KK** ['prɛfərəns] **DJ** ['prefərəns]　偏好
- uncommon **KK** [ʌn'kɑmən] **DJ** [ʌn'kɔmən]　不尋常的
- prioritize **KK** [praɪ'ɔrə'taɪz] **DJ** [prai'ɔriˌtaiz]　按優先順序處理
- appropriately **KK** [ə'proprɪˌetlɪ] **DJ** [ə'prəupriˌeitli]　正確的；適當的

❸ About the company　公司相關問題：

可經由航空公司網站、人力資源招募網站或服務於航空界的親友，收集應試公司的資料。

Q Why are you interested in our company?

你為何對我們公司有興趣？

Q Why do you apply to our company?

你為何來應徵我們公司？

Q Why do you want to work at our company?

你為何想在我們公司工作？

Q What do you know about our company?

對我們公司，你知道多少？

Q Why do you select our company over others?

為什麼你會選我們公司，而非其它公司？

A1. I look forward to working for the top airlines, and Airline is the one. I have learned that your company's core values are to promote safe and punctual flights, friendly and professional services and innovative, efficient operations. These are exactly what a great airline company should guarantee to their passengers.

我期待為頂尖的航空公司工作，而 航空公司名 便是這樣的公司。我知道貴公司的核心價值是提供安全準時的航班、友善專業的服務以及創新效率的營運模式。這絕對是一家優良航空公司應該向乘客許下的承諾。

• guarantee 🅚 [ˌgærənˈti] 🅓 [ˌgærənˈtiː] 保證

A2. I would like to be completely honest to you. I have done some research. Your company offers employees the best salary and benefit package among Taiwanese airline companies. I believe that it is the way to express how much this company values and respects your employees. I would definitely devote myself 100 percent to return for such honors if you could grant me the opportunity.

很坦白地說，我做了一些功課。貴公司提供的薪資和福利，是台灣航空業者中最好的。我認為，這是公司以此表達，對於員工的看重和尊重。如果您能給我機會，我絕對會盡自己所有的能力，回報公司如此的厚愛。

A3. Airlines are obligated to undertake the best effort to provide passengers safe and satisfactory transportation service. I think that airline company has been doing a wonderful job to accomplish this goal. Thus, you earn such a great reputation and become the top one on the list of most admired companies.

航空公司應該盡其最大能力，提供旅客安全滿意的運輸服務。我認

爲 公司名 一直以來，都做得非常好，也達成這樣的目標。所以，貴公司才能擁有如此優良的聲譽，成爲大家夢想進入服務的公司。

- obligate ㎞ ['ɑblə,get] ㎗ ['ɔbligeit] 使……負義務

A4. airline company is the first private-owned airline company in Taiwan with more than 60 years history. The amazing thing is that you continuously grow and upgrade yourself with active energy, innovative capabilities and multiplex characteristics. I can't think of any reason why I would not want to work in your company.

航空公司 是台灣第一家的私營航空公司，已經有超過60年的歷史了。讓人驚嘆的是，你們仍然持續成長及進步，充滿活力、創新能力以及多樣化的風格。我實在想不出有甚麼理由，會不想進入這家公司工作。

- multiplex ㎞ ['mʌltə,plɛks] ㎗ ['mʌltipleks] 多樣的

A5. My parents are your "Frequent Flyer" card holders. airline company is our only choice when traveling abroad. Your staff always provides us with efficient and sincere service, either on ground or in the cabin. I wish to join your company, because I would like to be the one who deliver such unforgettable memories to passengers.

我的父母都是貴公司的哩程酬賓計畫會員。 航空公司 是我和家人出國的唯一選擇。無論是地面或空中，你們的服務人員總是提供高效率又親切的服務。我希望能夠加入你們，因爲如此一來，我也可以是那個傳遞難忘回憶給旅客的服務人員。

❹ About the position　職務相關問題

Q Why do you want to be a flight attendant?

你為何想成為空服員？

A1. It provides me a great opportunity to travel around the world and explore the links between cultural diversity.

這份工作給我一個絕佳機會去環遊世界，和探索不同文化之間的聯結。

A2. This position suits my personality perfectly. I enjoy helping people and love to make friends from all over the world.

空服員一職和我的個性完全吻合。我很享受幫助他人的感覺，也喜歡和世界各地的人交朋友。

A3. The competitive salary and fringe benefits are no doubt attractive to me. Besides, I look forward to being a professional and working with well-trained teammates.

具有競爭力的薪資和附加福利當然很吸引我，除此之外，我期望成為一名專業人士，和訓練有素的組員一起工作。

• fringe **KK** [frɪndʒ] **DJ** [frindʒ]　邊緣的；附屬的

A4. Being a flight attendant means that I may well utilize my interpersonal skills to offer passengers satisfactory service. Furthermore, I have to keep up with the latest trends to continuously upgrade myself. This position is truly full of challenges.

成為空服員讓我有機會好好運用人際關係能力，提供乘客滿意的服務。尤有甚者，我必須持續進步，掌握最新潮流。這份工作真的充滿挑戰性。

• utilize ㏍ ['jutḷˌaɪz] ㏈ ['juːtilaiz]　運用

A5. Flight attendant job is definitely awesome. I may widen my vision and obtain much more opportunities than most of people to practice experiential learning.

空服員工作眞是太棒了！我可以拓展視野，也能比別人有更多的機會實踐經驗學習。

• awesome ㏍ ['ɔsəm] ㏈ ['ɔːsəm]　太棒了（口語）
• experiential ㏍ [ɪk'spɪrɪ'ɛnʃəl] ㏈ [iks'piəri'enʃəl]　經驗的

Q What are cabin crew's responsibilities?

空服員的職責爲何？

A1. Flight attendants represent the airlines. And they are obligated to conduct cabin service, monitor cabin security, and maintain safety in the cabin.

空服員常被視爲航空公司形象代表。必須執行客艙服務、監控客艙內所有保安相關狀況、維護客艙安全。

Duties and responsibilities of cabin crew members include:

空服員的職責舉例如下：

➢ Before passenger boarding　乘客登機前

- perform pre-flight check (e.g. check emergency and service equipment, cabin facility, cabin security, cabin cleanliness etc.)

執行飛行前檢查工作，如檢查緊急和服務用品、客艙設備、客艙安全及清潔檢查

- conduct ground preparation (e.g. double check with diverse groups of ground crew to make sure required quantity of meal, beverage, dry goods and duty free items being loaded on board)

進行地面準備作業，如與各組地勤組員重複確認餐點、飲料、服務備品、免稅品的數量

➢ Passenger boarding　乘客登機

- greeting passengers

迎賓

- help passengers locate their seats

幫乘客找座位

- help arrange the space for passengers' carry-on

協助乘客找到可放置手提行李的空間

- safety demonstration

緊急逃生示範

- safety check before take-off

執行起飛前安全檢查

➢ During flight　飛行中

- distribute forms (e.g. Landing card, Customs form)

分發入境表格、海關申報單

- meal / drink service

餐飲服務

- duty-free sales

販賣免稅品

- cabin cleaning

清潔客艙

- case handling

狀況處理

- seat belt check and final check

安全帶檢查及降落前安全檢查

➤ After landing　降落後

- farewell to passengers

送客

- cabin check

下機前客艙檢查

➤ Emergency situation handling　緊急狀況處理

- turbulence (clear turbulence)

亂流（晴空亂流）

- cabin fire

客艙失火

- decompression

失壓

- equipment malfunction

設備故障

- hijacking

劫機

- bomb threatening

炸彈威脅

Q What are the requirements for being a competent flight attendant?

成為一名稱職的空服員，需要甚麼條件？

A. Being a competent flight attendant means that you have to be well-prepared both the inner and outer aspects.

For example, you must be patient and independent, sincere to passengers and have a courteous working attitude. Also, you must have great intrapersonal and interpersonal skills. To communicate well with passengers, a high level of language proficiency is a must. Since cabin crew is viewed as airlines representative, a decent figure and pleasant appearance are required. In addition, flight attendants have to maintain physical fitness as cabin work is quite heavy.

成爲一位稱職的空服員，代表你必須內外兼修。例如：你必須有耐性又獨立，眞心誠意地對待乘客，且工作態度有禮。你也必須具備良好的自我調整與人際關係能力。爲了能夠與乘客溝通無礙，良好的語言能力是必要的。因爲空服員往往被視爲航空公司的代表，所以無論身形或外表，都應該維持一定水準。此外，由於客艙工作繁重，空服員一定要有健康的身體。

• courteous 🆰 [ˈkɝtjəs] 🆳 [ˈkəːtjəs] 謙恭有禮的

🆀 Why do you want to be an airline employee?
　你爲何想在航空業工作？

A1. The airline industry attracts my interest because it consists of a wide variety of job opportunities that I can be retrained in various fields.
　航空產業吸引我的原因，是因爲它涵蓋了多樣的工作機會，讓我可以在不同領域持續學習。

A2. Working in an airline company allows me to meet new people from all over the world and interact with them in a positive way.
　在航空公司工作可以讓我接觸來自世界各地的人，和他們良性互動。

A3. I am passionate about working in the airline industry, because young people like me may start the career with solid foundation and great potential.

我十分嚮往航空業的工作，因為那代表像我這樣的年輕人，可以有機會在充滿潛力和穩固基石的行業中，開始我的工作生涯。

A4. I want to work in the airline industry, because I can earn decent wages and have the opportunity to see the world.

我希望能在航空產業工作，因為薪水很不錯，而且有機會能看看這個世界。

A5. The airline industry is highly competitive. Being an airline employee means that I have to continuously make progress and improve various skills. I love its fast-paced work environment.

航空業是個非常競爭的行業。成為航空公司的員工，代表我必須持續進步、提升各種不同的能力。我喜歡這種步調很快的工作環境。

Q How well do you know about the airline operation?

你對航空業的運作了解多少？

A. Basically, an airline company provides air transportation services for traveling passengers and freight. The airline industry is viewed as a capital, manpower and technique intensive industry. It requires a wide variety of professionals to operate the airline business. The operation phase of an airline company may consist of demand forecasting, fleet assignment, aircraft routing, crew planning, airport facility and staff planning, revenue management, sales and distribution, and irregular operation management.

基本上，航空公司的任務即為提供旅客及貨物的空中運輸服務。航空產業一向被視為資金、人力、技術密集的產業，需要一群不同專業背景的人共同經營。關於航空公司實際運作端的部分，可以列舉一些重點如下：需求預測、機隊規劃、飛機排程、組員規劃分派、機場設備及人員規畫、收益管理、銷售及通路、異常狀況管理等

- capital <small>KK</small> ['kæpətl] <small>DJ</small> ['kæpitl] 資金
- manpower <small>KK</small> ['mæn,pauɚ] <small>DJ</small> ['mæn,pauə] 人力
- technique <small>KK</small> [tɛk'nik] <small>DJ</small> [tek'niːk] 技術
- intensive <small>KK</small> [ɪn'tɛnsɪv] <small>DJ</small> [in'tensiv] 密集的；加強的
- forecast <small>KK</small> ['for'kæst] <small>DJ</small> ['fɔːkɑːst] 預測

Q There are many kinds of airline employment opportunities. Please name the positions as much as you can.

航空公司不同種類的職務非常多，請盡可能的指出其中你所知道的。

A. Except the regular positions which also can be found elsewhere, airline jobs include cockpit crew, cabin crew, maintenance crew, airport staff, flight dispatcher, crew schedule coordinator and so on.

除了一般公司亦會有的職務之外，航空公司還包括了以下的幾種工作：機師、空服員、機務人員、機場地勤人員、簽派員、排班人員等等。

❺ Others　其它可能問題

5.1 School life　學校生活

Q Tell us about your school life, please.

請描述一下你的學校生活

A. So far, it's the most wonderful time of my life. I insisted on "work hard, play hard" principle. I worked on my best to get good grades and took the initiative to participate in a wide variety of extra-curricular activities. I also was on the school basketball team. I am confident to say that I never idled away my time when I studied at university.

到目前為止，這是我生命中最精彩的一段時間。我堅持「認真工作、再認真玩樂」的原則。除了盡力維持好成績外，我主動參加各式各樣的課外活動，而且我也是學校籃球校隊的一員。我可以很有自信地說，我完全沒有虛度在學時間。

- principle KK ['prɪnsəpl̩] DJ ['prinsəpl]　原則
- idle KK ['aɪdl̩] DJ ['aidl]　無所事事

Q What are your most liked and disliked subjects?

你最喜歡和最討厭的科目是甚麼？

A. My favorite subjects are English and International Etiquette. They both help extend my horizons. I cannot think of any subject that I dislike. I always enjoy learning new things.

我最喜歡的科目是英文和國際禮儀，兩者皆能幫助我拓展視野。我無法舉出不喜歡的科目，因為我一向對學習新事物很有興趣。

- etiquette KK ['ɛtɪkɛt] DJ ['eti'ket]　禮儀；禮節

5.2 Life and career planning　生涯／職涯規劃

Q If you are not selected, what other jobs would you like to give a try?

如果你沒被選上，還有甚麼工作是你想做的？

A. Working for an airline has been my lifelong dream. If I am not selected, first of all, I will try to find other customer service jobs to make a living and continuously enhance my service skills. Nevertheless, I will not give up on trying again.

進入航空公司工作是我一生的夢想。如果這次失敗了，我會先找其它服務業的工作，一方面養活自己，一方面增進服務技巧。但我不會放棄繼續嘗試的機會。

Q Can you briefly describe your career plans?

請簡略説明你的職涯規劃

A. Growing with this company is the ultimate goal that I look into. I will be dedicated and serious about the job, and achieve comprehensive growth on a professional level. It is my primary goal to master the art of doing in five years. The next step will be seeking and finding a pathway to become a leader. I look forward to continuously exploring my potential in a number of different roles and business areas within the company. Eventually I expect myself to be an expert on airline business.

和這家公司一起成長是我的終極目標。我會勤奮認眞地工作，以充分達到專業程度的要求。我的初級目標是在五年內，可以完全精熟工作內容，下一步則是往管理階層邁進。我期待能在公司的不同部門裡，持續學習並發掘自己的潛能，最終期許自己以成爲航空業經營管理的專家爲目標。

• comprehensive **KK** [ˈkɑmprɪˈhɛnsɪv] **DJ** [ˈkɔmprɪˈhensiv] 廣泛的；綜合的

5.3 Social phenomena 社會現象

Q In your opinion, what are the serious problems in Taiwan currently?

依你的見解，台灣目前有哪些嚴重的問題？

A. I consider that both political and economic issues are the most serious problems in Taiwan over the last decade. I am tired of the irrational fights between the KMT and the DPP. Also, Taiwan is facing the economic difficulty. Lots of developing countries have copied the success experience of Taiwan model and taken away many cheap-labor mass production OEM industries from Taiwan. Industrial transformation admits of no delay.

我認為政治和經濟是台灣近十年來最嚴重的兩個問題。兩黨之間無理性的爭鬥讓人厭倦，此外，台灣正面臨著經濟的困境。許多開發中國家，複製台灣的成功經驗後，從台灣企業手中，拿走許多需求大量廉價勞力的代工產業的生意。產業轉型已是刻不容緩的事了。

- political ㎅ [pə'lɪtɪkḷ] ㎙ [pə'litikəl]　政治的
- economic ㎅ ['ikə'nɑmɪk] ㎙ ['i:kə'nɔmik]　經濟的
- irrational ㎅ [ɪ'ræʃənḷ] ㎙ [i'ræʃənəl]　不理性的
- transformation ㎅ ['trænsfə'meʃən] ㎙ ['trænsfə'meiʃən]　轉型
- KMT Kuomintang (Chinese Nationalist Party)　國民黨

  DPP Democratic Progressive Party　民進黨

  OEM Original Equipment Manufacturer　委託代工

Q What will you tell passengers about Taiwan?

　你會怎麼向乘客描述台灣？

A. Taiwan, just like its former name "Formosa", is a beautiful island. Taiwan is definitely a great travel destination for people all over the world. It is famous for a wide variety of regional and international cuisines. Taiwan also excels in adventure travel. For example, hiking or biking in Taroko Gorge National Park will reward you with the astonishing scenery of white marble boulders lining the steep canyon walls.

台灣，就像它的昔日封號「Formosa」，是一座名符其實的美麗島。對於全世界的人而言，台灣絕對都會是個非常適合旅遊的目的地。台灣以各種不同的當地料理或各國美食聞名於世，台灣同時是個進行探索之旅的好地方。舉例來說，到太魯閣國家公園健行或騎自行車，你將可以看見鬼斧神工的天然景緻: 由白色大理石巨大石塊，排列成陡峭的峽谷山壁。

People here are friendly and always greet guests with warm and sincere care. I assure you that you will be too delighted to leave Taiwan by the end of the trip.

台灣人友好又好客。我向你保證，這趟旅程結束時，你一定會因為太開心了而捨不得離開台灣。

- regional KK ['ridʒən!] DJ ['ri:dʒənəl]　地區的
- cuisine KK [kwɪ'zin] DJ [kwi'zi:n]　美食
- excel KK [ɪk'sɛl] DJ [ik'sel]　勝過；突出
- adventure KK [əd'vɛntʃɚ] DJ [əd'ventʃə]　探險
- astonishing KK [ə'stɑnɪʃɪŋ] DJ [əs'tɔniʃiŋ]　驚人的
- scenery KK ['sinərɪ] DJ ['si:nəri]　風景
- boulder KK ['boldɚ] DJ ['bəuldə]　巨礫；大圓石
- canyon KK ['kænjən] DJ ['kænjən]　峽谷

5.4 Case handling　狀況處理

Q What would you do to calm down passengers if a flight was delayed?

　飛機延誤時，你會如何安撫乘客？

A. First I would sincerely apologize to all passengers for causing them trouble. Since passengers have the right to know what exactly happened and the approximate new departure time, I would provide the related information as soon as possible. If the case would take more than two hours to fix, I would serve passengers drink or snack.

我一定先向乘客致上誠摯的歉意。乘客有權知道發生的狀況和新的預訂起飛時間，所以我會盡快提供這些訊息。如果延誤的時間可能超過兩小時，會提供飲料和小點心的服務。

Q If you accidentally stained a passenger's shirt with juice, what would you do?

如果你不小心潑灑果汁在乘客的襯衫上，你會怎麼處理？

A. The passenger might get angry about the incident. However, what's done cannot be redone. The priority one is to solve the problem. After making an apology to the passenger, I would try to remove the stain with wet towels and soda water, if the passenger has another shirt to wear. In addition, offering the passenger cleaning coupons would be an alternative to handle such a situation.

乘客可能因此非常不高興，但覆水難收，第一要務應是解決問題。向乘客道歉後，如果乘客有其它衣服更換，我會拿濕毛巾和蘇打水洗掉污漬。此外，贈送乘客洗衣券也是另一種解決之道。

- priority 🅺🅺 [praɪˈɔrətɪ] 🅳🅹 [praiˈɔriti] 優先
- coupon 🅺🅺 [ˈkupɑn] 🅳🅹 [ˈkuːpɔn] 優待
- alternative 🅺🅺 [ɔlˈtɝnətɪv] 🅳🅹 [ɔːlˈtəːnətiv] 替代方案；二擇一的

● References 參考資料來源

- Aerospace Medical Association, Medical Guidelines Task Force, Medical guidelines for airline travel, 2nd edition, 2003
  http://www.asma.org/asma/media/asma/travel-publications/medguid.pdf
- Abdelghany, A. and Abdelghany, K. (2010). Modeling Applications in the Airline Industry. Surrey, UK: Ashgate.
- Airline Boarding Announcement Script
  http://airodyssey.net/reference/inflight/
- British Airways Health Services
  http://www.britishairways.com/health/docs/before/airtravel_guide.pdf
- British Medical Association, Board of Science and Education, The impact of flying on passenger health: a guide for healthcare professionals, 2004
  http://www.bma.org
- Cabin Crew Handbook
  http://evaflow.evaair.com/B7ISO/fileupload/f3e426e3-45f2-4f53-8887-90c86d81ff9c/0638d5f7-fcff-4cc7-9df6-199a0faa6404_PARTIII.pdf
- Cathay Pacific Airways
  http://www.cathaypacific.com/cx/en_HK/about-us/careers.html
- China Airlines
  http://www.china-airlines.com.tw/
- EVA Airways
  https://www.evaair.com/en-us/index.html
- In-flight HealthCare
  http://www.china-airlines.com/cn/check/service-6-1.htm

- Singapore Airlines

  https://www.singaporeair.com/jsp/cms/en_UK/global_footer/careers-at-sia.jsp

- TransAsia Airways

  http://www.tna.com.tw/

- Travel by Air: Health Considerations

  http://whqlibdoc.who.int/publications/2005/9241580364_chap2.pdf

- World Duty-free Allowance Guide

  http://www.worlddutyfree.com/information/customs-allowances.html

國家圖書館出版品預行編目資料

實用航空英語／陳淑娟編著. -- 二版. --
臺北市：五南圖書出版股份有限公司，
2018.04
面； 公分
ISBN 978-957-11-9649-7（平裝）

1.英語 2.航空勤務員 3.會話

805.188   107003898

1X54

實用航空英語

編　　著 — 陳淑娟

企劃主編 — 黃文瓊

責任編輯 — 吳雨潔

封面設計 — 謝瑩君

插圖繪製 — 凌雨君

出 版 者 — 五南圖書出版股份有限公司

發 行 人 — 楊榮川

總 經 理 — 楊士清

總 編 輯 — 楊秀麗

地　　址：106台北市大安區和平東路二段339號4樓

電　　話：(02)2705-5066　傳　真：(02)2706-6100

網　　址：https://www.wunan.com.tw

電子郵件：wunan@wunan.com.tw

劃撥帳號：01068953

戶　　名：五南圖書出版股份有限公司

法律顧問　林勝安律師

出版日期　2015年 5 月初版一刷（共二刷）
　　　　　2018年 4 月二版一刷
　　　　　2024年10月二版四刷

定　　價　新臺幣390元

經典永恆・名著常在

五十週年的獻禮 —— 經典名著文庫

五南，五十年了，半個世紀，人生旅程的一大半，走過來了。

思索著，邁向百年的未來歷程，能為知識界、文化學術界作些什麼？

在速食文化的生態下，有什麼值得讓人雋永品味的？

歷代經典・當今名著，經過時間的洗禮，千錘百鍊，流傳至今，光芒耀人；

不僅使我們能領悟前人的智慧，同時也增深加廣我們思考的深度與視野。

我們決心投入巨資，有計畫的系統梳選，成立「經典名著文庫」，

希望收入古今中外思想性的、充滿睿智與獨見的經典、名著。

這是一項理想性的、永續性的巨大出版工程。

不在意讀者的眾寡，只考慮它的學術價值，力求完整展現先哲思想的軌跡；

為知識界開啟一片智慧之窗，營造一座百花綻放的世界文明公園，

任君遨遊、取菁吸蜜、嘉惠學子！